THE FIRE WITHIN

THE FIRE WITHIN

A TALE OF ANCIENT POMPEII

CARMELA DOLCE

THE BAY OF NAPLES, AD 79

DIRECTION OF ASH CLOUD DURING THE ERUPTION OF MOUNT VESUVIUS.

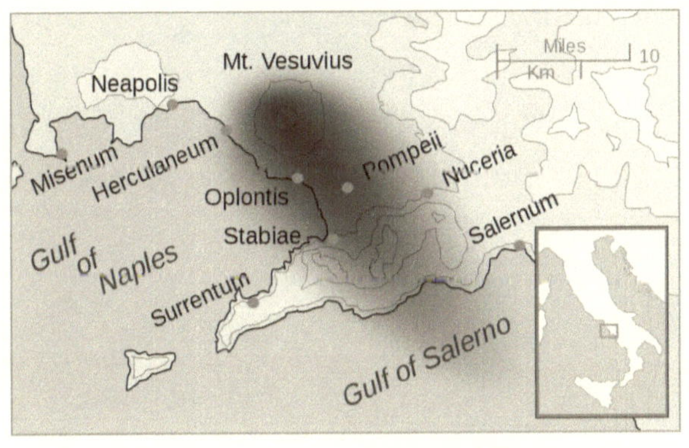

Credit: MapMaster

If you felt the fires of love,
mule-driver,
you would hasten to see Venus.
I love a charming boy;
I ask you,
strike the whip; let's go.
Take me to Pompeii
where love is sweet.
You are mine.

Graffito, Ancient Pompeii

CHAPTER 1

JULY AD 79

A love potion?

Aurora Fortunas fanned herself in the shade of the canine booth and thought it unusual for a medical scroll to encourage superstition. She reviewed the recipe once more for the Fiery Elixir:

Spoonful of spotted lizard ashes
Petals of one wild orchid
Bowlful of rocket leaves
Juice of one pomegranate
Handful of pine nuts
Pinch of pepper
Crush with mortar & pestle into fine paste
Mix with pure wine, drink
Doctor's note:
Increases fertility, sexual function and desire
Caution—a powerful love potion with physical effects,
may also be used with a love spell.

SHE UNDERSTOOD why a doctor might need to disguise a remedy in a clever way, especially to the common folk. Drinking a *fiery elixir* was much more exciting than simply taking your medicine. And many Roman doctors did believe that herbs, prayers, chants, and charms paved the way toward healing.

But a love potion? *Ridiculous.*

And if she thought a *love potion* might really work, she would have tried one by now. For if a man was ever going to fall in love with her, she knew by the gods it was going to take some magic to make it happen.

As unseemly as it was for an educated lady of the Empire to be unmarried at the age of eighteen, it was better to be fortunate and free than living under the thumb of a domineering man. At least that's what she kept telling herself. And thus far, she hadn't met a man worthy enough to challenge her belief.

Aurora laughed, rolled up the little scroll of herbal remedies her mother had given her, and tucked it into her bag. Each day she would endeavor to commit another one to memory.

Despite the heat, it was a beautiful morning. The sun was shining splendidly on the fertile, vine-clad slopes of Mount Vesuvius, the majestic mountain that dominated the Bay of Neapolis and ascended to the heavens just beyond the city gate.

She scanned the crowded forum and sighed. It was the day of Saturn, market day in Pompeii. She had come to buy a birthday present for her mother and to enjoy a morning of leisurely shopping. She really wanted to continue on, to explore the exotic goods that flooded into Pompeii from the East, but her brother wasn't budging.

Against her better judgment, she had allowed her little brother to accompany her. He had immediately spied the puppy vendor, and her morning of shopping had ended before it began. *I should have known better.*

The little imp had promised to just peek at the puppies, but peeking had turned into playing, and playing had escalated into laughing wildly with unabashed glee.

Moreover, and to her utter embarrassment, her brother wasn't standing in a dignified manner, as one of equestrian birth should; he was *lying down* on the dusty travertine floor of the forum, body shaking with mirth as the puppy stood on top of him. *Not exactly the behavior expected from the grandson of the prestigious surgeon of Pompeii.*

The puppy barked and nipped at her brother's nose, making him go into another fit of laughter. He laughed heartily, with all of his breath and soul, experiencing the moment with the pure and untainted joy of a child. Despite herself, Aurora smiled and laughed with him. *Ah well, let him enjoy himself a little bit longer.*

Like her beloved parents, she believed that life was a gift from the gods, and each moment should be savored like a fine Falernum wine.

And who doesn't love a puppy?

She turned her attention instead to the beautiful garlands interwoven with flowers, ribbons, and fruit that were on display in the next booth. She could smell the fragrant roses and lilies through the thick morning air, and she considered buying one for her mother.

Her eyes roamed over the people passing by, and her breath caught in her throat as she glimpsed the figure of a tall and dark-haired stranger in the aisle. *He must be a visitor from Herculaneum, or maybe Nuceria.* Suddenly, she felt very impatient. She stood up and fixed her eyes on her brother.

"Teo? It's time to go."

The little boy ignored her.

"I want to buy this puppy, Sister."

"We already have a dog, Teo. We are not getting another one!"

"Lupa will not mind," he protested, "and she will have someone to keep her company while she is guarding the door."

Every domus in Pompeii had a dog that slept lazily under the shade of the garden trees by day and watched vigilantly over the family by night.

She thought of Lupa running laps through the garden, then splashing through the water of the impluvium with abandon. The last thing they needed was another dog in the house. Aurora leaned down and tried to wrestle the puppy from her brother's hands, but he held on to it tighter.

"Father will never agree. Now give me the dog!"

"No!" He rolled his body away from her.

No wonder mother won't take him anywhere without his slave. How am I ever going to get him away from here? And what am I going to do? Drag him kicking and screaming across the forum? The city guards will fine us for disorderly conduct.

Though her mother and grandfather had given her abundant medical training, she was not prepared for dealing with an irascible child.

Aurora sucked in a deep breath and exhaled slowly, closing her eyes as she squeezed her forehead with her fingers. His tutor really needed to incorporate Seneca's teaching on stoicism into his lesson plan. This display of emotion was embarrassing. She smoothed her silk *palla* over her shoulder and considered her options.

"Looks like you've got a little problem, *puella*."

Aurora startled and turned toward the masculine voice that had addressed her respectfully as a young, unmarried woman. Her eyes widened at the handsome man smiling down at her. It was the same dark-haired man she had just glimpsed a moment ago.

He was muscular with deeply tanned skin. She could tell he was wealthy by the way he was dressed, and he spoke with just a hint of an accent. She knew he wasn't from Pompeii, as she had never seen him before. Still, there was something slightly familiar about him.

"Please excuse us, Dominus. My brother can be a bit insistent when he doesn't get his way." She felt her face flush red with embarrassment. "Are these your dogs?"

"No, I'm just here to see the canines myself. I need one to guard my vineyard." He smiled broadly, his clean white teeth lighting up his smile. "But perhaps I can help you with your brother." He glanced around. "No slave with you today?"

Aurora shrugged. How could she explain that she was independent and liked to do as she pleased? *And that her slaves were more like family who watched her every move.*

The captivating stranger brushed past her, toga flowing in the breeze, and kneeled down next to Teo. An aura of calmness surrounded him, and she stood entranced as his scent of fresh sea pine drifted over her senses.

"Hello there, little boy, may I see that puppy you're holding?"

Teo sat up, tears streaming down his cheeks, and grudgingly held out the dog to the stranger. He knew better than to disobey a dominus.

The man took the dog and cradled it in his large hands.

"Did you know that a puppy like this is going to grow up to be a very big dog? Look closely at the size of his paws." He held one up for Teo to examine.

Her brother looked at the dog's paw as if seeing it for the first time. He was now sitting cross-legged in front of the man, who was fully commanding his attention.

"Imagine a gladiator training with his *gladius* inside of your room."

Teo laughed loudly. "My bedroom is way too small for a huge gladiator!"

"Exactly, and a dog like this would be very sad if it were locked up inside a little domus."

Her brother nodded dejectedly in agreement.

Aurora watched as the handsome stranger massaged the puppy's little head with his long, fine fingers. His hands looked strong and capable, and she wondered indecently what it would feel like to have those magnificent hands massaging *her*.

He had large blue eyes and thick black hair that framed a handsomely sculpted jaw. She stood spellbound for a moment as she remembered how to breathe.

Suddenly, the puppy's mother howled loudly, giving them a start. She began to pace restlessly in her pen as the other dogs began to cry and whimper.

"Why are all the dogs so upset? Is it because we have the puppy?" asked Teo.

"I don't think so. Perhaps a storm is coming in over the bay," answered the stranger. They looked up to the sky, but there wasn't a cloud to be seen.

"Well, something is going on here," Aurora said. "The animals are acting strange, and that's a bad omen." She took her brother's hand. "We really should be going."

She looked up at the elegant man, who was studying her intently. His perusal made her thoughts scramble and her skin go up in flames. The last thing she wanted to do was walk away, but it was the only proper course of action.

"Good day, Dominus. I thank you for your help with my brother."

"Go in peace, *puella*."

~

As Aurora walked down the crowded colonnade toting her brother behind her, she felt strangely warm and energized. Thoughts of the handsome man ran through her mind. *Who is he? Where is he from?* She glanced stealthily over her shoulder, hoping to catch a glimpse of him again.

"Let's move along, Teo. We came to the market to buy a birthday present for Mother, remember? Do you think she would like a pretty blown-glass jar for her jewelry?"

Teo shrugged, his previously buoyant mood deflated.

"Come now, my lamb, let's stop first at the bakery for a honey cake."

They passed by tables filled with every manner of merchandise: leather sandals and coin pouches, silver platters and bronze cooking ware, and her brother's favorite, molded clay drinking mugs with silly faces carved into them.

One booth was filled with terra-cotta oil lamps in a vast array of sizes and shapes; some round, some oval, some decorated with pictures of lovers in various sexual acts. *You can never have too many of those,* she thought as she ran her finger over the top of a small lamp carved with an erotic scene.

Next came a booth filled with musical instruments, and she stopped for a moment to pluck the strings of a lyre. A sweet, bright sound vibrated through the air, and she closed her eyes to savor it.

"Just beautiful," she whispered, "mesmerizing . . . like the eyes of the stranger."

"Whose eyes?" Teo pulled at her scarf and huffed.

Oh gods, did I say that out loud? "No one, Teo."

"Sister, I'm hungry. I want to eat."

"Well, come on, then. Let's get that snack I've been promising you."

They started to walk toward the bread booth when a dark, swarthy man blocked their way. "Beautiful muse, come and see my treasures from Persia." He gestured to his stall that was filled with an astonishing range of merchandise. "Surely I have something special for an enchantress such as you," he lilted.

"Not today, sir. Thank you."

She tried to get around him, but he continued to block them.

"A magical amulet to protect you from the Furies? How about a beautiful bronze figurine of Venus to set beside your bed? A Persian rug to keep your toes warm in the winter?"

She ignored him, pushing Teo in front of her.

"Let us pass, sir, or I will call for the guards!"

"Perhaps another time, then." He stepped out of their way.

As they approached the macellum, where the food vendors were located, the smell of freshly baked bread wafted through the air.

"Do you smell that, Brother?" She inhaled deeply.

"The only thing I smell is stinky fish!" he grumbled.

They arrived in front of a counter that was piled high with round loaves of bread scored into wedges. "Good morning. Two honey cakes, please."

Teo jumped up and down with excitement.

"No, *three*, Sister, I want *two* of them for *myself*!" he emphasized as he tugged at her arm. He had a lopsided grin that she could never refuse.

"Three, please," she amended. She dropped some coins into the slave's hand and passed the honey cakes to her little brother.

"Let's find a place to sit."

They walked under the colonnade until they found an empty marble bench.

"All right, Teo. You may eat your cakes now."

He looked at her with honey dripping down his chin and smiled.

She shook her head at him. "You are an impatient and insubordinate child, but I love you nonetheless. Now let me have one of those cakes before you finish them all off." She took a big bite and closed her eyes as the flavors melted on her tongue. "Oh . . . these are . . . absolutely scrumptious!" she exclaimed, licking the honey off her fingers.

Most Pompeians shared her love of food, as was evident by the throng of men and women crowded around the food vendors, haggling cheerfully over the price of fresh fruits, vegetables, and seafood.

A friend of her mother's walked down the colonnade pushing

a large weaving loom, a basket of eggs hanging from her arm. "Good morning!" she greeted.

Many more friends passed by, some who were patients of her mother or grandfather, others who were clients of her father. Though the Empire was often known to be cruel and corrupt, she cherished the feeling of benevolence and goodwill that Pompeians shared with one another.

She turned her attention back to her brother.

"One more stop, Teo? But first let's rinse our hands in the fountain."

"I guess." Stomach satisfied for the moment, he was inclined to be agreeable.

THEY ARRIVED at an impressive stall where beautiful creations of blown glass sparkled in the bright morning sun. The wooden shelves were lined with wineglasses, flower vases, and tall, graceful pouring flasks for olive oil and garum.

Aurora spotted a cylindrical jewelry container. It was the color of translucent water and exquisitely crafted. "Mother would love this for her gold bracelets and precious stone rings."

The glassblower's wife laid the piece gently in Aurora's hand and opened the lid. "Yes, this beautiful glass pyxis was very finely crafted by my husband. The cost is twenty *asses*."

Aurora examined the delicate artwork, holding it up to the light. "It is definitely a stunning piece. I am sure it is worth twenty, but I have only ten with me." She handed the jewelry box back to the vendor and turned to leave.

The glassblower's wife stepped in front of her, blocking her way. "Fifteen. I will make a special price for you today of fifteen *asses*. Let me wrap it in wool to make sure it does not get broken on your way home."

Suddenly Aurora felt a strong vibration in the floor beneath her and heard a loud creaking noise. "Something strange is—" To her shock, the colonnade started to sway, and the clinking of glass on the shelves became intense.

Oh gods, an earthquake!

Teo lost his balance and cried out. Before she could steady him, he fell down as row after row of glassware smashed to the stone floor around him.

"Teo!" she shrieked.

She stumbled backward, tripped over a rolling terra-cotta amphora, and ended up in a heap on the floor. She curled her body into a ball and covered her head with her arms.

The sounds of panicked people and animals surrounded her. Dogs were howling, and mules were braying. Children cried and called to their mothers. Still, the ground trembled, making it impossible to stand up.

After a few terrifying moments, the shaking finally stopped. Aurora sat up and surveyed the scene around her. Tables were overturned, and merchandise was strewn across the forum floor. Shards of broken glass were everywhere.

She felt panic rise up in her chest and took in a few deep breaths to calm herself. She noted that her arms were scratched and her hip felt bruised, but other than that, she was fine.

Then she remembered her brother.

She turned to find him and saw two strong arms lifting him gently out of the broken glass. Her heart started to race as she saw blood oozing from Teo's leg and realized that he was injured. A large, jagged shard was sticking out of his left thigh. It threw her mind and body into action.

"Pick him up! Pick him up and hold him horizontally!" she cried to the man.

She struggled to take off her long silk palla as she made her way toward her brother, stumbling over debris. The man turned toward her, and she stopped when she saw his face.

"It's you!" she cried gratefully, her chest swelling with relief.

She ran toward him. It was the handsome stranger from the canine booth, but at this moment she couldn't allow herself to wonder how or why he had found them again, she just needed to help her brother.

She wrapped her scarf as tightly as she could around the top of Teo's injured thigh in order to staunch the bleeding. Then she pulled the piece of glass carefully out of his leg, eliciting a high-pitched scream from her brother.

"It will be fine, little boy, I've got you. And your sister seems to know what she's doing," the man soothed in his deep, calm voice.

"I need to get him home quickly!" she told the man, wrapping the rest of her long scarf around her brother's leg.

"We better take him straight to a surgeon. He's losing a lot of blood."

She nodded in agreement. "Just follow me. We'll take the back-streets to my house. My mother can take care of this."

The man looked at her for a moment, confused. "Your mother? What can she do? This is more than just a little cut."

Aurora was quickly growing annoyed. "My mother is a *medica*. So if you please, sir, escort us to our domus!"

"Fine," he agreed. "But *you* follow *me*." He gave her a look that told her he would brook no argument. He was obviously used to being obeyed, but she was no slave and wasn't accustomed to being ordered about by a man.

"And stay close behind me," he commanded. "The streets are filled with panicked people and animals."

He started to walk toward the north archway.

"Where are you going, Dominus?"

He stopped abruptly and gave her a withering look.

"The baths are that way, too many people," she explained. "Go toward the Marine Gate and pass the Basilica. When we reach the Temple of Venus, turn right."

He looked at her for a moment, but didn't move.

"Well?" she cried. "What are you waiting for?"

The man stared at her incredulously, and her brother began to sob.

"Sister, help me, my leg hurts. It huuuurts!"

Teo was dazed and bleeding all over the man's pristine white toga, and the situation in the forum was quickly deteriorating. Looters were running away with armfuls of merchandise, and she feared that people might turn violent.

"Quiet, my little lamb. I will take care of you," she promised. "If only this stubborn donkey's ass of a man would listen to me!" she yelled.

Now she was really upset. She needed to take care of her brother, and this man was wasting precious time.

He shook his head like he could bear no more of her disrespect.

"We'll go your way, then," he answered gruffly. He stepped over the broken glassware, taking care not to let the shards get into his sandals. "And for gods' sake, be careful where you step!"

She pulled up her *stola* and saw his eyes quickly appraise her ankles and calves. She gave him a disdainful stare that said *never in a hundred Roman years*, then began to tiptoe gracefully over the rubbish on the forum floor.

"You should be whipped!" he admonished under his breath, but she heard him and couldn't control her reply.

"Just try it," she dared.

CHAPTER 2

Aurora watched carefully as her mother wove the needle through her brother's tender skin, skillfully sewing up his leg like a precious silk scarf, one stitch neatly looping into the next. She knew that one day it would be up to her to take care of the medical needs of the household, but at this moment, she didn't know if she was strong enough to handle it.

"Squeeze my hand, Teo, it won't hurt so much," she offered. Her little brother was crying, his head shaking back and forth. His face and arms were covered with small scratches and cuts, but it was his thigh that had been sliced wide open during the latest earthquake to rock Pompeii.

The sight of blood didn't bother her, but she closed her eyes in sympathy as she remembered the thorn-like pain of the needle from her own childhood injuries.

She replayed the scene again in her mind, wondering what she could have done differently. *If only I hadn't rushed him through the market. If I had let him play with the puppies just a little bit longer . . .*

Her mother's firm command interrupted her thoughts.

"Aurora, hold the two sides of the wound closer together, like this."

Aurora did as she showed her, facilitating the stitches sewn by her mother's steady hand. Her brother's leg jerked involuntarily.

"Aurora! Keep. Him. Still."

It was amazing the way her mother could switch from doting parent to unaffected doctor in the blink of an eye. *How does she do that? How can she shut out her feelings so completely?*

A quote from Horatius came to her mind: *Remember when life's path is steep to keep your mind even.*

Perhaps when it was a matter of life and death, emotions couldn't be allowed to cloud your judgment. Maybe that's how soldiers operated too, just a mental shift, and they could leave their loved ones behind or kill another man without remorse.

Her mother had practically poured the poppy juice and honey down her brother's throat, barely waiting for it's numbing effect to take over before splashing vinegar into the ugly wound. The poor child had screamed from the burning pain, but her mother had carried on unflinchingly, determined to prevent disease from setting in. She knew her mother would not take any chances with Teo; he was her only surviving son.

Aurora tried hard to keep herself under control. It wouldn't help anyone if she burst into tears, especially not her brother. She knew her weakness well; she felt others' pain as if it were her own. And it wasn't just people she felt for, it was animals as well. At eighteen, she was still too soft.

At least that's what grandfather keeps telling me.

She took in a deep breath to calm herself and thought of the handsome stranger. Although he was as pompous and self-right-eous as every other man of equestrian birth, he had still come to her rescue.

Twice.

Who was he, anyway? He had appeared out of nowhere, *deus ex machina*, and lifted Teo to safety. His tall, strong body had passed easily through the crush of people in the narrow streets, and while she didn't want to admit it, she had felt safe following behind him.

Strange. It was as if the gods had ordained their meeting. Then she remembered the way he had ordered her about and felt her face flush with anger. She pushed him from her mind.

Giorgio and Pioppo, two young slave boys, were helping with the surgery. Giorgio was holding a small silver platter that glistened with steel surgical knives and instruments, all of which had been cleansed in boiling water.

Pioppo, his brother, was tearing clean sheets into narrow strips and placing them on a small table. The sheets had just come from the fuller that morning, scoured and soaked in urine to purge all impurities. Her mother was scrupulous when it came to cleanliness, as she believed that blood and dirt were the cause of disease.

And where is Apollonius when I need him?

Apollonius was the eldest slave brother, the one she leaned on for friendship and support. They had grown up together, and slave or not, he carried himself with the demeanor of a prince.

He and his brothers were natives of Greece and had been sold into slavery by the Roman military. She felt a twinge of sadness at their bad luck, but by the gods, what would her family do without them? He should have been back from her father's vineyard by now.

She looked down at her brother to assess how he was doing. He was only in his eighth year, still just a little child. She caressed his forehead, smoothing back the dark curls.

"Be still, *carissimus,* it will all be over soon. You can do it; you're tough like Hercules!" Teo groaned and turned his head to look at her, eyes glassy from pain and fear. But in those big brown eyes, she could also see his trust and love.

"Mother is almost done stitching you up. I promise you, soon you'll be playing in the garden with Lupa, and all this pain will be forgotten."

At the sound of her name, Lupa, a sleek black hunting dog from Laconia, howled from the hallway. She was chained to the front door of the house and, by the sound of her cries, was not happy about it. She was usually given free run of the domus except when there were patients in the sickroom.

Unfortunately, today it was Lupa's beloved boy who was lying on the bloodstained travertine table. They could hear her pulling fiercely on her chain, trying to free herself.

"Unchain her! Unchain her!" Teo cried weakly.

The dog let out a groan, and Aurora heard the sound of her body flopping down on the cool mosaic floor. Again, she thought of Apollonius. If he were here, the dog would be quiet and calm.

"As soon as we're done here, I will unchain her. We can't have her running in here, Teo. She will try to jump on you!"

"Pass me that hook," her mother ordered.

Aurora snapped back to attention and handed her mother a long, sharp instrument used for retracting the edges of a wound.

"Am I going to die, Mama?" Teo asked weakly. His voice was raw and full of fear. She saw her mother's spine straighten and her breath catch in her throat. She had lost Niketus just three years earlier despite all of the medical training she had received from her father. He had assured her that nothing more could have been done to save the sick child, but still, her mother felt that it was her fault.

"No, my precious boy, you are not going to die," she promised him with a firm voice. "But you must remain still if I am to do a good job of sewing up your leg."

Her mother turned away, but not before Aurora saw one fat tear rolling down her cheek. Apparently she *was* affected. Aurora continued to stroke Teo's hair until he was quiet and calm. The opium was taking over, and she could tell that he was on the verge of sleep.

"'Rora . . ." he croaked.

Aurora leaned over and kissed his face.

"Sleep now, my lamb. All will be well when you wake up. You know mother and I would never let you die."

He closed his eyes and passed into a deep slumber.

As difficult as he could sometimes be, she shared a special bond with her little brother and was with him always except for the hours he spent with his tutor. She sang him to sleep at night and made him laugh, just to ease the pain he felt over losing his twin brother. She had even carved a gladiator onto the wall by his bed to protect him while he slept. Her love for him was tender and protective.

She leaned toward her mother. "He's asleep. Are you all right, Mother?"

"I'll be better when we are done." She gestured to Aurora to pour more vinegar over the freshly stitched wound, and then she rinsed it again with boiled water.

"Grab the linen strips and tie them around his leg securely. We want to be sure the injury is carefully protected from the elements."

Aurora finished wrapping her brother's leg, making sure not to overtighten the bandages.

"All right, boys, it's your turn. Remember to be very gentle. Clean your hands first with boiled water and vinegar."

The slaves removed Teo's soiled clothes and the gold bulla from around his neck, which was splattered with dirt and blood. The bulla was a charm that distinguished freeborn boys from slaves, but most importantly it warded off evil spirits. Inside the bulla was a small gold phallus, another protective amulet. Her mother was obsessed with protecting Teo.

Her brother would wear his bulla until he was fourteen and celebrated *Liberalia*, the ceremony that marked the beginning of manhood. At this ceremony, a boy would burn his toys from childhood and exchange his purple-striped toga for the pure white toga of manhood.

Her mother plunged her hands into one of the buckets of clean water and began scrubbing under her nails with a sponge. "Giorgio, please dip the bulla in boiled water and take the bloody clothes to the fuller."

"What about his sandals, Domina?"

"See if the fuller can clean those too. If not, take them to the tanner for new straps. Where is Apollonius?"

"He went to the vineyard with Dominus Fortunas this morning," the slave boy answered, a note of concern in his voice.

"Well, hopefully the earthquake didn't cause too much damage outside the city walls. Aurora, come scrub your hands."

"Everything will be fine, Mother. Teo will be all right. The gods won't take them both from us." She washed her hands, then hugged her mother tightly despite their soiled dresses.

"Daughter, I lean on you more than you know. You are such a comfort to me."

"And you are amazing, Mother. I don't know how you do it. You stitch up skin like you're sewing a blanket. You don't even ruffle an eyelash!"

"I do it because somebody has to," she said wearily. "And I want it done right. There is too much death and disease in the world. I want to change that."

"So do I, Mother. I understand."

Her mother let out a long sigh and turned to Teo, placing a kiss on his forehead. "Let's pray there will be no fever. We can arrange for an offering at the Temple of Juno tomorrow. But for now, we better go talk with our guest."

They pushed open the wooden partition of the sickroom and entered the atrium, where the handsome man was sitting patiently, sipping a glass of fresh water. The dog lay at his feet, panting happily.

He stood up as they approached him.

"I want to thank you for carrying my son home today," said her mother, taking hold of the stranger's hands.

"Lady Lucina, how is the boy?" he asked, looking at her blood-stained clothes with concern.

How does he know my mother? Aurora wondered.

"He is fast asleep, and the wound has been cleaned and sewn."

The man looked relieved. He ran his hand through his thick black hair.

"I am glad. I am also amazed beyond words that the two of you were able to clean and sew that nasty gash." He glanced at Aurora, eyes lingering on her face.

She stared back at him defiantly, still angry with him for the way he had treated her in the forum. And curse him too, for being so attractive. He obviously had an old-fashioned attitude when it came to women, and she couldn't abide that.

He is amazed that we can clean and sew a wound?

She felt like a string on a lyre, overly tightened and ready to snap. She couldn't help the words that flew out of her mouth.

"Amazed that a woman could be a doctor or that a woman could be intelligent?"

He took a step away from her, obviously offended by her boldness. She could feel her mother's eyes boring into her with a warning. *Not now Aurora, don't you dare get into a speech on Roman female independence.*

Her mother smiled charmingly at the stranger.

"Please excuse my daughter and allow me to explain. My father is one of the greatest surgeons in Pompeii. I am his only daughter, his apprentice. He taught me everything he knows about caring for the sick. In turn, I am passing this knowledge on to Aurora. It may be unconventional, but it serves a woman well to have such uncommon skills, for one never knows what the Fates may bring."

Aurora's eyes flashed from her mother to the stranger, curious to see his reaction, and gods help her, she couldn't look away. He was a banquet of male beauty and sexuality. And even though she had never been with a man before, attributes such as his were highly valued in Pompeii.

He exuded confidence, strength, and dignity. He reminded her of Hector, the fearless prince of Troy, from her favorite book, *The Iliad*. Hector was a family man, a man devoted to his wife and child, but also a brave warrior who fought to save his city from the Greeks.

Hector represented all that was good in the world—strength, love, honor, and duty—and she wanted a man with those same qualities. In the end, he had died and Troy had burned, all because his brother had run off with beautiful Helen, another man's wife. Her father's warning rang through her ears. *Do not confuse a man's true nature with who you want him to be.*

The last thing she needed was an old-fashioned husband who believed that a woman should never leave the domus, shouldn't recline with men at dinner, shouldn't voice her opinions, and shouldn't do her own shopping.

She practically glared at him.

"Of course," he agreed congenially, looking at Aurora. "There are many female doctors these days. I didn't mean to imply that you . . . uh, it's just that I am quite impressed by your medical knowledge and skill."

Seemingly embarrassed, he looked down at the dog and scratched her head.

"She was crying, so I unchained her and let her sit with me. I hope you don't mind." An awkward silence descended between the two of them.

"*Cave canem?*" he asked, referring to the black-and-white mosaic of a dog in the entranceway. "Should I really beware?" he asked jokingly. "She doesn't seem too bloodthirsty to me." He smiled and ruffled the dog's ears.

Aurora narrowed her eyes at him.

Her mother looked back and forth between the two of them.

"Do you not remember each other?" she asked.

The stranger shook his head. "I didn't recognize her at all; everything was so chaotic at the market. The last time I saw her, she was just a child. But when we arrived at this house, I realized she was Aurora."

Though she was scowling at him, he took a step closer.

"Where did all your spit and vinegar come from? You were a fun-loving little girl when I left. But now I see that you are all grown up." His eyes traveled appreciatively over her body. "Amazing what can happen in ten years," he said in a low, smooth voice that sent flames down her spine.

Aurora raised her eyebrows and tried to appear unaffected. "We know each other?"

"Aurora, this is Maximus Evandrus Mercurius the Second," her mother explained. "His family used to live in Pompeii years ago. They moved to Corinth when you were eight. You used to see each other all the time at festivals and parties. I will remind you that we are hugely indebted to him after his kind act today. *Be nice.*"

Aurora looked directly into his deep blue eyes and felt heat break out over her skin. She stared hard at his face. No wonder he felt familiar to her. She did remember him vaguely, but she decided not to let him know it.

She took in the strong plane of his jaw and sculpted chin. She could still see the remnants of his younger self, but barely. His eyes were the only body part that hadn't changed dramatically. He had filled out and broadened in all the right places.

She tentatively held out her hands.

He took them and kissed them, sending tingles up her arms.

"You can call me Evander." He enclosed her hands warmly in his. "You have grown so beautiful, Aurora. And smart. You really don't remember me?" he asked, voice filled with hope.

"No, but I do feel a certain . . . familiarity about you," she answered. She looked up at him. "How did you grow so very tall? I thought your family was from Pompeii."

Evander laughed. "My mother is from the south, but my

father's family comes from Vindelicia in the north. He stands much taller than my mother."

"And by Hercules, you stand a whole head above us!"

The rays of the sun shining down through the open roof of the atrium illuminated his eyes. Beautiful, deep, expressive eyes, like the waters of the bay.

I could write music for those eyes.

He was the most handsome man she had ever seen, now that she had the chance to really look at him. She realized that he was still holding her hands, and she pulled them away.

"And where are you staying?" her mother asked.

"My family still maintains a house here, near the grand theater. We also own a villa and vineyard just outside the Herculaneum gate. Our slaves have tended our properties for years. My mother refused to sell off the land of her ancestors when she left Pompeii."

"Well, it is wonderful that you have come home, Evander, and at just the right moment, it would seem. Could I prevail on your kindness one more time?"

"You may ask anything of me Domina," he answered sincerely, but his eyes were fixed on Aurora.

"Would you mind moving my son from the sickroom into the cubiculum across from us? I am going to change out of these soiled clothes. Would it please you to dine with us?"

"It would please me greatly, Lady Lucina. But not today." He gestured to his bloody clothes. "I really need to get back home."

"Of course, then at least allow us to send you back into the street in a clean toga." With that, she turned and left the room, humming to herself as she walked away.

Evander picked up his glass of water and took a quick sip. "I've forgotten how sweet the water tastes around here."

Aurora nodded in agreement.

"The great Aqua Augusta still brings it into Pompeii from the surrounding hills?"

"Yes," she answered. "Although lately we have noticed a funny taste in the water."

Evander looked at her thoughtfully. "Hmm, well today it seems fine."

He set the empty glass on the marble table in front of the impluvium and walked quietly over to the sickroom. "Let's get your brother more comfortably situated."

Aurora pushed open the sliding wooden doors that divided the sickroom from the rest of the atrium. Pioppo was standing guard quietly at Teo's side.

"Thank you, Pioppo. You may go help in the kitchen now."

Evander gently picked up the sleeping child and followed Aurora into a small bedroom off of the atrium. He placed her brother on the soft wool mattress of the bed, then stepped back to the door to give Aurora some space to maneuver.

She felt him watching her as she covered Teo with a light blanket, smoothed back his hair, arranged the pillows around his head, and checked the olive oil in the terra-cotta lamps.

"May the gods protect you," she whispered as she kissed his cheek.

"You really love him," Evander whispered. "It's heartwarming to see the way you fuss over him."

She stood up and looked directly at him. Eyes locked on each other, they stood motionless for a moment, not knowing what to say.

Aurora's chest tightened when his attention turned to the fresco above the bed. Two little cherubs sat among the flowers of a garden, one holding a pomegranate in his hand, the symbol of the underworld.

"That one looks like Teo, but who is the other little boy?" asked Evander.

"That is Niketus, Teo's twin. He died three years ago."

"I'm so sorry. I didn't know he had a brother."

"How could you? They were born after you left Pompeii." As always, the mention of her deceased brother made her emotional.

"Forgive me," he said. "I shouldn't have asked about him."

Tears filled her eyes, and she swallowed hard as she tried to control her emotions. "Fortune is a fickle goddess. One day you are in her favor, and the next you are not. It makes no sense," she said hoarsely.

He took a step closer to her, eyes filled with compassion. "You're right, it makes no sense," he agreed, pulling down gently on one wayward curl. "But don't forget there is no darkness that does not come with some good."

"So you are a philosopher as well? I can't think of anything good that comes from someone dying," she answered bitterly.

She turned her back to him as the tears rolled down her face.

"Aurora, listen to me." His warm breath tickled the back of her neck. "There is no good reason why one child should die and another should live. I can only imagine the pain that it causes you. But we have to continue on and be strong for our family, like you were today in the forum."

She considered his words but kept her back to him, not willing to converse with him any longer lest she start to sob. She was tired of being strong, and this day had been too much.

"Dominus?" Pioppo peeked his head through the bedroom curtain. A room has been prepared for you to wash and change. Please follow me."

Aurora waited until he was halfway down the hall before she finally peeked her head through the curtains and called to him.

"Evander? Thank you for your help today."

He nodded politely, then turned and followed the slave into a small room.

～

AURORA SAT with her brother a little while longer while she

collected her thoughts and dried her eyes. A short time later, she shuffled quietly under the portico of the garden, heading for the narrow hallway that led to the upstairs rooms. She was eager to take off her soiled clothes and wash her face with cold water. Then she was going to throw herself down on her bed for a much-needed nap.

A fresh breeze blew in off the bay, blowing open the curtains of the garden rooms. She spied Evander through the veils and stopped midstride. He had removed his toga and tunic and was leaning over a basin, splashing water on his face and neck.

Dark, curly hair spread from the bottom of his throat, across his muscled chest, and down to his abdomen and beyond. Despite her inclination to dislike the man, her eyes lingered appreciatively on his well-defined body.

She turned reluctantly away, bumping right into Apollonius.

Caught.

He grabbed her by the arm and tugged her toward the stairs.

"Aurora, what are you doing? And if your father should see?"

"Apollonius! Thank the gods you are safe. I was so worried about you." She threw her arms around him and embraced him. "Is my father back as well?"

"Yes, he is here. Everyone at the vineyard is fine. But tell me, who is that man in the bedroom?"

She looked back at the garden room where Evander was washing. The veils were no longer blowing, blocking him from view.

"Apparently, he's someone that I used to know." She shrugged. "No one of importance. Now if you'll excuse me." She turned and walked up the wooden stairs to her room, fighting the urge to steal one more glance in Evander's direction.

CHAPTER 3

$\mathcal{E}$vander stood on the prow of his ship, face turned into the sun. The scenic Bay of Neapolis spread out before him like a glittering gemstone. The morning sun sparkled on the tranquil waters, and a southwest breeze blew over his skin.

He was heading to the coast of Cumae to visit a winery. He had high hopes that the winemaker would be interested in signing a contract, allowing him to export Falernum, a delicious and exceedingly potent white wine, to Greece.

The coast of Campania was one of the loveliest he had ever seen, with large seaside villas dotting the landscape between every town. The whole area gave the impression of a single city, from the promontory of Misenum in the north to the promontory of Surrentum in the south. Sailors referred to this area as the "Wine Bowl" due to its semicircular shape.

He knew these waters well; he had traveled them often with his father when he was a young boy. His father shipped goods from the Roman Empire to Greece, and from the Peloponnesian Islands back to the Italic Peninsula. He owned a fleet of fifty merchant ships, all adorned with pure linen sails.

Evander's family had lived in Pompeii until he was fourteen, when his father had relocated them to Corinth. Korinthos, as the Greeks called it, was a prime location for a shipping business, and his father had made a fortune there.

He loved Corinth for its beauty and cosmopolitan atmosphere. The city was known as the "Master of Two Harbors" since one harbor led to Asia and the other to Italy. It was also known for its fertile land and natural springs. Julius Caesar had colonized Corinth over a hundred years ago and made it the provincial capital of Greece.

Evander had spent the last ten years there, learning his father's business as well as studying history, philosophy, mathematics, literature, and rhetoric. He was fluent in Latin and Greek and could get by in many of the tongues spoken around the Mediterranean. He was as well educated as any senator's son, and at twenty-four he was now ready to assume a more prominent position in his father's company.

He should have been focusing on his upcoming meeting with the viticulturist, but his mind was completely overtaken by thoughts of the beautiful and feisty Aurora Fortunas.

When he noticed her in the canine stall the other day at the forum, he simply couldn't take his eyes off of her. She was a heart-stopping beauty with expressive brown eyes and dark curly hair. He had even made up that story about needing a dog as an excuse to go talk to her.

When he looked in her eyes for the first time, he had experienced a moment of exhilaration. It reminded him of the moment on his ship when the ropes were cast off from the dock and the sails caught the first wind of morning.

But maybe it was just the recognition of an old friend playing with his emotions. Who would have guessed she was the little girl he used to play hide-and-seek with behind the colonnade of the forum? He couldn't believe how grown-up she was.

Even when they were children, he remembered looking out for her. He'd held her hand when she was a toddler and taught her how to swim when she was five. He still remembered carrying her on his back through the city streets, her gentle arms wrapped around his neck. She used to bring him little presents like seashells and old coins. She had actually been quite fond of him.

But back then we were just children at play.

Everything was different now.

He was different now.

He looked at her through the eyes of a man. He felt the desires of a man, and although she probably didn't realize it, she affected him profoundly.

When he left Pompeii ten years ago, he'd been on the brink of manhood. He had been excited by the prospect of moving to a big city and meeting exotic women. He had been ready and willing to experiment with the opposite sex. And Corinth, with her Temple of Aphrodite high on a rocky outcrop overlooking the city, was a place dominated by love and pleasure.

The girls of Corinth were like no others. They were forward and fast and willing to indulge his every fantasy. He shook his head as he remembered how he had lost his virginity on his first night in the city. But now, looking back, he felt shame for some of the wayward things he had done. His father had even reprimanded him for his lack of wisdom and morality.

Did he have an eye for beautiful women? Absolutely.

But now, as a grown man, he was feeling tired of the same routine. He had whored himself too many times for the favors of powerful women, then ran away as they plotted to marry him to their daughters.

And now the risks were higher than ever. His father needed to safeguard their shipping business. Vespasian had died last month, leaving his son Titus as Roman emperor. Emperors could ensure your total success or your complete ruin, depending on their favor.

His father had made it clear that he should return to Pompeii in order to cultivate relationships with powerful men who could eventually introduce him to Titus. He had even suggested that a marriage of convenience be arranged between Evander and the daughter of a prominent Roman family.

Evander didn't agree with his father regarding an arranged marriage, but he was obliged to obey him, as Roman fathers always had the final say. He decided that he would do his best to work hard, make connections, and allow their business to prosper.

The rest would fall into place.

He had certainly missed Pompeii, the small-town culture, the friendly conversations at the fountains and street corners, the meeting up with friends at the baths or gym. But there was more to this homecoming than just the city, he thought, and it had to do with a certain girl. Something about Aurora made him feel like he was *home*.

But the girl was a mystery.

She was intelligent and self-composed, a student of medicine, yet she professed not to remember him. He could tell by the way she looked at him that he pleased her. At the same time, she showed no compunction about defying him, and a woman should know her place; she should never contradict a man, especially in public.

If this was her strategy for catching a husband, he understood why she wasn't married yet. He had wanted to throw her over his knee and spank her like an errant child when she had argued with him. He sighed. They had obviously gotten off to a rough start.

And yet, an invitation to dinner had arrived at his door the other day, neatly written on a small scroll of papyrus. The Fortunas family was hosting a dinner party, and he was to be the guest of honor. He was looking forward to the dinner more than anything he had looked forward to in a very long time.

Would Aurora be happy to see him too, or would she burn him with her fiery tongue?

Perhaps he should bring her a peace offering, a little gift to smooth things over. Although she had deserved it, he had spoken to her harshly.

He wondered how a girl could inflame his passion as well as his displeasure to such a degree. She had touched something inside of him that he couldn't explain. Perhaps it had been her determination to see her brother survive, or the tender way she had cared for him in his bedroom after the surgery.

He thought back to the moment in the forum when she had run to him as one who runs to shelter from a storm. He had felt needed, important, and something more . . . he didn't know, but as long as he lived, he would never forget that moment.

He looked out to the unfathomable depths of the sea. *And it's strange,* he thought, *how a single moment can change your entire life.*

IN THE DISTANCE, just off the shore of Herculaneum, something caught Evander's eye. A small fishing boat was in distress. The fishermen were struggling to pull a man on board who seemed to be injured. He called to his slaves to steer his ship in their direction.

They dropped anchor as they approached, and Evander and a few of his slaves climbed down into a smaller boat and rowed over to the fishermen.

"What is happening?" Evander called out.

"Our companion dove into the sea for a swim. When he surfaced, he was screaming—something about the water burning him!"

"Burning him?" Evander dipped his hand in the sea. It was warm, unusually so, but certainly not hot enough to burn anybody. *The man must be drunk.* When Evander was close enough to the fishermen's boat, he climbed on board. He kneeled down next to the injured man, who was moaning in pain.

"Can you tell me what happened?" He looked at the man's legs and torso. His skin was red and beginning to blister.

"The bubbles . . ." The rugged fisherman's voice quivered with pain. "They came up from underneath me. Scalding hot, like a pot over a fire . . ." He closed his eyes and grimaced.

Evander looked at the other men. "And what about the fish? Have you caught anything this morning?"

"Not even one. But we have seen many dead ones floating on the surface."

Evander reached down and pulled some coins from his leather pouch. "It seems that he has been stung by some angry sea creature. I know some women who can help him. They are healers. Take him to the harbor of Pompeii. From there, hire a litter to carry him to the Fortunas household. Tell the women that Evander sent you. I would escort you myself, but I am due in Cumae this afternoon for a business meeting."

The weatherworn fishermen thanked him heartily for his help, and one grabbed his arm as he was turning to climb out of the boat.

"Evander is your name? Yes, you are a good man indeed."

"A fire has broken out on the north side of the city, in the taverns near the Nola gate. I have been sent to fetch your mother to help with the people who have been burned. Is she here?" The messenger bent over, put his hands on his knees, and tried to catch his breath.

"My mother is not in. She is working with my grandfather today. She left just after another tremor struck," Aurora answered, springing into action. "But I can help, I am a medica as well. She looked at her brother, who was lying down on a couch. "Teo, you stay here with Pioppo and rest. I'll be back shortly."

"But what if there is another tremor, Sister?"

"Then I will come straight home, I promise."

She motioned for the slave to follow her as she rushed down the hall toward the storage shelves that held the medical supplies.

"What was the cause of the blaze?" she asked, stuffing bandages into a satchel.

"A large oil lamp spilled and ignited in the back room of a tavern during the quake. The owner didn't realize what had happened until the wooden shelves were aflame and it was spreading to the second floor. There were children asleep in the loft upstairs!"

Aurora gasped in horror at the thought of children being caught in a fire. Her eyes ran quickly over the labeled jars of tannic acid, pig fat, pine resin, and honey. "I will need all of these," she said as she shoved the satchel into the messenger's arms. "Start packing it up. I need to find more bags."

She ran down the hall to the slaves' quarters. "Myrrhine! Where are you? I need your help."

AURORA and her escort of slaves walked briskly down the street, arms filled with bags of medicine. They passed the fountain and had just turned the corner when they saw Evander coming toward them. He quickly advanced and took the satchel from Aurora's arms.

"Where are you hurrying off to?" he asked, full of concern.

"There is a fire on the north side of town. Children have been injured."

"May I accompany you?"

Aurora thought back to the forum, how he had contradicted her, and wondered if he would get in her way. At the same time, she didn't know what she was about to encounter, and he certainly had been helpful with Teo. She nodded to him. "As you wish."

"I came to inquire about the fishermen I sent to you yesterday. Did they find their way to your house?"

"Yes. Strange situation. The injured man said the bubbles in the water had burned him." They crossed deftly over the large stepping-stones that connected one street with another.

"So what was your assessment? Have you ever seen something like that before?"

"Well, I have seen many rashes and blisters caused by the sting of sea creatures, but never in that pattern. My mother said the man had truly suffered burns all over his body, but how or why, she could not ascertain." She glanced up at him, and their eyes caught and locked. "But now I need to focus on the crisis at hand." She swallowed nervously as she saw the black smoke rising from the buildings.

The messenger led them to a large domus one block from the fire.

"Here," he pointed. "They were bringing the victims into this house."

Aurora looked with regret down the street toward the burning taverns. The entire area was filled with noise and commotion as the Vigiles worked hard to put out the fire.

She was led down the hall and into a large atrium. Her steps faltered as she saw at least thirty victims, with various burns and injuries, lying on the mosaic floor around the impluvium. Suddenly she felt very small and foolish, as if she had overestimated her own abilities. *How am I ever going to help all of them?*

Evander nudged her forward. "You can do this, and we are going to help you. These people need you."

His words of encouragement gave her the push she needed. She found the children, two girls and a boy, and hastened over to them, motioning for the slaves to put down all of her supplies. The parents and children were crying, and it broke her heart. The children's arms and legs were covered with blistering red welts, and their hair was singed. Their faces had been spared with only mild burns, as they had probably shielded themselves with their limbs.

She thought of her mother, of her incredible strength and focus. She wanted to be like her, and she knew she could do it. She looked at the distraught parents confidently. "I am a trained medica. My grandfather is Vibius Popidius, respected surgeon of Pompeii. I can help your children."

She looked through the supplies she had brought and grabbed

a large wooden mixing bowl and spoon. "Evander, you are going to stir vigorously as I add in each ingredient." She pushed the bowl and spoon into his hands.

"Myrrhine, hand me the honey and the pig fat. She opened the top of each jar and scooped out the amount she needed with a small spatula.

"Now for the pine resin."

Myrrhine pulled off the top of the sticky glass jar, releasing the pleasant smell of the forest. Aurora leaned into Evander as she scraped the resin into the bowl. "Keep mixing; the burn ointment is almost ready."

Lastly, Aurora poured a good amount of tannic acid into the thick mixture. She and her mother had made it by soaking the bark of sumac trees in wooden containers filled with river water. Combined with the rest of the ingredients, it made a powerful healing balm for burns.

"Hand me a small towel. I am ready." She wiped her hands and looked sternly at Myrrhine and Evander. "I will need you both to hold down each child as I apply the ointment. They will not like it; they will most likely scream and kick and cry. But remember, we are doing this to heal them. Don't lose heart."

Her words were as much for her own benefit as for theirs.

"Let's begin."

She kneeled down next to one of the little girls. "*Pupa?* Little doll, can you hear me?"

The girl opened her eyes and looked anxiously at Aurora.

"I am going to help you. I must apply some medicine to your burns so they don't become putrid. This will help you heal very fast. Do you understand?"

The girl nodded, but her face wrinkled up, and she began to cry. Behind her, the child's parents held on to each other for support. Aurora gave the signal to Evander and Myrrhine. She scooped out some of the burn ointment, then smoothed it as gently as she could over the girl's arm. The child screamed in pain, and it was difficult for Aurora to take. She could only imagine the agony this child was feeling. She stopped abruptly and signaled to some of the slaves.

"Take the herbs in the smallest satchel to the kitchen. Boil a large pot of chamomile and valerian flowers, then add a few dried poppy straws to the infusion."

She looked at Evander and Myrrhine. "Burns are excruciating. We will give this herbal pain remedy to the children a few minutes before we apply the ointment. It should also help with the anxiety. In the meantime, let's take care of the adults."

She worked her way around the patients in the atrium with an inner strength that she was only just starting to recognize. The people blessed her as she worked and promised to repay her kindness one day.

When they returned to the children, they found them peaceful and resting quietly. Her herbal brew had worked better than any charm. She skillfully applied the burn ointment to their injuries. The parents showered her with praise and gratitude, and it left her feeling overcome with emotion. She left them with a large jar of burn ointment and agreed to come back to check on the children's recovery.

Through it all, Evander remained by her side, following her directions and never once contradicting her orders. After a few hours, she felt fatigued, but she continued on until she had seen everyone.

They received word that the fire was finally extinguished, and they all let out a sigh of relief. Aurora was proud of herself for a task well done. She packed up her bags with the remaining medical supplies and stood to leave.

Evander insisted on escorting her back home. They were silent as they made their way across town, over the stepping-stones, and along the narrow sidewalks. She motioned for the slaves to return through the side entryway.

When they were just inside her front door, Aurora leaned

against the wall and closed her eyes. Her mind retraced the treatments she had given, and she hoped that she hadn't made any mistakes. Evander touched her arm.

"You did very well today," he lauded. "I'm afraid to say anything more for fear you'll get upset with me."

She let out a small sigh. "Will you concede that a woman can be every bit as competent as a man? Or are you still *surprised*?" She waited for his reply.

"I'm not only surprised, I'm amazed."

"You can say that to me after what I've done today?" She felt her face prickle with heat.

"If you would allow me to finish . . ."

"Go on, then." She folded her arms over her chest.

"I am amazed at the *level* of your competence. That is hard to find, even among male medics. The way you took control, the brew and ointment you prepared, even the way you spoke to the children and parents. You inspired confidence in your patients, and I was impressed. *Not* because you are a woman, but because you are truly great at what you do."

Aurora relaxed her body and gave him a genuine smile. "Thank you." She gazed at him for a moment and decided that he wasn't so bad. "I am very pleased with the work I did today, but I will confess to you that I still have a long way to go."

"Don't underestimate yourself. What you did took a lot of courage."

She reached out and touched his hand. "I appreciated your help, you know. You didn't have to stay with me, but I'm glad you did." She looked into his deep blue eyes and felt her heart softening toward him.

"I will see you at the dinner party tomorrow evening." He bent down and kissed her cheeks good-bye, then walked out, leaving her staring at the panels of the painted wooden door.

CHAPTER 5

The house buzzed with excitement as everyone prepared for the dinner party. Aurora had just come from the baths and was standing in the atrium. She could hear the cook yelling orders from the small kitchen down the hall, losing his temper the way he always did before a party. The aroma of roasted meat, cumin, and nutmeg wafted through the air, making her mouth water.

Slaves had been brought in from her father's vineyard, and they rushed about in groups of two, intent on accomplishing their various tasks. Some were standing on ladders hanging flowered garlands across the colonnade, other's were draping clean linen sheets over the couches, while still others were setting out polished silver bowls filled with fresh fruit or nuts.

Aurora noticed that two pillowed couches had been moved into each wing of the atrium for those who wished to recline more privately. A round marble table, balanced on three lion legs, had been placed in front of each couch and decorated with flowers and a bowl of fruit. Tall, candelabras stood in each corner. Each wing looked cozy and inviting. She imagined herself reclining there with Evander, then scoffed at her thoughts.

What would he say to me? Would he lecture me on the virtues of being a quiet, submissive woman?

The dog seemed to sense the excitement in the air. She raced around the garden trees, through her father's office, then jumped into the impluvium, splashing water over the newly cleaned mosaic floor.

"Will somebody get that dog!" her mother cried out from the upstairs balcony, and Apollonius rushed in to fetch her.

"Sorry, Domina. I'll clean it up," he called to her.

He saw Aurora standing by the couch and walked over to her as Lupa did a few more laps around the atrium before settling at his feet.

"Aurora, may I speak with you for a moment?" His dark eyes looked worried.

"What is it?"

The handsome slave shrugged his shoulders.

"It's a bit awkward," he admitted as he clipped on Lupa's leash.

He cleared his throat, and Aurora looked at him expectantly.

"I know that you have a romantic interest in the man who carried Teo home the other day."

"Apollonius!" She blushed bright red. "I can assure you, I am not interested in him!"

"Hear me out, Aurora. I may be your slave," he lowered his voice, "but I'm still a man." His eyes searched her face. "And I care about you."

"I care about you too, Apollonius. And slave or not, we treat you like a member of this family. So why are you concerned?"

"We have grown up together, and you know that I would protect you with my life."

She rolled her eyes at him. "Trust me, I don't need protecting."

"But you do!" he said emphatically. "I know you *think* you can take care of yourself, but the reality is that you have led a very sheltered life."

"Oh please!" she huffed.

"Pompeii is a small city by the sea, and we take care of our own. Men like Evander sail into town, have a little fun, and sail back out before anybody even knows what happened."

She could feel heat rising into her face. "Why would you think—"

"Because I'm a man, and I understand these things," he interrupted. "Evander has spent the last ten years living in Corinth, a city known for its licentiousness. He travels the Mediterranean Sea, he's worldly and smart and probably used to women throwing themselves at his feet."

"And how do you know so much about him?" she snapped.

"Slaves talk, Aurora. He's the most exciting thing to sail into the port of Pompeii in years. And he's rich too. Did I mention that?"

She felt like someone had dropped a ballista stone into the pit of her stomach. "So what are you suggesting that I do? Refuse to talk to him? Ignore him? This is outrageous!" she cried.

He moved closer to her, his voice barely a whisper. "I'm just asking you to be careful, that is all. I don't want him taking liberties with you once the wine starts flowing."

She shook her head at him. "My parents will be here. You know they wouldn't let anything happen to me."

He glanced around. "Your parents are hoping that you will land right into this man's lap. They would be thrilled to see you married into a wealthy family with powerful connections."

"That doesn't matter to them." She crossed her arms defiantly.

"Oh, don't you think so? You're eighteen years old, not twelve. They want to see you settled. They won't be around to protect you forever. And I . . ." he paused for a moment, "well I'm just your slave."

Her heart softened as she looked at the handsome young man who had always been her protector. "No, Apollonius. You are so much more than that. You are my family," she told him.

"And you are mine, but I have no power over a freeborn Roman citizen. If he hurts you, there is nothing I can do about it."

"I will be careful. I promise you." She squeezed his hands and kissed his cheek, then walked away completely flustered.

~

AURORA CLIMBED up the stairs to her room to get dressed for the party. After coming from the baths, she had been feeling calm and refreshed until Apollonius gave her his warning speech. Was there any truth to what he said? Was she romantically interested in Evander? Would he seduce her, take advantage of her, then sail away and break her heart?

Myrrhine, mother of the slave boys, came in to help her dress. Together they chose a yellow silk stola that hung completely off one shoulder and a flowing, pale blue palla for accent. She sat down at her vanity table as Myrrhine styled her hair.

The matronly woman smoothed back the curls from her face, twisting and twirling the long strands until they were piled high on her head. Aurora handed her two pearly white seashell combs and a headband, but unruly curls sprang out everywhere, and she put her head in her hands and sighed. She fought down the nervous feeling in the pit of her stomach. Why was she reacting like this? It was only Evander and a few other families that were coming over for dinner.

Only Evander.

Evander, a childhood friend, had come back home. But there was no trace of the lanky boy that she remembered. His tall frame was now muscular and well proportioned. She hadn't been able to keep her eyes off of him as he carried her brother home from the forum. And yesterday, as he had faithfully worked beside her, she had wondered more than once what it would feel like to be wrapped in his arms.

"What is the matter?" the slave woman asked. "Why are you so uptight?"

"Oh, Myrrhine, I feel like such a fool! I've treated someone poorly, and now I think that I was wrong about him."

"*Him?* Are you referring to the man who helped you yesterday during the fire?"

"Yes, Evander Mercurius. And although I've tried hard to deny it, especially to myself, he captivates me. But Apollonius is right. I am no match for him. He's probably just being nice to me out of respect for my parents."

"My son told you that you are no match for Dominus Mercurius? He is wrong. You are a perfect match for him! If only you could see yourself as others see you. You are intelligent and articulate, and you look beautiful tonight, especially with those curls cascading down your neck."

Aurora gave her a doubtful look. "Thank you. I will try to remember that as I melt into a puddle of wax when he walks through the door."

THE BRASS DOORKNOCKER clanked on the heavy wooden portal, and Lupa ran to the front hallway, barking frantically. Teo limped behind her, chain in hand, and Aurora took in a deep breath as she tried to control the fireflies in her stomach.

"Not so fast, Teo!" her mother yelled from the atrium. "Do you want me to have to stitch up your leg again?"

Teo shook his head dramatically as he clipped the chain onto Lupa's collar.

Aurora and her family gathered in the vestibule, and Apollonius appeared behind them, calm, clean, and dignified. He quickly arranged her father's toga, then opened the front door and greeted their guest. As he walked away, he took the dog from Teo

and gave Aurora a discreet look that said, *Remember what we talked about.*

Evander stood at the threshold of their house, smiling.

"By Hercules! You have grown more handsome than you were a few days ago!" her mother exclaimed as she rushed to his side. She looked stunning in a red silk stola, her long dark hair flowing over her low-cut dress. Evander stepped into the hallway. "Lady Lucina, it is a pleasure to see you once again. You are looking quite beautiful this evening." He leaned down and kissed her on both cheeks, then held out his hand to her father.

"Dominus Fortunas, it is wonderful to see you again."

"Well, look who it is!" her father said with a friendly shout. "My gods, how you've grown. You're a man now!"

He gave Evander a hearty hug. "So you've come home to Pompeii after all these years. Welcome back. I can't wait to hear all about Corinth and your shipping business."

"Let him come in, Aurorus! Don't keep him standing in the hall." It was only when Evander's large frame had stepped out of the doorway that they realized someone was standing behind him, holding an armful of packages.

"Well, let your door be wide open to one bearing gifts," her father exclaimed.

"This is Manolo." Evander introduced the slave holding the packages. The slave bowed respectfully, trying not to drop anything.

"This one is for you, Lady Lucina," he said, handing her a gift. "And this heavy one is for Dominus Fortunas."

He leaned down and, with much exaggeration, said, "And this one is for Teo. I see that you are getting along quite well now, after your little accident. You know good things come wrapped in small packages, don't you?"

Teo's eyes grew wide as he snatched the gift from Evander. "Can I open it now?" he asked as he started pulling at the linen wrapping.

Aurora finally stepped forward. "Wait until we have properly greeted him, Teo."

She looked up at Evander and smiled. "Welcome to our home again, and I hope it will be under better circumstances than the morning of the tremor."

She thought of the chaotic flurry of activity, the shrieks and cries and yells that had gone throughout the household when Evander came through the door holding her brother, clothes covered in blood. It had looked much worse than it actually was.

Evander stepped forward, took her hands in his, and kissed her cheeks.

Aurora blushed at the touch of his lips and was sure that his kisses had lingered on her skin for an extra moment. His silky black hair brushed her face, and her heart started to pound.

"This one is for you," he said softly. He took the last gift from Manolo and placed it in her hand.

"Thank you," she said quickly, noting that her parents were watching them closely.

"Come, children, let's sit in the garden before the rest of the guests arrive and open our gifts." Her mother took Evander by the arm and escorted him outside. "It is such a beautiful evening for a party, don't you agree?"

"Yes, it is quite a beautiful summer night, Lady Lucina, and may I compliment you on your house, so welcoming and beautifully adorned with flowers and garlands."

Aurora took her father's arm and walked behind them to the garden. She watched Evander as he moved fluidly through the domus. His long legs were dark from the sun and covered with a dusting of black hair. Even his feet were handsome and clean inside his expensive leather sandals. He wore a fine linen tunic with a gold belt and a bright white dinner toga draped over one shoulder and around one arm.

She couldn't take her eyes off of him.

Her father looked at her and smiled knowingly.

They sat down on marble benches in front of the bubbling fountain, her mother making sure that Aurora sat on the same bench as their guest.

She folded her hands gracefully in her lap and tried to appear calm. It was easier to be around him yesterday when she was focused on a task—and still holding a grudge against him.

He was so close to her she could smell him. She inhaled deeply, reveling in his masculine scent. He reminded her of a breezy night down by the sea.

Evander gestured with his arms. "Please open your gifts."

"Finally!" Teo cried as he pulled at the wrapping, revealing a small ceramic dog. It was painted black and had a red collar around its neck. "It's Lupa!" he squealed, kissing the ceramic dog on the nose.

Teo wobbled over to Evander, who embraced him warmly. He cradled Teo's little head in his large hands, reminding Aurora of the way he had held the puppy.

Her mother leaned forward and took Evander's hand. "I will be forever grateful to you. If it weren't for your help, Teo could have been taken from us, just like his twin, Niketus. You will always be a welcome guest in our home."

"Thank you, Domina. I look forward to visiting often."

Her father put his arm around her mother's shoulders. "Beautiful wife, let us not talk of loss or sadness. Tonight, let us be thankful for all the goodness in our lives." He smiled warmly at her. "Now open your gift."

Her mother unrolled the linen wrapping, revealing a pretty glass pyxis the color of sea foam.

Aurora's jaw dropped as she turned to Evander.

"How did you know?"

"How did he know what?" asked her mother.

"That is exactly the present I was going to buy for your birthday when the earthquake struck." She looked questioningly at Evander.

"I went back to the forum yesterday to meet with some potential clients. The glassblower's wife recognized me and asked how the little boy was doing. She brought me to her shop and said that she lost a lot of her inventory but happened to save this piece because she was holding it in her hand at the moment of the tremor. She said you had wanted to buy it for your mother. So happy birthday, Lady Lucina."

"It's absolutely beautiful! Thank you." Her mother held it up and examined it in the light.

"Thank your daughter," Evander said with a chuckle. "She picked it out."

"My turn." Her father pretended to weigh his gift in his hand. "It's heavy; what can it be?"

"Hurry, Father, just open it!" cried Teo.

"All right, all right!" He laughed and unrolled the linen to reveal a small sculpture of a man holding a lyre riding on a dolphin's back.

"Corinthian bronze," he remarked as he turned the sculpture over. "Is this Arion of Corinth?"

"Yes, it is," Evander said.

"The famous lyre player who composed the first *dithyramb*?" asked Aurora.

"Exactly. The legend is well known in Corinth, as you can imagine."

Teo pulled at his mother's dress. "What's a diddy ram?"

"It's an ancient Greek hymn sung and danced in honor of Dionysus," she explained. "But the legend of Arion is said to be true."

"Tell me the story, Mother," Teo begged.

"Well, why don't we all take a turn?" she suggested. "It's a wonderful tale."

Everyone nodded in agreement, and so her mother began, just as Myrrhine arrived to pass out glasses of spiced honey wine.

"A long time ago in Greece, there was a man named Arion

who was known to be the best lyre player of his time. He had spent some time in Italy and Sicily singing and performing his music, and had made a small fortune. When he was ready to go back home, he hired a group of Corinthians, who he trusted above all other men, to sail him back to Corinth. But when these men learned that Arion was a wealthy man, they conspired against him and ordered him to kill himself by jumping overboard."

"Wait—why did they want him to kill him?" asked Teo, a confused look on his face.

"So they could steal his money," answered Aurora.

She continued where her mother left off. "So Arion of Corinth begged them not to kill him, but they wouldn't change their minds. He agreed to jump overboard only after they allowed him to play a song on his lyre. He was sure that he could win them over by the beauty of his music."

Her father cleared his throat. "He dressed up in his musician's clothes, stood up on the deck, began to play the lyre, and sang them the most beautiful song he had ever written."

"Did it work?" asked Teo.

"No," answered her father. "When he was done singing, they made him jump overboard. But lo and behold, a beautiful dolphin came along and told him to get up on her back. Arion climbed up, holding on to his lyre, and the dolphin took him on a ride through the sea, delivering him safely to the shores of Cape Taenarum."

Aurora laughed at the expression on Teo's face; his eyes were as wide as dessert dishes.

"And what happened to the evil men? Were they killed in the arena?" asked Teo.

"My turn to tell the tale," said Evander.

"Arion went to Corinth and told Periander the Tyrant, the ruler of the city, what had happened. But Periander didn't believe him! He kept Arion under guard and wouldn't let him leave the city until the evil men returned to port. When they finally arrived,

Periander asked them if they had news of Arion. They lied and said that Arion was well and living in Sicily!"

"Imagine their surprise when Arion appeared before them wearing the same clothes as when he had jumped into the sea! The men were punished, but Periander, believing a miracle had happened, erected a beautiful bronze statue of Arion and the dolphin at Taenarum."

"Wow!" said Teo. "Can a dolphin really do that? Carry someone on its back?"

"Many people believe so," answered her father. He looked at Evander and pointed to his new gift. "Thank you, son. This is a great piece of art to display on my desk in the tablinum. As a matter of fact, I'm going to place it there now." He shook Evander's hand and walked out of the garden, examining the beautiful sculpture.

Evander looked at the unwrapped present in Aurora's lap.

"You're the only one who hasn't opened her gift. I hope you like it."

She untied the ribbon around the linen wrapping. A beautiful yellow palla with gold threading slipped out. She held it up, allowing the silky material to glide through her fingers. "It's exquisite. Thank you." She wondered if he realized that buying clothing for a woman was a very romantic gesture in Pompeii.

"Well, your other palla was ruined when you used it to bandage Teo's leg. I thought you might like a new one, and yellow goes so nicely with your skin tone."

Skin tone? She looked at him with raised eyebrows.

"I grew up with three sisters," he said, as if he knew what she was thinking.

She saw her mother watching, so she changed the subject.

"How is your family in Corinth?"

"My father is very busy, as usual, with his shipping company, and my mother has her hands full running the household. My two eldest sisters are both married, and Sabina is expecting her first child."

"And how is your younger sister?" asked her mother.

"Helena is giving my parents quite a difficult time. She has her own idea of a woman's place in the world, her own notion of how she should spend her days, who she should marry . . ."

"I think this is a common theme in the Empire right now. Don't you agree, Aurora?"

"Mother, please!"

Evander laughed and rested his hand over Aurora's. "In fact, my sister will be arriving in Pompeii in a few days' time. I was hoping I could introduce you to her."

She nodded her approval. "I would like that very much. I think your sister and I will get along just fine."

Someone was knocking at the door again, and it was perfect timing. Her mother stood up and told them to relax in the garden while she went to greet the other guests. Giorgio and Pioppo rushed in to gather up her brother, the presents, and discarded linen wrappings from the ground, then shuffled away to prepare for the party.

When the flurry of activity settled down, Aurora realized that she was alone with Evander. His deep blue eyes rested on her face, and he drew his finger softly over her shoulder.

"I'm sorry I yelled at you the other day in the forum. I didn't know who you were, and when you refused to listen to me, I just thought you were being stubborn."

Aurora watched his eyes as he spoke and knew that he meant what he said. She felt like a dog with its tail between its legs. "And I'm sorry that I insulted you, threw *pugiones* at you with my eyes . . . my behavior was unacceptable."

He held her hands in his, "You were throwing *pugiones* at me?" he asked, amused.

"Small ones. No larger than a kitchen knife." She laughed, and he squeezed her hand.

"You did what you had to do to save your brother. If you want to know the truth, I thought you were amazing, just as I told you yesterday."

"You thought I was amazing?"

"Truly. So . . . can we call a truce between us?"

"Truce."

He gazed at her intently.

"Why are you looking at me like that?"

"Because you are beautiful," he answered simply.

She took in every detail of his face, the way his eyebrows framed his eyes, the fullness of his bottom lip. She looked down at her hand, now intertwined with his. Unfamiliar feelings flooded her, and she wasn't sure how to deal with them.

A poem by Sappho came to her mind, and she recited it silently, *When I look at you, my tongue is silent, a flame runs under my skin . . .*

"We're not children anymore, as I'm sure you've realized."

She blushed at the implication of his words.

"Do you still play the lyre?" he asked.

"I do."

"Will you play for me later?"

A vision of him reclining on her couch while she played music for him drifted through her mind.

"Evander—" Her eyes locked with his. She wanted to tell him that there was little she could refuse him. Instead, she stood up gracefully from the bench and smoothed down her dress. "Let's go join the party."

CHAPTER 6

Trebius Valens, one of two senior magistrates of Pompeii, stood like a triumphal column around which all the other guests were gathered. He was tall and robust with curly blond hair and had a charismatic and engaging personality. His booming voice echoed through the atrium, and it was no surprise that he was always the life of the party.

"They say that one drinks better in Nuceria, but they have never tasted the wine from the Fortunas Vineyard! And tonight, if our gracious host, Aurorus Fortunas, will allow me to be the master of revels, I will gladly determine the correct ratio of wine to water."

Abundant cheers mixed with groans went out from the guests.

"Oh, Trebby! You will have us drunk before midnight, and I so want to enjoy this party!" cried one of the women.

Marcus Tibertinus, the quiet and handsome *aedile* in charge of public works, held out his arms. "We all know that while Trebby does an outstanding job of upholding the law and order of our city, he should NOT, I repeat NOT be in charge of the wine!"

The guests roared with laughter and exchanged stories of past dinner parties that had gone awry, for Trebby loved his wine and loved it strong.

The laughter quieted when they realized that Aurora was standing in the entranceway of the atrium with an unknown man. A quiet murmur went up from the guests.

Aurora's father beckoned them over. "Now here is a man whom the fates have smiled upon. May I introduce everyone to Maximus Evandrus Mercurius the Second, of Mercurius Shipping & Trading. You may remember that his family lived in Pompeii before moving to Corinth ten years ago."

"Evander is our guest of honor tonight," explained her mother. "The goddess Fortuna placed him in the forum, close to my children, on the day of the earthquake. When my son was wounded, Evander carried him swiftly home. I was able to sew up the wound before my son had lost too much blood and all hope was gone. My husband and I are indebted to him for his kind act. Tonight's dinner is given in his honor."

The guests clapped enthusiastically for Evander. Lady Julia, wife of Marcus, stepped forward. She was beautiful and virtuous and sparkled like a gemstone. Aurora had always admired her for her strength and dedication to her family.

"Welcome home, Evander, and what a fine man you have become. We remember your parents well, and your sisters too. We are anxious to hear how everyone fares in Corinth. But first, tell us in your own words. What happened at the forum on the day of the earthquake?"

The circle of guests shuffled away from Trebius Valens and formed a semicircle around Evander. All eyes were on him now, eager to hear his story. Aurora stepped back and stood off to the side with her parents. This was an important moment for him, a reentry into Pompeian society, and she wanted to give him the stage.

"Mother, what do you really think of him?" she whispered, throwing a discreet look in Evander's direction.

Her mother smiled approvingly. "I think he is quite strapping. Intelligent, determined, confident—you may have found your match, Daughter."

"Hmm. I'm sure he suffers no lack of female attention."

She could see the men nodding in agreement as he told of the strange behavior of the animals and how it had been a portent of what was to come. She could also hear the sighs of the women as he recounted how he had pulled Teo out of the shattered glass. She realized that the women were completely infatuated with him. They didn't merely listen to him; they ravaged him with their eyes from head to toe. The women were in awe, as if a veritable god were standing before them.

Lady Claudia, wife of Trebius Valens, leaned close to her. "Watch out, dear girl, the she-wolves will be fighting over this one." Her loud, scratchy voice grated on Aurora's nerves, but she nodded politely and smiled. *No doubt your daughter will be one of them.*

Apparently seeking to reclaim the attention that had been stripped from him, Trebius Valens pushed his way forward. "Welcome home, Evander! Do you know that Rome is charging an exorbitant tax on unwed daughters of marrying age? Well, I have two of them! Please, won't you consider helping out an old man?"

Evander chuckled and held out his hand. "Pleased to meet you, sir."

"Likewise, and I welcome you back to the celebrated city of Pompeii. I hope you plan on attending some of our town meetings."

Evander spoke in a voice that exuded confidence and strength. "I certainly do plan on participating in city government, sir, and getting reacquainted with the good citizens of Pompeii."

"That's right," Trebby encouraged. "Never underestimate the power of the right contacts when considering how to promote your business." He held Evander's eye for an extra moment to make sure he had understood his meaning. "In fact, you and I should discuss your business plans more in depth at my home. I do have private baths, you know, and the most spectacular garden triclinium in all of Pompeii, shaded by a beautiful pergola."

"It sounds marvelous," said Evander.

"Now let me introduce you to my eldest daughter, Valentina. She will knock the sandals right off your feet." He scanned his eyes over the group of people in the atrium. "Valentina, come here, my dear. I want to introduce you to this impressive young man."

Aurora was galled, but not surprised. Trebby was always using his eldest daughter as bait for his business transactions. She and Valentina had never been more than passing friends because they could never find anything in common. Valentina resented Aurora for her brains as much as Aurora envied Valentina for her beauty.

Valentina sashayed slowly toward Evander, throwing a spiteful glance at Aurora. She was tall and voluptuous with long blond hair and seductive green eyes. She reminded Aurora of an evil sea nymph. Her turquoise dress was gorgeous, and she was adorned with sparkling jewelry from head to ankle. She held out her hands to Evander.

"Pleased to meet to you, Valentina," he said, kissing her hands.

"The pleasure is all mine, *Evander*." She sounded like a siren, sweet and alluring. It made Aurora sick to watch, and she looked away.

Everyone knew Valentina was an opportunist like her father, and her father was eager to marry her off before she deflowered herself with some hapless fool. Roman women of good birth and education were expected to be virgins on the night of their wedding; otherwise, they would shame their family. After birthing a few children, the laws relaxed. If a married woman wanted to find pleasure in the arms of a discreet man or handsome slave, so be it.

As Aurora looked at Valentina's ample bosom and low-cut dress, she found it hard to believe that she was still a virgin. In fact, she knew that some of Valentina's friends had come to her mother for remedies to terminate unwanted pregnancies.

A stab of jealousy pierced Aurora's heart. She didn't want another woman stealing Evander's attention from her, especially not someone as malicious as Valentina. She tried to appear composed, but her mood was quickly souring as she realized the dinner party was marred by the presence of a beautiful and conniving woman.

She hadn't anticipated competition. She had imagined that Evander would give her his undivided attention. Why she thought this, she couldn't say. Perhaps she had misread his interest in her. *Silly girl.*

Apollonius was right. Evander was most likely a rogue, a wealthy man with promiscuous habits. He probably sailed the Mediterranean, indulging himself at every port with the company of ravishing women. She could never hold his interest. She let out a sigh and tried to lose herself amongst the guests.

She wandered through the atrium, playing the part of hostess. Several guests were still talking about the earthquake and the smaller tremor that had followed it yesterday.

Lady Julia called her over. "Aurora, what a beauty you are tonight! Come and chat with us," she invited, kissing her on both cheeks.

Marcus and Bertus, her two strapping sons, leaned in and kissed her as well. Both Tiburtinus brothers were athletic, handsome, and educated. They had thick brown hair, hazel eyes, and bulging biceps. They were excellent discus throwers and had performed in many of Pompeii's athletic competitions. Unfortunately, Bertus, the younger brother, was wearing a sling around one arm.

"Aurora, you look stunning tonight," he complimented.

"Thank you, Bertus, but what happened to your arm?"

"A piece of the ceiling fell on me during the tremor. My shoulder was dislocated."

"I'm sorry to hear that. Was anyone else injured?" she asked.

"Father was near the Nucerian Gate and was almost thrown from his horse."

"It's a miracle that I didn't fall off and break my neck!" Marcus Tiburtinus the Elder said. "The ground just tossed me around like a boat on the water."

"Father, tell Aurora *why* you were near the Nucerian Gate," Marcus the Younger prompted with a mischievous smile on his face.

Lady Julia gave her son a hard look. "It is hardly appropriate dinner conversation."

"I am not easily shocked," replied Aurora. "You can tell me. What is it?"

"Some malefactor defaced the wall of the Nucerian gate with all kinds of anti-government graffiti," Marcus the Elder explained.

"That's not so unusual . . ."

He leaned forward and whispered in Aurora's ear. "And then defecated on the grass, as if to punctuate his words."

Aurora made a face of disgust. "All the tax money we've given to Vespasian to pay for public baths, and some fool does that?"

Lady Julia quickly tried to change the subject, all the while giving her husband and son a look of stern disapproval. She gently took Aurora's hands.

"I was sitting in the frigidarium at the Stabian Baths when the earthquake struck. The water tossed and churned, but the walls held up well. Unfortunately, some people took a fall on the slippery floor. Still, the earthquake wasn't as bad as the quake of seventeen years ago."

"I've heard a lot about that one . . ." Aurora trailed off as she glanced in Evander's direction.

"Of course you don't remember, dear, you were only a baby. Marcus the Younger was just a toddler, and I thought the very walls of the house were going to crumble." She shuddered as she remembered, then looked at her husband and sons. "I'm telling you all, these tremors are getting stronger!" There was a note of hysteria in her voice.

Trebius Valens walked over to their circle, placing his large hands on Lady Julia's shoulders. "Now, Julia, the decurions are holding a town meeting tomorrow afternoon at the basilica to discuss the frequency of these tremors. We are going to find the best way to safeguard our homes and businesses. Don't you worry, you know that Rome has the best city engineers in the whole Empire."

Trebby looked around the atrium. "Attention, everyone! The meeting at the basilica tomorrow will commence at the seventh hour after sunrise. I encourage you all to come."

Aurora's father walked over and looked at them gravely. "Something is not right. There are strange things happening in the city and at the water's edge. Have you not noticed how warm the water has been this summer? And whole sections of my vineyard have completely dried up and withered. That has never happened before."

Aurora's mother laced her arm through her husband's elbow. "Now, Aurorus, you know it has been a very hot summer. I see nothing strange about the water being warmer than usual. And enough talk of the earthquake! This is a dinner party—it's supposed to be fun!" She looked at the Tiburtinas family. "I think a little music and wine will take the edge off of all of us."

As if on cue, the musicians in the garden started to play a soothing hymn to Apollo. Myrrhine entered the atrium. "Dinner is served. Elders, please follow me out to the summer dining room."

Aurora gathered the younger guests to her with a sweep of her arms. "Our illustrious guest of honor, Evander Mercurius, will be reclining with us this evening."

A round of cheers went up for Evander. Everyone seemed energized to be in his presence, especially the Tiburtinas brothers, who were just a couple years younger than him.

The young men smacked him affectionately on the back, and the girls smiled and leered at him, especially Valentina, who told him in her siren voice what an honor it was to be dining in his distinguished presence.

Apollonius appeared, handsome and dapper in his best dinner attire, and asked everyone to follow him to the indoor dining room. His eyes quickly darted from Aurora to Valentina.

Evander held out both elbows. "Allow me to escort you two gorgeous ladies into dinner." Aurora painted a smile on her face and laced her arm through his, enjoying the warm, smooth feel of his skin. Valentina did the same, but crossed her free hand over to rest on Evander's large bicep and squeezed.

"I hear you have been living in Greece," she cooed.

"Yes, I have spent the last ten years at my family's home in Corinth, studying with a tutor and learning about my father's business."

"I have always wanted to visit the Greek Isles. You will tell me all about them at dinner, won't you?" she asked, her voice dripping with honey.

Aurora knew without a doubt that Valentina would recline on the same couch as Evander. She gritted her teeth. The seating arrangement would work to Valentina's advantage because, as the hostess, Aurora had to sit on a different couch than the guest of honor. There was no way around it.

Pioppo and Giorgio awaited them in the dining room with clean white towels in hand. Apollonius reminded everyone to step over the threshold of the dining room with their right foot first for good luck.

The couches were arranged around a short marble pedestal where the *mensa* or tabletop was to be placed.

Each couch was covered by a clean white sheet and adorned with plump red pillows, inviting the guests to recline and relax comfortably. Several oil lamps hung from the ceiling, casting soft shadows over the entire room, and incense was burning on a small shrine built into the wall behind the couches. The mood was set perfectly for dinner and romance.

"What a beautiful dining room!" exclaimed Priscila, Valentina's younger sister. "So romantic." She sighed as she looked around at the red-and-black wall panels and frescoes depicting the great love affairs of the gods.

There was Venus with Mars, who was donning his great war helmet, Jupiter and Io stealing illicit moments before he changed her into a white heifer, and Apollo with Daphne, her arms turning into the outstretched branches of a laurel tree.

The slave boys removed the guests' sandals, then washed and dried their feet with cool, perfumed water. It was considered bad manners to step up onto the couches with unwashed feet.

Apollonius knelt down before Aurora. "Allow me, Mistress." He unwrapped her laces from her calves to her ankles, removed her dinner sandals and began to wash her feet. When he was done, he stood up, leaned forward, and whispered in her ear, "Don't let *her* rankle you. You are a beautiful woman."

He had warned her to stay away from Evander, so what did it matter? She didn't understand his reasoning for saying that, but she nodded her thanks and squeezed his hand.

When she turned to lie down, she saw that Evander was watching her with an annoyed look on his face. Well, she didn't need to explain to him that she shared a close friendship with the eldest slave brother. It wasn't his concern.

She gestured to him to lie down on the couch closest to her, reserved for the guest of honor. Nobody could sit between them, and as custom dictated, host and guest of honor could easily converse. The problem was that someone could still lie close *behind* him.

"Come, everyone, there's plenty of room on the couches. Make yourselves comfortable," Aurora invited.

Marcus the Younger reclined next to Aurora, and Bertus lay on the third couch between Priscila and a girl named Stefania, the fuller's daughter. The town fuller was a client of her father's and was often invited to dine with them. Priscila, who was always in the shadow of Valentina, couldn't have been happier, for Bertus was an outgoing and handsome young man, and with his injured shoulder would need a little help with dinner.

Finally, and with as much panache as she could muster, Valentina stepped up onto the second couch. Aurora fumed inwardly at her new adversary, who was now devouring Evander with her eyes. She examined every bare stretch of skin and muscle from his toes to his thighs. Then, with a quick glance at Aurora, she smugly sank down on the couch behind him, her sumptuous breasts nearly popping out of her bodice and into his back. She ran her hand seductively through her long blond hair and gave everyone a brilliant smile.

Valentina certainly knew how to attract the attention of a man, but Aurora thought her ignorant and shallow, always wanting to be the center of attention like her father, Trebby. She wondered what was going through Evander's mind and whether or not he liked that kind of girl.

Of course he likes that kind of girl.

What was she thinking? Men were men, and when it came to women all they seemed to notice was a pretty face, big breasts, and an ample bottom to hold on to. She wondered if intelligence even entered into the equation.

The fireflies in her stomach returned as Evander's soulful blue eyes connected with hers. It was as if he was trying to tell her something.

Meanwhile, slaves brought in *mulsum*, a sweet wine boiled with honey and spices, and gave a delicate glass to each of them. As they sipped their drinks and conversed cheerfully, Apollonius entered the triclinium and began to play the lyre. Aurora closed her eyes to enjoy the sweet sounds made by the plucking of the strings—and to will herself into a better mood. The music reverberated off of the dining room walls and echoed through the domus, enchanting as a tale from olden days.

Next came the *gustatio*. Hot ash-cooked eggs surrounded by green olives and an assortment of cheeses, all arranged beautifully on a large silver platter. Aurora began the dinner by picking up olives and small pieces of cheese and setting them on her plate. This was the signal that the other guests could now serve themselves as well.

"Evander, what was life like in Corinth? Did you like it better than Pompeii?" Bertus asked. He popped an olive into his mouth, removed the meat with his teeth, then spit the pit onto the floor. "I heard that they don't like Romans in Greece, is it true?"

Evander finished the cheese he was eating and washed it down with a sip of wine. "The truth is, I love Corinth. It is a modern city filled with people from all over the world, but mostly Romans, Greeks, and Jews. There is always something interesting going on, whether it be theater performances, musical concerts, or athletic competitions. It is an exciting place to live."

Aurora's heart sank. He would never be happy in a small town again. "Did you ever miss Pompeii?" she asked.

"Of course I missed Pompeii. But remember, I was only fourteen when I left."

Aurora saw him stiffen ever so slightly as Valentina ran her finger down the middle of his back. "And what about the girls?" she murmured. "I hear they are not as pretty as the Romans."

"There are many pretty girls in Corinth, but none as beautiful as all of you." Evander gestured to the young women with his wineglass, then made a toast.

"To the prettiest girls," he said as he winked at Aurora.

"To the prettiest girls," the men echoed.

The girls giggled and blushed at the compliment. Valentina finished off her glass of wine and turned her attention to the fuller's daughter. "Stefania, it must be such a nice treat for you to eat dinner in a house that doesn't smell of urine."

"And it must be nice for you to eat in the company of people who have good manners," Stefania shot back. They all laughed heartily at her witty retort, but Valentina was offended.

"Come now, Valentina, it's all in good fun," Aurora said. "You can't dish out insults and not be prepared to get one in return. Stefania's father may not run the city, but he makes a good living as the town fuller."

Evander looked over his shoulder at Valentina. "Would you like to hear more about Greece?" he asked, obviously trying to distract her.

"Oh, Evander," she said, suddenly demure, "why, yes, I would love to hear you tell me all about it." She smiled and rested her jewelry-clad hand on his shoulder.

"Well then," he began, "Greece is a land of great beauty that will steal your breath away. There are majestic white temples reaching up to the skies of Olympia and sapphire waters, bluer and clearer than you could ever imagine." He paused for a second and looked around at their rapt faces.

"There are dolphins that jump out of the sea and race with the boats of the fishermen, and at sunset the sky is painted a glowing orange-red. Some of the islands have white sand, some have black, and some even have fire mountains that spit out molten rock."

Everyone sat and listened, almost without breathing, trans-fixed by the incredible description that Evander gave of Greece.

"I've heard of those fire mountains," said Bertus. "I would love to have the opportunity to see one up close."

"Yes," agreed Marcus, "I imagine it must be exciting to watch fire roll down a mountain. I mean, we have Vesuvius here, but the only thing rolling down its flanks are olives and grapes."

Everybody laughed at his comment.

The second course was now being served, and the aroma of slow-roasted meat filled the air. Mouthwatering chunks of wild boar rubbed with spices were piled high in the middle of a painted ceramic platter. Roasted onions, beets, and parsnips surrounded the meat, and all had been drizzled with olive oil and garum, the salty, fermented fish sauce that infused everything with flavor.

Aurora called Pioppo over to her. "Why has Teo not come down for dinner?"

"He says that his leg is hurting him, Mistress. In other words, he wanted to eat dinner in his room with the dog."

Aurora sighed. "That boy does whatever he pleases, and Mother lets him get away with it. Please tell him that I will come to check on him later." She turned her attention back to her dinner guests and smiled. "How do the Corinthians feel about education?" she asked.

"They place a high value on education, as most Greeks do," Evander answered. "They value virtue, beauty, and the stable equilibrium of the soul."

Aurora was intrigued. "What exactly is the stable equilibrium of the soul?"

"It is the state of being balanced so that one can choose an action knowingly, and for its own sake."

They wrinkled their eyebrows at Evander, prompting him to give a better explanation. Valentina moved closer to him, pretending to be interested in a philosophical discussion.

"Aristotle believed that being virtuous must be expressed through actions and that a person should strive for the highest moral character by doing good works."

"In other words," explained Marcus, "it is not enough to *say* you are a good person or *think* you are a good person, you must *manifest* it through your soul, through your decisions and your habits. Aristotle was a brilliant teacher."

"Yes," Evander said. "As was Plato before him."

He took the loaf of freshly baked bread, broke off a chunk, and soaked up the olive oil left on his plate. "But many of the Greeks resent the Romans for colonizing their cities, stealing their art, and exploiting their resources," he added.

"Resent us? They should love us!" Marcus exclaimed with a sweep of his arm. "We have contributed so much to their cities. Great Augustus, gods rest his soul, brought peace and stability to the whole Empire. We have built solid roads for trade and travel and constructed aqueducts that bring fresh water to all. Not to mention our beautiful baths that keep people clean and free of disease!"

"All true," said Evander. "The Romans are great city planners, but Greek civilization was flourishing long before the Romans arrived. The Greeks didn't need our help. The Romans needed them. We have taken their doctors, philosophers, teachers, art, and religion."

"And we have improved on all of it!" Marcus countered.

Aurora cleared her throat. "As Horace once said, *Captive Greece captured her rude conqueror.* That is to say, we *have* borrowed much from the Greeks. But as Marcus said, we have also given back much in return. Although we shouldn't be so egocentric to assume that everyone loves the Romans, or our way of life."

Evander looked at Aurora with respect in his eyes and nodded. "Well said."

Valentina's face turned red. She could never compete with Aurora intellectually, so she tried another strategy. "Evander, what about the wives?" she asked sweetly, rubbing his calf with her pretty toes. "I hear that the Greek men keep them locked inside their houses."

Evander shifted subtly away from Valentina and moved his leg. "It's true that Greek women don't enjoy the same freedom as Roman women. Greek men tend to keep their women on a short leash. But at least everyone strives to educate themselves, even the women," he answered, looking over his shoulder. "There is competition among the families to procure the best tutors and gain entry into the finest schools, although women are usually educated in the home."

Aurora made a satisfied sound. "Thank the gods for that!

There can be no progress for women without education. It is the only platform that truly elevates the civility of a society. Without it, we are barbarians."

"So you think girls should be educated as well, beyond basic reading and writing?" Priscila asked.

"Absolutely! We have plenty of women right here in Pompeii who have taken their place in society. Look at Eumachia, patroness of the cloth trade, and Lady Faustilla, the moneylender."

"And what about your mother, Lady Lucina? She is a trained medica, and you are following in her footsteps. That's very impressive," Evander said.

Aurora appreciated his compliment. Yes, she was educated, and she was glad he approved. She could speak Latin and Greek better than many and had studied a fair share of Greek and Roman literature, but suddenly she was feeling inferior. Evander was worldly and intelligent, as Apollonius had said. He had been living in a large, bustling city for the last ten years. What could he possibly want with a girl from Pompeii?

Dinner ended with a bowl of fresh figs drizzled with honey, and Aurora could tell that the guests were feeling the relaxing glow of the wine. Bertus was flirting shamelessly with Priscila and Stefania, and Evander and Valentina were laughing at a joke told by Marcus. Overall, it had turned into a very nice dinner party.

Aurora closed her eyes as she savored a sip of wine.

Evander brushed his fingers over her arm. "Let's take a walk around the peristyle." He sat up and called for Manolo to put his sandals back on, then picked up hers. "Allow me," he said with a twinkle in his eye. "No need to call your slave boy." He glanced at Apollonius, who was still playing the lyre.

Valentina tried desperately to get Evander's attention, but he pretended not to hear her. Marcus moved swiftly over to her couch and began lathering her with silly compliments.

Aurora sucked in her breath as Evander's warm hand came around her bare ankle. He took his time lacing up her sandal straps, his strong fingers tickling the sensitive skin of her feet and calves. By the time he was finished, her heart was throbbing and her body felt flushed. He held out his hands to help her up but pulled a little too hard, causing her to bump right into his chest. She giggled, and he put his hands around her waist to steady her.

"I like you when you've had some wine; you're more relaxed, fun even," he told her.

"Are you saying that I'm a bore otherwise?"

"You could never be boring, but you are too serious for a girl of your age."

She gave him a cheeky look. "Well then, why don't you show me how to have a little fun?"

CHAPTER 7

urora felt light-headed and happy from the wine as she looped her arm through Evander's and leaned on him for support. They walked into the colonnaded garden, where a refreshing breeze rustled through the leaves of the olive trees.

The floor around the peristyle sparkled in the moonlight, and they strolled leisurely over the black-and-white mosaic pieces that were arranged in delightful geometric designs.

She loved the way the light of the flickering oil lamps danced all around them, mimicking the twinkling of the stars in the black sky. A soft and enchanting melody echoed through the garden, and it gave an aura of mystery to the summer night.

She also loved the fact that Evander had chosen to stroll with her alone and had not invited Valentina to join them. *Perhaps Apollonius was wrong, after all.*

Arm in arm, they continued slowly down the narrow promenade of the garden. Aurora couldn't help the smile that spread across her face.

"What are you grinning about?" he asked her.

"I am taking pleasure in a magical night." The wine had loosened her tongue, and she glanced up at him.

"And what is so magical about it?" He tilted his head toward her, waiting for her response.

She chose her words carefully. "All is right with the world tonight. Family and friends surround me, we have just eaten a delicious dinner, and now we are enjoying a leisurely stroll through the garden. The music, the stars, it is all so . . . enchanting. Don't you agree?"

They were at the far end of the peristyle now, the trees and bushes blocking them from view. He let go of her arm and leaned against a column, pulling her to him.

"Do I not factor into your list of what is right in the world?"

She looked at him curiously in the flickering lamplight. "Well, of course you do. You've captivated us all with your stories of Corinth. Valentina was hanging on your every word."

"Yes, but I wasn't trying to impress *her*."

She gave a little shrug of her shoulders.

"I want to be *more* than a friend to you, Aurora, surely you can see that."

More than a friend? Her soul began to soar. But what were his true intentions?

"What I'm trying to say is that I would like to spend more time with you, just the two of us. I want to get to know you again." He searched her eyes for answers. "Do you feel the same way about me?"

"Well, I—"

But before she had a chance to answer, his lips came down on hers, and he wrapped her in his arms. He felt solid and strong, and his kiss turned her insides to fire.

She lost her breath as his tongue swirled inside her mouth, and heat broke out over her skin. She kissed him back, her tongue gently dancing with his. He tasted of sweet wine and honey.

She could feel his hardness through her stola, and his scent was unimaginably arousing. He smelled like a mixture of sea pine and musk, and she felt more intoxicated by him than by the wine she had drunk.

He ended the kiss and leaned his head against the column, eyes fixed on her face. "I haven't stopped thinking about you since the day I saw you at the market." He pulled on one of her long curls, then released it and watched it bounce back into place.

She tried to gather her wits. "Tell me the truth: Were you following me that day?"

"Yes."

She threw back her head and laughed. "It is true what they say, then, a drunk man cannot lie."

"Who says I'm drunk? I'm far from it." He kissed the side of her neck and nibbled playfully on her ear. "But at least I am honest."

"So much for the fair goddess Fortuna placing you close to the children . . ." She giggled and looked at his muscular chest, well defined beneath his tunic. The base of his neck was exposed, revealing a patch of dark hair, and she reached out to touch it. She smoothed her fingers over his warm skin, across the top of his chest, and down one arm, realizing that she wanted more of him.

"Seriously, Evander, why were you following me?"

"I had to know who you were."

"Why?"

"Because I thought you were beautiful, and I couldn't let you slip away."

Warmed by his words, she pulled him closer. Her lips found his, and they kissed each other again in the darkness. She felt her body loosen and melt into his. He was aroused, and she was the object of his desire. She was amazed at the furious way her body responded to him.

"When you came to help me in the dog booth, I was intrigued by you," she admitted.

"And why was that?" He loosened his hold on her.

"Your eyes seemed familiar, and there was something about you . . . something that made me feel safe."

"You feel safe with me," he echoed, taking her hands.

"And I liked the way you handled Teo."

His eyes caught the flicker of an oil lamp. "There's nothing more you want to tell me?"

"What do you want to hear?"

He tipped her chin up and kissed her sweetly. "How do you feel when we're together?"

She stared at him silently. *I fear that nothing will ever be the same again.*

He waited patiently for her reply.

"I appreciate that you are cultured, intelligent, and you seem to be a man of good morals. Aristotle would be proud," she finally answered, dodging his question.

"And you, Aurora of the rosy-fingered dawn," he paused for effect, "you are educated, accomplished, well-spoken—and able to handle rude dinner guests." They both laughed at his reference to Valentina. "Did I mention beautiful as well?" He trailed wet kisses down her jaw and neck.

She was falling under his spell, and if she didn't stop this soon, she might give away more of herself than she wanted to. She gave his chest a little push. "The wine has made you amorous. Tomorrow, I will not believe a word of what you have said to me tonight."

"Then I shall scratch a verse upon your wall, and you shall read it in the morning and know that I have been true."

She humored him with a smile. "Let's go listen to Apollonius play the lyre."

"Apollonius, your very handsome *slave boy*?" he said a little too loudly.

"Yes, him. We are very close. I consider him family, and he always watches out for my best interests."

"I see."

"Come, now. Let's go find some laurel wreaths to wrap around our heads before the wine gives us a headache," she urged.

"I don't want to put on a laurel wreath, Aurora. I want to feel the wine in my blood and you in my arms," he protested, embracing her again. "Don't you know how that old adage goes? *Whoever loves, let him flourish. Let him perish who knows not love . . ."*

They gazed at each other for a moment, then he gave her one last, lingering kiss. *"Let him perish twice over, whoever forbids love."*

~

THE MUSICIANS HAD SWITCHED from relaxing dinner music to the rhythmic beating of African drums, causing the dinner guests to dance shamelessly around the domus. They had formed a line with Trebius Valens at the head. He was leading them out into the garden and around the colonnade.

Lady Claudia, Valentina's mother, pulled on Evander's arm.

"Come, Evander. You must dance with us!" she cried in her loud, scratchy voice. "It would be a crime if you didn't spend a little time indulging your elders. We would like the chance to talk with you also." She winked at him, then put his hands on her ample hips and obliged him to follow her.

The line of drunken dancers swayed and trotted to the music. They soon broke into hysterical laughter as they danced around the garden paths, bumping hips and breasts and bottoms.

"Neptune's big, hairy balls! Who taught you how to dance, Trebby?" Marcus the Elder shouted above the music.

"Your wife!" he shot back, and they all broke into loud laughter again at the implication that the lovely and virtuous Lady Julia had dabbled with the notorious Trebius Valens.

But Lady Julia, warm with the glow of wine, was now behind Evander. She grabbed on to his fine hips and squeezed. "I've got me a fine piece of meat right here, Trebby. I don't need your fat ass to dance with anymore!"

"Aw, come on, Jules, you know you're hot for me!"

They howled with laughter as they continued snaking around

the garden insulting each other. They were half dancing, half holding on to each other to stay upright, but living this moment to the fullest, even if they might regret it in the morning.

Aurora stood at the garden entrance watching the scene play out before her. Her stomach hurt from laughing. She was enjoying herself immensely, something she always found hard to do. Evander was right. She was much too serious for a young woman of eighteen, especially since her brother had died. She knew that it was important to mourn those who were gone, but maybe just for a little while.

It was also important to go on living, to squeeze every last drop of joy out of each moment. Hades chariots would come soon enough. *The wine urges me on, the bewitching wine . . .* She grabbed on to Marcus the Younger's hips as the line of party revelers passed by and joined in the dancing. It was high time she had a little fun.

CHAPTER 8

*E*vander was once again the center of attention, exactly what he didn't want to be. But he decided that socializing with the elders was the right thing to do, even though he would have preferred to recline on a comfortable couch in a private corner of the atrium with Aurora. He did have a business to promote, after all.

He saw that Aurora had joined in the dancing, and she looked like she was truly enjoying herself. He had monopolized her attention tonight after dinner, and he supposed that he should give her a little space. Maybe he was being overbearing and presumptuous, but he couldn't help it. Something about her drew him to her, like Odysseus to the siren's song.

She delighted him for reasons that he never knew were important. She was passionate, educated, and philosophical. She knew how to navigate a social function, and she had much to contribute in the way of intellectual conversation. She knew who she was, she stood up for her beliefs, and she didn't need a man to define her.

And by Hercules, she was beautiful. Not the kind of beauty

that was painted on with sticks of kohl and powdered colors. No, she had the kind of beauty that radiated out from her soul.

He wanted to be important to her.

She listened to him, scolded him, and didn't seem to care if it offended him.

He found her irresistible.

But his father had sent him home to rub noses with the business owners and city leaders, hoping he would make a match that would solidify his shipping routes in this part of the Mediterranean. *Money is money, and love is love, and the two don't always agree.*

No matter how much he cared for Aurora, he knew that his father would have the final word.

After another hour of singing and dancing with the elders in the garden, he decided it was time to go home. He said his good-byes to everyone, but he couldn't find Aurora. She must have gone upstairs to check on her brother, or perhaps she was already asleep. He walked quietly through the atrium to the front door.

A woman moved in the dark shadows of the vestibule.

"Aurora? Is that you?"

Her hands came around his neck, and she pulled him down for a kiss like she had done in the garden. She bit his lip and thrust her tongue into his mouth, surprising him with her boldness. He wrapped his arms around her, then realized that everything felt wrong. This wasn't Aurora's body or her unique, alluring scent. He leaned back and strained to see her face in the darkness.

"Come on, Evander. Don't be such a prude!" The woman laughed and kissed him hard on the lips again. Just then an oil lamp illuminated the hallway, and Apollonius appeared like a pillar of stone, his eyes cold and accusing.

Evander disentangled himself from Valentina and stomped toward Apollonius. "It's not what you think," he said under his breath.

The handsome slave kept quiet, his face frozen like a marble statue.

"If you tell Aurora, you'll only hurt her. Now please tell Manolo that I am ready to go." He glanced back at Valentina. "That was a dirty trick."

"What do you see in that dormouse, anyway?" she hissed.

Evander turned and stalked out of the domus, his long, angry strides carrying him briskly through the narrow streets to the home of his ancestors. His family had lived there for hundreds of years, just down the street from the large theater.

He entered the hallway, stalked through the atrium, and out into the garden. He turned right and entered the library, his favorite room. A fresco of Minerva, Goddess of Wisdom, looked down at him from the wall.

He thought of Aurora and the misunderstanding it would cause between them if the slave boy revealed what he had seen. He had been caught kissing another woman in a dark and empty hallway, just hours after he had kissed Aurora in the garden.

Not wise at all.

Valentina had tricked him. But how could he have been so stupid?

Manolo entered the room, flustered and flushed as though he had run the whole way home. "Dominus?"

Evander let out a frustrated sigh. "I've been played for a fool."

The slave removed his sandals and toga, and Evander fell into his favorite sleeping couch, his body exhausted but his mind overflowing with thoughts of Aurora.

The cool night air blew quietly through the silky curtains of the library. He thought he felt the earth rumble beneath him as he fell asleep, but decided he was too tired to care.

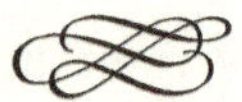

CHAPTER 9

The next morning, Aurora woke slowly and relished those moments between dreams and waking. Her thoughts turned to Evander, and images of him flowed through her mind. She remembered the feel of his skin as they strolled arm in arm through the garden, the way he had embraced her, the sensation of his warm lips on hers. She sighed deeply and contentedly as she thought about the special moments they had shared together in the garden last night.

He had told her that he wanted to be more than her friend. *What does that mean?* Did he really want to pursue something long-term? Now that the wine haze was clearing, she could think about everything coherently. She stepped down from her bed feeling a little like she was floating.

"Myrrhine, is there fresh bread yet?" she called down from the balcony.

"Yes, Mistress. Apollonius just returned from the bakery. A table has been set for you in the garden," the slave woman answered.

"Thank you, I'll be right down." She slipped on a light cloak and her morning sandals, then looked at her reflection in the polished silver mirror on her bedside table. "By Hercules, I need to get to the baths!" Her curly hair was a tumbled mess, and her eyes were puffy from sleep and wine.

She stepped carefully down the wooden stairs to a small *latrina* that sat inside the kitchen, separated by a thin divider. A pot of water was boiling on the hearth, and four round loaves of freshly baked bread sat on the kitchen shelves.

When she was done, she walked through the narrow arched hallway that led from the kitchen to the garden, a passageway usually used by the slaves.

A table had been set up under the portico in the shade. Apollonius was busy setting out bread and a glass bowl of fruit. She sat down on a cushioned chair to enjoy her breakfast. A thrush sang merrily on the branches of a strawberry tree, then swooped down to eat some scraps left on the ground from last night's dinner.

"I've brought you some fresh water from the city fountain." Apollonius's voice sounded tired. "Hold out your hands." He poured clean water over them, dried them with a napkin, then filled up her glass. She sipped at the water and made a face.

"It tastes like rotten eggs."

Apollonius sighed. "I'll bring you something else to drink."

She picked up a wedge of bread and took a bite. *Delicious.* The crust had just the right amount of crunch, and the inside was still soft and warm from the oven.

Ah, Priscus, what would we do without you? His bakery was one of the largest in Pompeii, and his wood-burning oven could hold over eighty loaves of bread. He often called on her mother for special ointments to heal the burns his slaves suffered from the hot embers.

Teo loved to visit his bakery in the afternoons, either to buy a sweet treat or to pet the donkeys as they rested in their stall after a long morning of turning the mills that ground the wheat into flour.

Apollonius returned to the garden and handed Aurora a

ceramic mug filled with a mixture of wine, honey, and spices. She promptly dipped her piece of bread into the hot drink and ate it.

"Delicious. Where are my parents?" she asked between bites.

"Still asleep, Mistress."

"And Teo?"

"Pioppo took him and the dog for a walk down to the harbor to see Dominus Mercurius's ships. They did not want to wake you."

He spun on his heel and left the garden as if her questions were annoying him. It was then that she realized he was upset. Had he seen her kissing Evander in the garden last night? Was he angry because she hadn't heeded his advice?

Apollonius returned and set a small platter of fresh apricots in front of her. They had been cut in half and drizzled with honey. She took a bite out of one.

"Quite a dinner party, don't you think?" She licked the honey off her fingers and looked up at him. Dark circles under his eyes showed that he had gotten little sleep.

"One that I would rather forget," he said flatly.

"Are you going to tell me what's bothering you?"

"No, I am not." His eyes were downcast, avoiding her probing gaze.

"Apollonius!"

"Please, Aurora, do not push me! It has not been an easy night."

"You just don't want to see me with him!" she cried, "And I don't know why!"

Myrrhine walked into the garden and gave her son a hard look.

"Are you ready to go to the baths, Aurora?"

"Yes." She stood up and looked at Apollonius, trying to figure him out. "You and your brothers may take it easy today. Get some rest," she ordered. Apollonius glanced at his mother, then bowed and took his leave.

Aurora grabbed a few pieces of fruit and walked over to the

lararium. She set the fruit on the altar, closed her eyes and prayed to the Lares and Penates, the guardian deities of the household, to protect her family as they went about their day.

Myrrhine waited patiently, holding Aurora's bath sandals and a wooden box. Inside were clean strigils, a container of massage oil infused with lavender, nail clippers, and a comb.

"You might want to wrap a scarf around that hair, Mistress. But don't worry, you are beautiful even when you are a mess." Myrrhine laughed. "Let's go, or soon it will be time for *prandium!*"

"Yes, just give me a moment." She walked out into the garden until she came to the column where Evander had kissed her for the first time. Sure enough, she saw a new scratching in the plaster. *Meus es. You are mine.*

AURORA STEPPED out onto the narrow street feeling like it was the first day of the world. Her chest was filled with joy, and she reveled in the colors surrounding her: the multicolored marble stones of the sidewalk, the red cinnabar paint of the houses, the frescoes that adorned the building walls. Everything seemed brighter, more vibrant, more alive.

She walked to the end of her street and stopped at the corner fountain to splash cool water over her face.

"What a glorious morning! Don't you think so, Myrrhine?"

The slave woman nodded. "It's wonderful, Mistress. Especially for one who has been struck by Cupid's arrow after long last."

"That's not true."

Myrrhine rolled her eyes. "Oh, you don't think so?"

"Definitely not." But Aurora couldn't fight the feeling that everything seemed new to her, as if she were experiencing it for the first time. She felt exhilarated, energetic, and refreshed.

Is this what love feels like?

She smiled and hummed to herself as they continued down the

cobblestone street to the Stabian Baths. But an unhappy thought nagged at her.

"Myrrhine, why does Apollonius dislike Evander?"

"I'm sure he doesn't dislike him, Aurora. He just doesn't want you to get hurt. And perhaps he feels that he is being replaced."

"Replaced? No one can ever replace Apollonius."

"Listen, my child, now that you are grown up and seeking a husband, it is no longer appropriate for you to have such an attachment to your slave."

Tears sprang to Aurora's eyes. "He is not just my slave, Myrrhine, and neither are you. He is like a brother to me, and you are part of my family."

"Yes, my sweet girl, but in the eyes of society we are still just your slaves. And as hard as that may be to accept, especially for me and my boys, you know that it's true."

"It doesn't mean that I like it."

Myrrhine looked at her kindly. "Do you remember when your father first brought us to your home? You were just a little girl. You and Apollonius were like two peas in a pod, always together, always laughing."

A lump formed in Aurora's throat. "I wish it could be like that forever."

"But it can't. Don't you see? Everything is coming full circle. If your heart tells you to be with Evander, you must move toward him and away from my son. Perhaps Evander is the one you have been waiting for."

"And Apollonius?"

"He will find his path as well, don't you worry."

Aurora pondered over everything Myrrhine had told her, feeling a bit like she was being torn in two. When they arrived at the Stabian Baths, Myrrhine handed a few small coins over to the female attendant for the entrance fee. *"Bene lava,"* she wished them. "Enjoy your bath."

They walked along the east side of the palaestra, under a long portico, and entered into the women's changing room. The air inside the baths was hot and humid and filled with the calming scent of lavender.

Beneath a vaulted ceiling, the walls were decorated with elaborate stuccowork, and diamond-cut mosaics decorated the floor. All around the room were niches for one's personal belongings, and under the shelving was a marble bench that ran along the sides and back of the room. A small, cold pool sat at the other end.

Aurora walked to an empty cubicle and stripped off her clothes.

"No exercise today?" Myrrhine asked as she folded the clothes and set them on the shelf.

Aurora thought about the three glasses of Falernum wine she had consumed last night and shook her head. Trebius Valens, who had been in charge of the wine-to-water-ratio, had left out most of the water.

"Just the baths today. I will go for a walk along the beach later."

The baths were crowded, but she didn't mind, for she felt a happiness this morning that she hadn't known since her brother died.

"I want to start with a hot bath." She slipped her feet into her wooden bath sandals. Together they walked through the rooms of the bathhouse until they came to the caldarium, the hottest bath of all.

Myrrhine took the pins out of Aurora's hair, and she kicked off her shoes. She stepped carefully into the large bath and let herself sink down into the steamy depths of the water. She closed her eyes. Leaning her head back on the marble edge, she let thoughts of Evander drift through her mind. She pictured him in his white toga and remembered his fresh, clean smell.

Most of all, she remembered his eyes. Piercing and intensely blue, they made her forget the world when she looked into them. She sighed just thinking about those beautiful eyes.

Evander was cultured and refined and needed a woman who

complemented him. She was the granddaughter of a great surgeon, and her mother was a doctor as well. Her father was a wealthy, equestrian landowner with vineyards and estates all around Pompeii.

But she was quiet and introspective, never the life of the party. And although she was educated, did it even matter? Most men wanted an exotic woman who dressed like an Egyptian but followed their commands like a slave.

She became aware of a group of women who had entered the caldarium. They were laughing and gossiping about men in the usual manner. She kept her eyes closed and didn't pay attention to them until she heard Evander's name.

"He arrived a few weeks ago . . . ten painted ships . . ."

Her ears pricked to attention as she strained to hear them better.

". . . wealthy as King Midas . . ."

". . . my father saw him in the baths, hung like Africanus . . ."

The women erupted into a fit of giggles at the mention of his manly attributes. Aurora smiled, a blush breaking out over her neck and face. Their conversation continued.

"I've reclined with him at dinner . . . gorgeous as Apollo . . . will dine with him again this day of Venus . . ."

What? Who is going to see him again on Friday?

She felt jealousy streak through her. She opened her eyes and turned her head to see who was speaking. Valentina and her friends! The girls had their backs turned to her, and she quickly turned around and sank down lower in the water.

"He's come home to find a wife," Valentina explained, "and my father told me that we are just the kind of family he is looking to marry into."

Aurora bit her tongue. As she put the pieces together in her mind, the situation started to make sense.

Emperor Vespasian had died a month ago, leaving his son Titus on the throne. But Titus was in love with the Jewish Queen

Berenice, and the Romans mistrusted her. The senatorial and equestrian classes were unsettled. They would never accept an outsider as empress of the Roman Empire.

The transfer of political power always brought uncertainty, and that was precisely why Evander had come home. He had come to protect his family's wealth and prosperity on this side of the Mediterranean.

She wondered how much Evander had actually discussed with Trebius Valens and how much Valentina was exaggerating to her friends. Still, he was planning on eating dinner at her house? When did this transpire? Leave it to Valentina to feed into all of her insecurities. She always had.

Aurora climbed out of the water and marched over to her.

"You obviously know that I was with Evander in the garden last night. Did you also know that I was behind you in the bath, listening to every word?"

Valentina looked surprised, then scowled disapprovingly at Aurora's naked, dripping body. "You really should eat more. You're much too thin to ever please a man; he would have no flesh to sink his plow into." The group of girls broke out laughing. "And if you think a few kisses matter to a man like Evander, think again."

"Ugh!" Aurora spun on her heel and stalked out of the caldarium.

"Mistress! You're going to burn your feet!" Myrrhine ran after her, waving the wooden sandals in the air. Aurora grabbed her shoes, threw them down at the entranceway, and stuffed her feet into them, not caring who she was blocking.

"I think I'll take a cold bath now," she announced. A group of ladies stopped abruptly to let her pass.

"You really shouldn't do that, it's too much of a shock for your body!" cried Myrrhine.

Aurora was so angry that she didn't even feel the chill of the water as she slid down into the pool, submerging herself to her neck. The water was cold and dulled all her senses.

Did Valentina really have the kind of family he would want to marry into?

Had she misunderstood Evander's intentions?

A young man of Evander's education and wealth would want to position himself strategically, perhaps even becoming a member of the senate one day. Although her family was of equestrian class, they had no real ties to the emperor. She came from an old Samnite bloodline that had deep roots in Pompeii, long before the city became a Roman colony.

Perhaps Evander wanted to be with her, but only temporarily. Perhaps he just needed her family to help reintroduce him to Pompeian society. She cupped handfuls of cold water over her face. Gods, she felt like a fool. The man had given her a kiss, not an iron ring.

Shivering, she stood up silently and let Myrrhine wrap her in a bath tunic. It was time to clean her skin. She must have had quite a scowl on her face because women moved out of the way when they saw her coming.

She entered a warm, dry room and headed straight for one of the massage tables. A bronze brazier filled with burning charcoal stood at the end of the room, giving off pleasant heat. A young female slave spread out a clean, dry sheet, then took the wooden box from Myrrhine and extracted the tools she needed.

She rubbed Aurora's skin with fragrant lavender oil and massaged her. Aurora's muscles began to relax and her anger began to dissipate. It was replaced by sadness and yearning, and she started to cry.

"Why are you crying, Mistress?"

"Why am I not married yet, Myrrhine?"

"Because no one is good enough for you."

Aurora snorted. "You sound like my mother. Really, Myrrhine, I'm eighteen years old. I should have three children by now!"

"But you have said no to every suitor, remember?"

"Because I can't bear the thought of someone touching me that I don't love."

"And your parents are a bit protective of you since your brother died."

"Yes, yes, I know. But still, I'm not daft or deformed in any way. One would think that it wouldn't be so hard . . ."

"The gods have their reasons, Aurora. Sometimes we don't understand, but later the reason becomes apparent."

The bath slave began to scrape the oil and dirt from Aurora's skin with a metal strigil. Aurora closed her eyes again, enjoying the gentle scrape of the smooth instrument over her soft skin.

She was beginning to think that she would never find a husband, not the kind she wanted, anyway. She wanted a man of good character, and that meant he needed to be kind to others, the way her father was kind to their slaves. He also needed to be intelligent or she wouldn't respect him.

Most of all, she did not want a man who was boastful or arrogant. She couldn't bear to be with someone who longed to hear his own voice all night long. She wanted a man who had the courage to stand up for what was right, to show compassion for those in need.

She wanted a man like her father. He was good and just and treated her with respect. And when he reprimanded her, he did it gently and wisely, and she knew that she had deserved it.

Could Evander be the man she had been waiting for? He had been in the forum that day for a reason. He had helped Teo. It was a good omen, a sign that they were supposed to meet again.

So what were the gods up to?

She didn't know, but she would be cursed if she let a girl like Valentina outsmart her. *Fortune helps those who help themselves,* she decided.

She walked home from the baths so quickly that Myrrhine could barely keep up with her.

"By Hercules! What has gotten into you?" Myrrhine cried as she slipped off of a stepping-stone and into the filth of the road, soiling her clean dress.

~

"FATHER, MAY I SPEAK WITH YOU?" She entered her father's tablinum and sat down on a handsomely carved bench.

"Daughter, what ails you? Your face is flushed. Grandfather warned you about sitting too long in the hot bath." He sat behind his large wooden desk with a stylus, several scrolls and wax tablets spread out before him.

"Yes, Father. I've just come from the baths, but I did not sit too long in the hot water." Her voice started to quiver. She looked at the beautiful bronze sculpture Evander had given to him. *Perhaps I misinterpreted the gifts as well.*

Her father came out from behind his desk and stood in front of her. "You look troubled. What has happened?"

"I heard Valentina talking in the baths. She didn't know I was listening . . ."

"Did she insult you in some way?"

"Yes, but I don't care about that."

"What, then?" He looked down at her hands and saw that they were twisting nervously in the silky folds of her stola. "Ah. This is about a man."

She could see his mouth twitch with pleasure. "Oh, Father, don't look so pleased. Evander has been invited to the Valens household for dinner this coming day of Venus."

"And this upsets you?" His eyes were wide, his eyebrows raised high. "You know he needs to promote his business. This is normal."

Aurora cleared her throat. "Yes, Father." She shifted uncomfortably on the bench. It was killing her to admit that she was this bothered over a man, and her father knew it. "But I feel there is more to it. I think Trebius Valens will try to encourage a match between Evander and his daughter."

"This is also normal," her father said with a shrug.

"Perhaps so, but is there nothing we can do about it?" she asked earnestly.

"You say Evander is going to dine with them on Friday?" He pulled at his beard.

"Yes."

"Then we will invite him for prandium on Thursday."

Aurora hugged her father gratefully, a broad smile spreading over her face. "Thank you, Father. All I've ever wanted is a man like you."

"Daughter, a word of advice. If you are truly interested in this man, you will have to tame your tongue and soften your beliefs about a woman's place in society. He won't have you if you are unpleasant—no man will."

"But I can't be someone I'm not, Father. I'm an educated woman. I do not wish to be dominated by a man."

"No, you are perfectly entitled to a free marriage. As long as I am alive, you will remain under my legal authority. But there is something called a compromise. The choice is yours. Do you want to have a family one day, or do you want to be alone? Show Evander who you really are, your goodness, your kindness, and your intelligence. If he chooses Valentina, he wasn't the man for you."

"I just don't trust the Valens family."

"Don't worry about them, they are looking out for their own interests. It's Evander you need to think about. Send Apollonius to invite him for Thursday."

Aurora sighed. "Does it need to be Apollonius? He's a bit protective of me."

Her father winked at her. "All the better, Daughter, all the better."

CHAPTER 10

This can't be good.

Evander's chest tightened as Apollonius was escorted into the atrium. Had he come to say that the Fortunas family wanted nothing more to do with him? He stood up tall and straight.

"What can I do for you, Apollonius?"

"I have come to invite you to the Fortunas residence for prandium this coming day of Jove." The slave kept his eyes on the floor.

A jolt of relief streaked through his chest. *He didn't tell her.* "It would be my great pleasure to dine with the Fortunas family once again."

Apollonius nodded respectfully.

Evander walked in a slow circle around him. He was handsome and classically Greek in appearance, with dark features. He was just the type of boy his younger sister would swoon over. Although, he must admit, the slave seemed wise for his age. "How old are you, slave?"

"Eighteen, Dominus."

"Please advise the Fortunas family that I will be bringing two guests. Why do you suddenly look worried, slave boy? Who do you think I am bringing?"

Evander turned to his slave and dismissed him. "My sister arrives tomorrow from Corinth. I would like her to meet Aurora and her family. As for the other guest, well, let's just say it's a friend for Teo."

Apollonius looked relieved. "I shall tell them, Dominus."

Evander regarded the slave more closely. He really wasn't a boy, he was a man, a very handsome man, and he seemed to care greatly for Aurora, which bothered him. But the fact that he hadn't told her about the fiasco with Valentina bode well for him.

"Apollonius, set your mind at ease. You think you saw me kissing Valentina, but in fact it was she who was kissing me."

The slave's eyebrows rose ever so slightly, and Evander let out a sigh.

"I thought I was kissing Aurora. It took me only a moment to realize that it wasn't her waiting for me in the darkness, that everything *felt* wrong and even *smelled* wrong, but then you were there illuminating my folly with your oil lamp."

Apollonius swallowed hard. "I humbly beg your pardon for trespassing on your privacy, Dominus."

"No apology needed. Just understand that my intentions are honorable when it comes to Aurora. I would never hurt her intentionally. I like her—a lot."

Apollonius pushed his shoulders back and looked Evander in the eye, risking punishment for his impertinence. "I have cared for her since we were children, and you should know that I would protect her with my life."

Evander was silent as he considered the slave's brave words. "Well then, she is lucky to have such a dedicated guardian. Until Thursday."

"Until Thursday." Apollonius bowed, then retreated from the atrium.

As he watched the handsome slave quit the domus, he became

aware of an uncomfortable feeling pervading his chest. Was he really jealous? *Of a slave?* He suddenly couldn't wait to see Aurora again.

CHAPTER 11

*A*urora stood in front of the gurgling fountain and stared at the statue of the chubby baby sitting on top of a little dolphin. The sound of the water pouring out of the dolphin's mouth relaxed her.

She heard a knock on the front door, Lupa barking, and her mother crying out for someone to get the dog. If she were not so nervous, it would have been funny, as the same scenario played out each time someone came to the door.

Her stomach was tied in knots at the thought of seeing Evander again. He hadn't said good-bye to her on the night of their party, and she wondered if he had regretted kissing her in the garden. She had only gone upstairs to say good night to Teo, and when she returned, he was gone.

What's more, Valentina's words had been eating away at her, and four whole unbearable days had passed since she had last seen him. Who or what had been taking up all of his time?

She heard her mother tell him that she was in the garden, then the shuffle of sandals and fabric on the mosaic floor. She closed her eyes and took one long, deep breath before turning around.

When she opened her eyes, she couldn't have been more surprised at what she saw.

Evander stood before her, tall and imposing. Beside him stood a lovely blue-eyed girl of about fifteen, holding the little black puppy from the forum. Despite her youth, the girl was elegant and refined, and her arms were adorned with gold jewelry.

Aurora's heart skipped a beat before she realized that the girl was his sister. She looked back and forth between the two of them, noting a strong family resemblance.

"Aurora, you look lovely, as always." Evander held out his arms to her and embraced her affectionately. The knots loosened as she let herself sink into his warm embrace, her senses overcome with his comforting touch. Memories of him kissing her in the garden swept through her mind. They were interrupted by the funny sound of the puppy's wee bark, and they laughed as they reluctantly let go of each other.

"I present to you my sister Helena."

Helena handed the puppy to Evander and took Aurora's hands in hers. She looked Aurora over approvingly and kissed her on both cheeks.

"Brother, she is as beautiful as you have described her."

"And you, Helena, are a most welcome surprise! I am so happy to make your acquaintance. We will have much to share and talk about."

"Of that, I am sure." She looked at Aurora knowingly, then back to her brother and smiled.

"But what of the puppy?" asked Aurora, reaching out to hold him.

"He is mine now," answered Evander. "I brought him along for Teo to play with, as I know how much he wanted to buy him."

The puppy licked her neck and got tangled in her scarf. Aurora sighed as she realized how quickly she could be reduced to emotion and whimsy. "You're just a furry little love ball, aren't you?" she cooed, rubbing the puppy's soft ear between her fingers.

It was going to be a splendid afternoon, in the company of this handsome brother and sister who radiated such love and good-will. Her heart swelled with happiness. "Well, Teo will be thrilled, but good luck getting the dog away from him when you leave!" She laughed merrily.

Evander wrapped his arm around her flirtatiously and whispered in her ear, "Then maybe I'll never leave here, Aurora of the rosy dawn."

His lips were close to hers, and she inhaled ever so slightly, hoping he would kiss her. Just then her family came around the garden partition, led by Apollonius. Teo launched for the puppy with squeals of great delight and promptly absconded to the far end of the garden. His slave followed him, pulled by Lupa, who was now leashed and crazy with excitement.

Her father gave Evander a hearty pat on the shoulder. "Welcome again to our home. We hope you enjoyed yourself at the dinner party last weekend."

Odd, why did Apollonius just throw the evil eye at Evander?

"I had a most enjoyable evening, thank you, Dominus. I had planned to come calling on you earlier, but my sister arrived. May I present to all of you Helena Mercurius."

Her father gave Helena a hug and a pinch on the cheek. "Well, well, you were just a little girl when we saw you last!"

Her mother lavished the girl with kisses and complimented her beauty. "I am filled with great joy that you are here with us. And hello to you, Evander, we missed you this week," she scolded, kissing his cheek.

"Please forgive me for not calling on you sooner, Lady Lucina. I was busy touring the newest garum factory in Neapolis, and I also visited a vineyard renowned for its Falernum wine. I was able to successfully negotiate a deal, and so I will start to ship both of those products back to Greece and the Adriatic."

"Well done," said her father.

Her mother put her arm around Helena. "And you, my sweet

girl, I can't wait to hear about all the wonderful things you have been doing in Corinth."

Evander coughed and rolled his eyes.

"Lady Lucina, there is really nothing to tell." She threw her brother an indignant look. "I mostly have just been trying to stay out of trouble."

"Yes, Lady Lucina, that is precisely why my father has sent her back to Pompeii," Evander added jokingly.

Her parents laughed and fawned over Helena. "You just stay here with us, my girl. We will take care of you. Our home is your home. Now let us give thanks so we can eat!" said her father.

Off in the corner of the garden, incense and candles were burning on the altar of the lararium. Small bronze figurines that represented the household gods were placed at intervals behind the candles.

They all stepped over to the altar, and her father led them in a quick prayer of thanksgiving. Her mother placed a small bowl of fruit on the altar and bowed.

When their devotions were done, Apollonius escorted them through the garden to a wooden table that sat peacefully beneath a shady arbor laced with grapevines.

In the middle of the table sat a large, long-stemmed silver bowl overflowing with apricots, peaches, and pears. Four wide benches adorned with cozy cushions beckoned them to sit comfortably and eat.

The garden was full of well-tended shrubs and shady fruit trees, blooming flowers and medicinal herbs. Several criss-crossing paths intersected at a fountain, and led to various outdoor rooms, including the large summer dining area.

The garden was the heart of the home, and it was here where the family spent most of their time during the warm months of the year. A statue of Venus stood in the corner amidst the greenery, watching over everyone.

"This is a such a beautiful dwelling. It inspires a feeling of peace and tranquility," Helena said.

"Thank you," her mother replied. "It's my favorite part of the domus."

"Lady Lucina, you are needed in the sickroom right away," Myrrhine called from inside the house. Her mother told them to go ahead and eat, then excused herself, hurrying inside.

Aurora hesitated. "Perhaps I should go help Mother."

"No, no," said her father. "Just sit and eat. She'll call you if she needs you."

Aurora and Evander sat together on a bench with her father and Helena across from them. Teo showed up at the table looking grumpy, obviously annoyed that he had to leave the puppy for a while. Evander tried to cheer him with little tickles.

"Teo, what are we going to name the dog?"

Her brother's face lit up. "What? You mean you haven't named him yet?"

"No, I was waiting for you to help me. So what do you think we should call him?"

"Hercules, of course!" shouted Teo.

"Of course!" Evander laughed. "Hercules it is, then."

Apollonius came around with a small flask of perfumed water and washed everyone's hands.

"Apollonius, would you care to play some music for us?" asked her father.

"I would be pleased, Dominus. Please give me a moment to go and tune my lyre."

Myrrhine appeared with a beautifully etched silver platter piled high with round, flat patties. Hot steam was rising off of them. She set it down in the middle of the table.

"What are those?" asked Evander, sniffing at the aroma. "They smell delicious!"

"Those are my cook's famous cabbage patties," her father answered proudly, plucking one fat patty off the platter. "Oh, look at that, they are fresh from the pan," he mumbled, licking his lips. "Thank you, Myrrhine."

Myrrhine bowed politely. "I'll be back in a moment with some olives and cheese. Enjoy your meal." She left the garden and returned to the kitchen.

Aurora felt pride as she looked at her father. He was kind to his slaves and supported his clients well, as a proper *patronus* should. His only flaw was that he could lose his temper in a fit of anger. But other times, he could show incredible sensitivity, tearing up at the sight of a newborn baby. Regardless of his outbursts, he was much loved by his household because he never treated those beneath him with disrespect.

Apollonius returned, sat down near the fountain, and began to play a sweet-sounding melody.

Evander watched the slave with a peculiar look on his face, and Aurora wondered why he seemed to have something against him.

Her father closed his eyes as he listened to the music.

"Ah, how that music relaxes me. Great job, Apollonius! Keep playing!"

"Is he one of Myrrhine's sons?" inquired Evander.

"Yes, he is the eldest. He is an honest, hardworking boy. I found them at a slave market in Greece ten years ago. They were half-starved, half-naked, and in chains. Poor Pioppo was still just a suckling babe."

"And so you purchased *all* of them, Dominus?"

For a moment her father looked uncomfortable.

"Myrrhine's husband was a Greek noble who came to an unfortunate end. I could tell she was a well-bred woman of fine bloodlines. Her expensive clothes were tattered, and one of her sons looked very sick and in need medical attention. I took pity on them and bought them all so they could remain together."

Aurora nodded. "I have very generous parents. Myrrhine and Apollonius run this household better than any of us. I don't know what we would do without them. They are truly part of our family."

"So what happens when they have enough money to buy their freedom?" asked Evander.

"They would probably return to work for us," her father said proudly. "Around here we respect their humanity and their bodily limits. If they are sick, they rest. If they are hungry, they eat. They are not abused or tortured."

"That is very admirable, Dominus." Evander looked thoughtful as he took in her father's words. Aurora wondered what he was thinking, and if his own father was very different.

Evander had shown compassion and tenderness toward her and Teo on the day of the earthquake. He had also supported her efforts on the day of the fire. She couldn't imagine him abusing a slave, but she really didn't know him at all. She frowned and looked down to her lap, suddenly concerned.

Helena touched her on the arm. "I know what you're thinking," she whispered. "Don't worry, my brother is a good and generous man, as I'm sure you will find out." She smiled reassuringly, and Aurora marveled at the girl's ability to read her so well. Was she really that transparent?

Her mother returned to the table looking flustered, which was odd for a woman who always displayed so much self-control.

"What is going on, Mother?" Aurora asked, alarmed.

Her mother looked around the table at them, as if deciding whether to tell them something.

"I just tended to a sheepherder who works for a farm up on Vesuvius. Something very strange happened to him this morning. He heard a rumble, then saw a cloud rising up from the earth. He says it enveloped part of the mountain, and the herd of sheep as well."

She stopped and frowned, as if she didn't quite believe what she was about to say. "When the cloud dispersed, all of the sheep were lying in the field, dead."

"Oh my gods!" cried Helena. "What does it mean?"

"Wait, there's more," said her mother. "The man said he was overcome with fear and ran to his horse, who was grazing at a distance down the hill. He began to feel dizzy, and then his legs were burned as hot air blew up from the ground around him."

They all started to shift nervously on the benches.

"What in Hades is going on?" Evander looked very concerned.

They all stared at each other, stunned, while they tried to make sense of it.

"It's like the fisherman who was burned by the water," said Aurora.

"Ahem." Her father looked annoyed, as he didn't like any disturbances during his mealtime. "I'm sure the man was just caught in a brush fire. And as for the sheep, the smoke from the fire must have made them sick. It sounds to me like the sheepherder had too much to drink last night if he can't figure that out."

"I don't know, Aurorus. He has also been vomiting and complaining of chest pains. He is beside himself, saying that there are *giants* roaming up on Mt. Vesuvius. I had to give him a good dose of valerian root to calm him down."

"Lucina, you are the medica. You know how a person's imagination can get the better of one's mind. I'm sure there are logical reasons for what happened. Do not worry yourself—or anyone else—unnecessarily."

Her mother sighed. "You're right. There must be a rational explanation. I'm sorry for the interruption, children, please continue eating." She tried to sound cheerful.

But her mother didn't fool her for a moment. Aurora could tell that she was very unsettled by this bizarre series of events.

Evander picked up a loaf of round bread and broke off two wedges, handing one to Aurora. Then he tore pieces for everyone else and passed them around the table.

"Dominus, I have noticed an unusual amount of dried and

withered vines in my vineyard. I wonder if this summer's heat has contributed to these unusual events."

"Very probable. I have also noticed many dead vines in our vineyard. But what can we do? Hopefully, we will still get a good grape harvest this year."

Her father brushed some freshly cracked nuts onto Helena's ceramic dish and changed the subject. "So your parents are grandparents now. We should be so lucky, eh, Aurora?"

Aurora turned bright red and looked at Helena, who burst out laughing.

"Does your father like to embarrass you too?" Aurora asked, mortified.

"All the time! Don't worry, all parents put pressure on their daughters to marry. My father has been trying to find me a husband since the day I was born, so much trouble did I cause!" Everyone at the table laughed, but Aurora noticed something flicker over the young girl's face.

"Well, you are very pretty, Miss Helena. I will marry you if you need a husband," offered Teo.

"How very sweet of you," she answered kindly. "I will take your offer into consideration." Everyone started to laugh again, including Apollonius, who seemed to be watching the pretty girl as he strummed his lyre.

Evander swallowed some wine, then cleared his throat. "I have been invited to the Valens house for dinner tomorrow night. Do you have any advice for me regarding how I should deal with Trebby? He seems to be a bit overbearing."

Aurora clanked her spoon down on her dish as she thought of her encounter with Valentina in the baths.

Her father snorted. "Yes, that's Trebby. Just be polite and don't let him intimidate you. You are already an established businessman."

Evander threw a quick glance at Apollonius, who promptly looked down at his lyre.

What is going on between them?

She forgot her concerns as a slight earth tremor shook the table, causing the dishes to rattle. It was over after a few moments, and they all breathed a sigh of relief.

"It was just a small one," said her mother. "Don't get nervous, Teo."

"How often are there earthquakes in Pompeii?" Helena asked, looking shaken.

"They are very common here in Campania. Usually, we feel a tremor every few months," answered her father. "But lately they are happening more frequently."

"Does Neapolis get them as well?" she asked.

"Yes, from Misenum to Surrentum, the tremors can be felt around the entire bay," answered her mother. "The common people believe that Neptune is bowling; others say he is angry. But our friend Gaius Plinius, a very learned man, believes that the tremors are a force of nature unrelated to the gods."

Evander nodded in agreement. "Oftentimes the Greek isles shake with tremors as well, but no one can really say why. The tremors are as mysterious as the fire mountains. There is one on the island of Sicily. Have you all heard of Mount Aetna? And there are many more throughout Greece. Usually, they just blow a little smoke and fire into the air, but sometimes fire runs down the flank of the mountain."

"And what do the people do if the fire comes toward the village?" her mother asked.

"The fire moves very slowly, Lady Lucina. It usually doesn't make it all the way down to the town."

"Interesting," her father said, rubbing his jaw. "The Greek geographer Strabo wrote that Vesuvius looked like it had been on fire in the distant past and that is why the land around the mountain is so fertile."

"Do you think Vesuvius is a fire mountain?" Evander asked, intrigued.

Teo's eyes opened wide. "That would be sooo exciting!"

"You mean horrifying!" Aurora cried. "Vesuvius is right outside our door!"

Her father gestured with his arms. "Calm down, children. I have lived here all my life, and my father before me, and his father before him. If ever there was fire within Vesuvius, it burned out a long, long time ago."

The conversation continued congenially until half of the food had been eaten.

"Now we shall stroll together under the portico while Myrrhine and her sons take their meal," her father announced. He held out his arm to Helena. "Come and walk with me, my dear. Lucina, my love, you too."

Evander held out his arm to Aurora. "That leaves just you and I since Teo is walking with the puppy."

She linked her arm through his, and they ambled under the shade of the portico.

"Your sister is truly lovely, Evander."

"Yes," he whispered, "but I have to watch her ever so carefully."

"What for?"

Evander glanced at his sister to make sure she was out of earshot. "She is always up to something, that one. Why do you think my parents sent her here? She was at the root of several scandals in Corinth."

"Your sweet little sister? Are we talking about the same girl?"

"You'll see, just give it time. In fact, there is a reason I wanted Helena to meet you. I was hoping you could give her some guidance and direction. Be a good influence on her."

He pulled her behind a flowering oleander bush and stole a kiss. His warm lips burned longingly into hers.

"I have been wanting to do that for days now. I've missed you. I've just been so busy."

"I've missed you too. And I would love to spend time with your sister. I think she and I will be fast friends."

"I know you will." He pulled her close and held her tight for a few moments, rubbing his hands over the bare skin of her arms. "I would like to invite you to come to the theater with me next week. *Dyskolos* by Menander is being presented."

"*The Grouchy Old Man*? I would love to see that with you, but I don't want to take you away from your work."

Evander laughed and put her arm through his. "You will be a welcome distraction. You always are." They started to stroll again.

Although she knew she shouldn't say anything, she couldn't help herself. She cast him a sly glance. "And what about the Valens's dinner party?"

"I don't want you to worry about that. There is nothing between me and Valentina."

"I know that you must find her attractive, as most men do."

"Yes, she is pretty, but I'm not interested."

She stopped walking and looked into his eyes. "Well, something is going on. Every time Valentina's name is mentioned, you and Apollonius exchange glances, like you are keeping some kind of secret."

He exhaled and looked away, then led her to a private spot in the garden behind the statue of Venus. "Valentina was very forward with me at your dinner party. I tried to ignore her advances as best I could without being rude."

"And what about Apollonius?"

Evander brushed his hand through his hair.

"He saw me with her. She was waiting for me in the dark hallway as I was leaving your house that night." He put his hands on her shoulders and kissed her on the top of her head. "Trust me, she means nothing to me."

"I heard her bragging to her girlfriends about you in the baths the morning after the party. She said many upsetting things."

Evander dropped his head. "So you know that we kissed."

Aurora gaped at him. "You kissed her! After spending the

whole night charming me, you kissed *her*? No wonder you didn't say good-bye to me!"

"Let me clarify." He tried to take hold of her shoulders again, but she knocked his arms away. "*She* kissed *me,* and it was dark, and I thought *I* was kissing *you*. I know it sounds ridiculous, but that's how it happened."

She shook her head at him, her eyes burning with anger, her chest so tight she could barely breath. She began to walk away. *She kissed* him? *Does he think I am that naïve?*

"Aurora, wait—" He grabbed her arms.

She let out a frustrated sigh and disentangled herself from him. "And still you would go to her house for dinner?"

"You know I must go to promote my father's business."

Her eyes lingered on his face for one last brief moment. "I'm sorry, Evander, I just don't know what to believe."

As she passed the statue of Venus, she sneered at the inscription below: *Allow me pure wine, then may Venus who guards the garden love you.*

Venus, protector of gardens and lovers, had apparently been distracted on the night of her dinner party.

CHAPTER 12

*E*vander walked briskly over the cobblestone sidewalk of the main thoroughfare of Pompeii, his faithful slave Manolo following close behind him.

He stopped at the entrance of a grand house. "This is it," he announced.

The bottom of the house was painted in faux black marble, and the top of the façade was covered in all sorts of electoral graffiti. There were also two old advertisements for gladiatorial games in Pompeii's amphitheater. One promised an animal hunt with an awning to protect the spectators from the sun; another promised that the games were to be held at no public expense.

The name of the ostentatious owner of the house appeared on the wall no less than five times: Trebius Valens. *What kind of a night am I in for?* he wondered.

Trebby had specified that tonight's dinner be for men only. No doubt he wanted to ensure that no other women were around to distract him—that is, no other women besides his own daughters.

He was sure that a man like Trebby would spare no expense on the food or entertainment, especially if he had a strong political agenda.

Evander knew that this night was going to cost him in more ways than one. It was easy to figure out that Trebby was looking for donations for city projects and ways in which he could benefit from the vast Mercurius shipping and trading business. No doubt there would be many offers made, but only after Trebby had plied him with wine; it was a symposium—drinking party—after all.

Unfortunately, he knew that tonight was also going to cost him with Aurora. She was not a girl to trifle with. She was sharp and perceptive and would not put up with indiscretions or trivialities. He already had one mistake against him, and coming here tonight would certainly not please her, but it was something that he had to do. This was the world of business and politics, a world she knew little about despite her fine education.

He raised his arm and rapped on the front door. He was quickly ushered in through a short hallway, from which he could see straight back to the garden, where a festive affair was being held. Manolo was directed to the kitchen to help prepare and serve the food.

The atrium was appropriately decorated with busts of dead ancestors, and the lively beat of two African drummers reverberated off of the ornately painted walls. He followed a slave out to the garden where Lady Claudia, Trebby's wife, acknowledged him with a loud hoot.

Is that supposed to be a greeting?

She lavished him with compliments and nonsensical flattery.

"Evander! How fine you look tonight," she gushed, revealing a space between her two front teeth. "Yes, you really are the perfect and most prime example of the embodiment of the, uh, male corpus," she stuttered.

She stared blatantly at the dark hair on his chest, as he wasn't wearing a tunic, only a toga that wrapped around his body and over one shoulder. He felt like he was being examined the way a cook might assess a piece of meat for dinner.

"Thank you, Lady Claudia. It is an honor to be invited to your house tonight." He looked around the garden. It was beautifully decorated with fruits and garlands, flowering bushes and olive trees.

"Your domus is quite beautiful."

"Thank you," she beamed. "We are just delighted to have you here tonight."

He saw Valentina and Priscila standing in front of a pretty semicircular fountain. "Your daughters are attending the symposium?"

Lady Claudia gave an embarrassed chortle, then put her arm around his waist and led him over to where her daughters were standing.

"Of course we're not going to be out here for the entire evening; it *is* a men's drinking party," she explained in her raspy voice, "but I wanted you to see the girls. You remember Valentina and Priscila?"

"Of course, I could never forget them, Lady Claudia."

He smiled graciously and kissed each one on the hand. But Valentina flipped her hand over and grabbed onto his fingers before he could pull away.

"I've missed you, Evander," she said in a silky, sweet voice. She smiled seductively and slithered closer to him the way a viper might before attacking its prey. Her long blond hair cascaded down one shoulder, and he wondered why she didn't wrap it up on her head in the latest Roman hairstyle.

"I hope you will enjoy the party. And if you get lonely," she squeezed his hand and paused for dramatic effect, "I won't be far."

She stood close to his chest, her full bosom revealed by the low cut of her colorful dress, her nipples erect and pressing through the thin fabric.

She was certainly beautiful, he admitted to himself, but in a base and sleazy way. A woman like her would scheme to ruin him at every possible turn, getting tangled up in scandal after scandal.

In the past, he would have taken her to bed and enjoyed all of the ways he could extract pleasure from her. But now? She just wasn't worth it.

His days of philandering were over. He was ready for a *real* woman and a relationship that inspired him, not just empty nights with girls who were shallow half-wits.

She finally let go of his hand, but not before trailing a slender finger full of jewels down his chest. He looked around the garden. Where did her mother and sister go, anyway? She leaned in close to his ear, and he was afraid she might bite him.

"A man like you needs a woman like me, who knows what to do with all those . . . manly parts." She glanced down at his hips suggestively. "Not a schoolgirl who reads poetry and plays doctor when her mother isn't around."

Evander's eyes opened wide at her bold words, but he was spared from replying when her father appeared.

"Well, it looks like you two are getting cozy already. Welcome to my home, Evander. I have a most entertaining night planned for my guests. Come, let me make some introductions for you. You will meet many men here who are in positions of power. They can help you spread your shipping empire into the Bay of Neapolis and north to Ostia and Rome. I actually have an interesting deal to propose to you myself, but all in good time, my son, all in good time. Come, let's have a drink together."

He dismissed his daughter, telling her that it was time for the women to quit the party, and, as promised, began introducing Evander to the other guests.

An hour later, they were seated for dinner and a section from Virgil's *Aeneid* was read to the men. Slaves served scrumptious appetizers on large silver platters and placed them on the table in the middle of the dining couches.

Trebby's outdoor dining area was quite unique in that the wall behind the dining area was decorated with small multicolored panels, and there was an opening in the side wall through which the slaves retrieved platters of food from the kitchen.

Evander helped himself to some raw oysters and sea urchins that were drizzled in garum and began to converse with the other men on his couch. The food was absolutely delicious, and he stuffed himself accordingly.

Next came a hilarious reading from the *Satyricon* of Petronius, the section entitled "Dinner with Trimalchio." The men laughed heartily as the main course arrived: sow uterus stuffed with leeks, pine nuts, cumin, and pounded pork meat. Incredible! Trebby really knew how to throw a party, he mused as he held up his glass for more wine.

Suddenly, the sound of castanets filled the garden, and four scantily dressed dancing girls from Hispania appeared. They had long, silky black hair, olive skin, and dark, almond-shaped eyes. They began to dance and undulate their hips to the most sensual and rhythmic music Evander had ever heard. He smiled despite himself. *I could get used to this,* he thought shamefully.

Meanwhile, the wine kept flowing, and he tried not to drink too fast, but he had to admit he was enjoying this lively dinner. And what was good food without good wine?

Trebby had spared no expense, just as he had predicted. The question now was what did he want in return? Nothing was ever given freely in the game of Roman politics, and it was important to keep a clear mind.

He stretched out on his couch feeling supremely relaxed and happy. His head was spinning just a little, but nothing he couldn't handle.

Two musicians entered the garden, male and female, and began to play the lyre. They sang a beautiful love song that made him ache for Aurora. He closed his eyes and imagined caressing her body tenderly, running his fingers through her rich, dark hair. *If I could, I would hold her in my arms and kiss that soft, soft skin . . .*

He felt himself grow hard.

He could almost imagine her nipples brushing against him, her warm lips dropping kisses like honey over his bare skin.

He became aware of a new scent.

He opened his eyes and was surprised to find a very pretty woman, dressed as an Egyptian, lying next to him on the couch. She was gently stroking his chest. He looked around in confusion and wondered where the other men had gone. How much time had passed?

There was a large group of high-class prostitutes who were now mingling with the men. Seductive murmurs filled the garden, and he saw some of the girls leading the men away to more private chambers.

The pretty woman picked up a small cheesecake and fed it to Evander. A drop of honey fell on his chest, and she leaned down to lick it from his skin.

"Don't." He pushed her gently away.

"Just relax. Enjoy this beautiful evening. There is nothing to be concerned about," she assured him, slipping her hand under his toga. She stroked his cock, causing him to inhale sharply.

He couldn't let this happen. This was not what he wanted.

Not because having sex with a prostitute was unacceptable, but because it would weigh on his conscience every time he looked into Aurora's eyes.

She was kissing his neck now, his member still firmly clasped in her hand. She teased him, tickled him, and nipped at him with her teeth, all the while fondling him expertly under the folds of his toga.

It would be so easy to just give in, to feel the intense pleasure and release. His muscles tightened in anticipation. *Should I take her to a private room?*

The physical pleasure was overriding his rational mind. He was hot and aroused and halfway to doing something he would really regret. He struggled with his emotions.

I don't want to do this, and yet I do . . . because it's mindless and feels so good and doesn't really mean anything to me other than a physical release.

But it would mean something to Aurora, and he knew that well. If she ever found out, it would come between them, just as that ridiculous kiss with Valentina had come between them. And this was much more than just a kiss.

He abruptly pushed the woman away and shook his head, then sat up and straightened his toga. Suddenly, Trebby appeared.

"She is not to your liking?" he asked, gesturing to the prostitute.

"On the contrary, she is very pretty and appealing," he replied, not wanting to offend his host. "But my head is swimming, Trebby. Your wine is very strong."

"Come, then, and take a stroll with me. It will do you well, and we can have that little chat I mentioned earlier."

A slave laced up Evander's sandals and helped him stand up from the couch. When he finally found his balance, he nodded to Trebby. "I must compliment you on your beautiful garden. Any god would be happy here."

"Thank you." Trebby looked pleased as he looped his arm through Evander's.

"And how did you find the food this evening?"

"Delectable. The best I've ever had. You really know how to throw a party."

"And this is only the beginning of the indulgences I can offer, Evander. You know that I would like very much to enter into a . . . business partnership . . . with you."

Here it comes, Evander thought through his haze. "What do you propose?" he asked.

"Well, let's say for example that you commissioned a public building and statue in my honor. You know, something like that annoying priestess Eumachia erected. She has her name plastered all over the forum."

"And how would *I* benefit from building you that?

"Well, to begin with, the Garum Producers Union and the Fruit and Vegetable Vendors have agreed to let you have sole distribution rights of their products exported from Pompeii to Greece."

"That is a fantastic and generous deal, but I will have to confirm with my father before I agree."

"And of course you would share a small percentage of your profits with me for arranging it all for you."

"Of course."

"And I'm sure you and your father have been wondering how you can procure an introduction to Titus, the new emperor, and protection from pirates by the navy?"

"It has crossed our mind. The emperor's favor is important when trying to solicit business contracts, and protection from pirates is always a benefit."

"Well then, consider it done. You and I can travel to Rome together next month. If the emperor approves of you, your success in business is guaranteed."

Evander reeled at the extraordinary offers Trebius Valens was laying at his feet. His father would negotiate the profit sharing, and financing a building and statue in Trebby's honor would not be too difficult.

"There is one more requirement . . . ahem, request," added Trebby.

He walked Evander over to a secluded part of the garden and looked him straight in the eyes. "If I am to do all this for you, you must first promise to marry my daughter Valentina in return."

And there it is, he thought sourly. He was being manipulated by a master.

He looked at Trebby soberly. "I cannot agree to that request."

Trebby's eyebrows shot up. "Don't you want Rome to know who you are?" he hissed. "Would you throw away everything I am offering over a pretty piece of ass? Now I understand that Aurora is the daughter of one of my friends, and a lovely girl at that, but her family doesn't have the right connections, as well you know."

Welcome to the world of politics and business, he fumed silently.

Trebby put his hands on Evander's shoulders and softened his tone.

"Now listen, my boy. There is no law that constrains you from enjoying the fruits of just one woman. Look around you! All of these men have lovely wives at home. Their wives understand what happens at these parties. They also understand that a man needs more than just one garden to sow."

"You are suggesting that I take your daughter as my wife and keep Aurora as my *mistress?*"

"Of course, but this is only natural. You are young. In time, you will understand that you must be willing to rearrange some of your . . . priorities . . . in order to get ahead in life."

Evander looked at him incredulously.

"Enough talk for tonight. I want you to take some time to think about all we have discussed here. No rush. You know where to find me. Now I hope you will enjoy the rest of the party." He slapped him on the back and walked off toward a group of men who were telling bawdy jokes and cackling loudly.

Evander stood in the shadows of the garden and wondered how rude it would be if he walked out. Would he be seen as less of a man for leaving early? Less virile for not having sex with the prostitute? Weak for not drinking until he vomited? Would the men think of him as just a boy? The pressure that existed at this party was daunting. It had been completely different at the Fortunas party last week.

He had a strong moral code of conduct and was not willing to compromise himself for anybody. Nor would he *rearrange his priorities*, as Trebby had suggested. His father had warned him before he left Corinth that being in a position of wealth and power was not an easy path to navigate.

A woman approached him, and he cringed inwardly. It was Valentina. He could see that she was upset, even in the shadows of the garden.

"Evander?"

"Yes, Valentina. It is I. Why are you out here? Your father might not approve."

"My father promised me that another woman wouldn't touch you!"

"Why would he promise you that? Am I not a man in charge of my own volition?"

"I saw what she did, how she caressed you . . ." she lamented, reaching out to touch his shoulders. He could smell the wine on her breath. *She is drunk.*

"What is your point?" he huffed. "And why were you watching? That is completely inappropriate!"

Valentina looked hurt. "Don't be upset with me. I would do anything for you, Evander." She threw her arms around his neck, pressing her voluptuous body to him. "Even give you my virginity," she whispered.

He tried to pull her off of him, but he had to tread carefully because to offend Valentina was to offend her father, and an awful lot was at stake.

"I'm not happy about what you did."

"Are you really upset about a little kiss?" she asked.

"It was your deception that bothered me. What is it that you really want from me, Valentina?"

She looked him in the eye. "Please, Evander. You *must* save me. My father is going to force me to marry this summer, and if I don't marry you, if you don't agree to his plan, he will marry me to an odious and aging senator. And I despise that old goat!" She threw a glance in the direction of a man he assumed must be the senator. He was reclining on a couch in the garden as two prostitutes pleasured him. One looked to be no older than a child. *Lecherous old man.*

"I'm sure you suffer no lack of male suitors. There must be other men who would agree to marry you."

"Of course there are!" she answered haughtily. "But no one

that my father approves of. They are not rich enough, or powerful enough, or they don't have the right connections."

Tears clouded her eyes, and he almost felt sorry for her.

"You're the one I want, and I'm used to getting what I want. You know that we would make the perfect match." She ran her hand across his chest seductively.

"I'm sorry, Valentina, I'm not the man for you," he said, removing her hand.

"You are going to regret this, Evander Mercurius!" Suddenly, she bent forward at the waist, her arm around her abdomen. "I'm not feeling so well."

"I think you're just upset."

She cried out and clutched her stomach again. "I'll be back—" She ran off in the direction of the kitchen, bumping into Manolo as she hurried past.

The slave quickly approached Evander. "It's time to go home, Dominus. Come."

"Yes, please get me out of here."

He was so annoyed with everything that had transpired tonight he wanted to punch someone. They walked quickly down a dark corridor and out into the back alley of the house, where the cloak of night obscured them.

Helena was waiting in the atrium for his return.

Manolo bowed to her. "It went as planned, Mistress."

Helena nodded back to the slave.

"What are you up to now, Sister?" Evander asked.

"Nothing," she answered cryptically, then kissed him on the cheek. "You reek of expensive wine and cheap perfume," she chided. "Rough night?"

"You have no idea," he answered darkly as he headed upstairs to his bedroom, and to his wonderfully cool and empty bedsheets.

CHAPTER 13

"*A*urora? May I come in?" Helena rapped several more times on her bedroom door. "Don't you want to know what happened at the dinner party?"

Aurora opened the door slightly and peeked her nose through the crack. She couldn't exactly leave Evander's sister standing in the hall.

"What is going on?" Helena pushed through the door and looked around at the messy room, which had clothes strewn over the bed and chairs.

"Are you *pouting*?" she asked, crinkling her nose.

Aurora let out a huff. "I do not *pout*, Helena. And I am offended that you should even suggest it!"

"If this is about Valentina, you need to learn how to beat that girl at her own game." Helena walked over to her vanity table and picked up a jar of donkey milk lotion. "May I?" She began to spread the luxurious cream over her hands before Aurora even answered.

"I do not play games, Helena. If your brother prefers Valentina over me, there is nothing I can do about it." She sat down on her bed and stared at a poem she had once scratched into the plaster of the wall.

Helena walked over to her. "My brother told me everything that happened at your party last week. He doesn't prefer her to you, and you know that. Your pride is just bruised."

"My pride? Bruised by that silly siren?"

"Absolutely. What do you think she was really trying to do by kissing my brother?"

Aurora raised her eyebrows to the naïve girl. "Do you need me to explain?"

"Listen to me." Helena sat down on the bed next to her. "From what I know of that night, I would say that Valentina wanted to drive a wedge between you two, and her tactic worked."

"Do you really believe that she tricked your brother into kissing her?"

"I have seen the way he looks at you. My brother is not a liar, I can assure you of that. He is honest to a fault. And as for Valentina, he seemed very relieved when she took ill last night."

"How do you know that? You weren't at the symposium."

"I have my sources." Helena smiled mysteriously.

"Well, what happened to her?" Aurora was ashamed that she was happy over another's illness, but honestly, Valentina deserved a little bad luck.

Helena stood abruptly and walked around the room. "Apparently, she developed stomach pains after dinner."

"Did the food make her sick?"

"No, my brother said the food was quite delicious. It sounds like she may have had cramps."

"Cramps?" she echoed. Aurora looked Helena over and didn't like what her body language was saying. The girl wouldn't look her in the eye, and her arms were crossed defiantly against her chest.

"Helena?"

"Yes?"

"Did you have something to do with Valentina's sudden illness? I seem to remember my mother giving you some cleansing salts the other day after prandium."

"Me?" She spun around, her face looking as innocent as she could make it. "I wasn't even at the party!"

Aurora stared her down.

Helena laughed nervously. "Oh, all right. I cannot lie to you. She deserved it."

Aurora's jaw fell open. "Oh gods! You didn't!"

She stood up and grabbed Helena's hands. "That was a terrible thing to do!" she whispered vehemently. "Never, ever tell this to your brother! And promise me you will never do something like this again! Poisoning someone is a crime!"

"Now, now, I didn't poison her. I just had Manolo put a little something in her wine to help her digest her food. There is a big difference, you know. I can't help that she drank so much wine."

As awful as it was, Aurora threw herself back on her bed and laughed as she imagined Valentina sitting on the latrina, sponge in hand, instead of flirting shamelessly with Evander. "I can't believe you did that, *but I love you for it*!" She stood up, threw her arms around Helena, and squeezed her tight.

Helena giggled and looked over her shoulder as she walked away. "What good is being rich if you can't take care of some minor irritations? Now get yourself ready; my brother is on his way to see you." She blew Aurora a kiss and was gone. Aurora stared blankly at the wall for a moment.

And I thought I was supposed to take care of her.

A FEW MINUTES LATER, Evander stood in the atrium holding up a wreath of flowers. "Peace offering. Can we talk?"

She took the wreath and led him to a room off of the garden with a comfortable couch. It was a breezy July night, and a small brazier had been lit inside the room, giving off a cozy glow. She sat down on the couch and gestured for him to sit next to her.

He sat down and held her gaze. It was the first time she had seen dark circles under his eyes. He looked weary and depleted of his usual vigor.

"So I assume the symposium went on all night?"

"I don't know. I left before midnight." His voice sounded strained.

"And Valentina?"

"She was the same. Flirtatious, shameless, base."

Aurora frowned and looked away.

"I tried to confront her about what happened at your party."

"She is who she is, Evander, and she will never apologize."

He nodded his head in agreement. "You're right."

"The point is I have to be able to trust you. *You* asked *me* to be more than your friend. I wanted to give you a chance. But if there is no trust, there is no point."

"I know. And I want to be that man on whom you can rely. But there is something I need to tell you." He stared down at his feet.

"Did something else happen?"

"There were prostitutes at the party last night."

Aurora put her hand over her mouth and felt sick.

"Oh my gods! Did you . . . ?"

He looked her straight in the eye. "No, Aurora! No, I did not."

"Why are you here, Evander? I think you should go. I want no part of this."

"Aurora, listen to me. I came here for a reason. I wanted you to hear about last night from me, and not secondhand through the mouth of a slave."

She looked at him, confused, and he reached out and took her hand.

"I learned a lesson last night. I learned that there will always be men who want to trick me and take advantage of me, men who will do anything to get at my father's wealth. But I have to be a step ahead of them. I won't let them manipulate me."

"I'm not sure what you are referring to, but it has obviously upset you."

He kneeled down on the floor in front of her and twined his arms with hers.

"Aurora, I don't want anything more to come between us, and I fully blame myself for what happened with Valentina at your party. If I had been in better control of my senses, it wouldn't have happened."

"But it did," she reminded him.

"I know, and last night at Trebby's symposium, he tried very hard to catch me in a compromising position."

"With a prostitute?"

He swallowed and looked away. "I knew I couldn't face you if I allowed anything to happen. I pushed her away before it went too far. I'd be lying if I said it was easy. It was not."

Aurora inhaled, trying to calm herself. A bitter stab of jealousy pierced her chest. The thought of another woman touching him was too much for her to bear, and her eyes started to burn.

Was he expecting her to comfort him? To tell him it would be all right? She couldn't fathom what he expected her response to be. And what did he mean, anyway, *before it went too far?* That implied that something intimate had transpired.

He had revealed very private information to her, and she needed time to digest it. The worst part was that in the eyes of society, he had done nothing wrong. Unfortunately, for a woman, it was a betrayal of the worst kind.

But here he was, kneeling in front of her, exposing his soul. She wanted to believe that he was telling her the truth. That he hadn't sought out Valentina at her party, that he hadn't slept with the prostitute.

It had taken a lot of courage for him to come here tonight and admit everything to her. He could have just lied. Why did he care so much about what she thought of him?

"So you've come here to tell me that you *almost* slept with a prostitute at the Valens's dinner party, and I'm supposed to pat you on the back and tell you I'm fine with that?" she asked.

He looked at her with those piercing blue eyes that seemed to see right through her.

"I came here to tell you that you are a woman who inspires me. A woman who makes me want to be a better man. Because of you, I have found an inner strength that I didn't know was there, and I want you to believe that you can trust me."

"Trust has to be earned, Evander."

"On both sides, Aurora. I need to know that you will not scourge me with that tongue of yours as you did on that day in the forum. I will not have it, especially in public. You will speak to me with respect or we will end this here and now."

He was asking her to control her tongue and defer to him in public, the same as her father had suggested. But what if she didn't agree with him? Would he allow her to speak her mind in private?

One thing she knew for sure, it would be torture to ever walk away from him. She wrapped her arms around his head and pulled him close to her chest. The warmth of his body comforted her, and she felt reassured in her heart that he was an honest man. He stroked her back with his capable hands, and she inhaled the fresh scent of his hair.

She would do what he asked and speak to him respectfully.

But how would she manage the parties and prostitutes and women like Valentina?

He was struggling to bear the incredible burden of his father's business, and she was learning that having a relationship with a man was much more emotionally demanding than she had originally believed.

CHAPTER 14

Chaireas: What, Sostratos? You saw a freeborn girl
crowning these statues of the Nymphs with flowers,
and you fell for her like that?
Sostratos: I fell for her at once.
Chaireas: Fast work! I'll bet you left the house to fall in
love on purpose!
Sostratos: Stop joking, Chaireas! I'm the one who's
suffering.
Chaireas (Glancing at the bulge in Sostratos's tunic):
Oh, I believe it!

Evander laughed at the scene being played out in front of him. Although he had read Menander's play before, he had never seen it performed. He was sitting closely to Aurora, leaning into her as he laughed.

He could tell that she was still upset with him by her slightly cool demeanor. He didn't blame her. He was the fool who had been caught kissing Valentina, and then he had told her about the prostitute as well. Maybe he shouldn't have said anything, but he didn't want there to be lies between them, and most importantly, he didn't want her to hear about it from someone else.

One thing he would not tell her, however, was the demand from Trebius Valens that he marry Valentina in exchange for his help. He was going to have to work that problem out on his own. But how? He wanted everything that Trebby had to offer, just not his shallow, disreputable daughter.

When he arrived at Aurora's house this evening, she had smiled and looked pleased to see him. He had kissed her cheeks and greeted her warmly, trying to reassure her of his feelings and good intentions toward her. He had even brought her a small gift.

"What is it?" she had asked, examining the little blue glass bird. "There is liquid inside."

"It is perfume. You must break off the tail of the bird to extract it."

"Oh, very clever!"

"Allow me." He had taken the delicate bird and quickly snapped off the end of the tail. Then he had poured out a drop of the fragrant liquid into his palm and held it up to her nose.

"Beautiful." She had inhaled deeply. "It smells like lilies."

"Come closer and look toward the wall." He had gently rubbed his palm over her neck, transferring the fragrant liquid to her soft skin. For a moment, they had gazed intensely at each other, but then she had turned away before he had the chance to kiss her.

The scent of her perfume drifted over him as they sat on the marble bench watching the play, and he hoped that this evening would give him the opportunity to make things right between them.

Aurora laughed again, and Evander glanced at her, relieved to see she was enjoying herself. She looked stunning in a sea-blue stola with the yellow silk palla he had given her wrapped around her shoulders. He felt that by wearing his gift, she had let him mark her in some way. He wanted to mark her in other ways as well. He wanted to kiss her and make love to her all night long. He wanted to protect her and keep her safe.

He had thought about Aurora continuously since the day of the earthquake. She aroused him both mentally and physically, and lately, he felt like he was burning up. He reached out and took her hand in his.

Throughout the play, she became more responsive to him. He could tell by the way her eyes lingered on his face when they spoke, the way she leaned in close to hear what he was saying, the way she looked at their intertwined hands.

As for himself, he was becoming aware that his feelings for her were deepening. Even though she was untraditional for a woman, her intelligence and dedication to something greater than herself made him respect her immensely . . . and eager to take things further.

When the play ended, they walked through a vaulted corridor to a staircase that descended into the beautiful Triangular Forum. It had been built over two hundred years ago, when the city planners had restored the theaters and temples of the city.

This forum was more of a garden filled with flowering oleander bushes and tall cypress trees. But most impressively, ninety-five Doric columns surrounded the forum except on the far end, where it opened up to a breathtaking view of the river flowing into the sea.

They walked arm in arm under the portico.

"Do you remember when we used to play here as children?"

She smiled and glanced up at him. "I do."

"So you're finally willing to admit that you remember me?"

"Yes, I admit it. I remember you. You were sweet and you used to watch over me."

"And now? Do you not desire the protection of a man?"

Her face became serious. "Not if it means that I lose my independence."

He frowned at her for a moment but instead of engaging her

on a subject that upset her, he decided to talk about Menander's play.

"So they finally convinced the girl's father to agree to the marriage even though he didn't want his daughter to marry a rich man."

"Yes, but for all of his grouchiness, he still had good morals and despised the evil of the world. Reminds me of my father," Aurora joked. "Grumpy, but loving nonetheless."

"The play was actually a satire on the differences between the rich and poor," he mused, "the message being that the poor have better morals and a better work ethic than the rich."

"Although Menander poked fun at the country folk too, with their sunburned faces and lack of good manners," she added.

They passed an ancient Doric temple dedicated to Hercules and Minerva, then arrived at the end of the forum, where a semi-circular stone bench looked out over the Sarnus River. It was decorated with lion's feet on each side, and behind the bench sat a large sundial.

"Beautiful!" he said, taking in the view.

"Sometimes I come here to sit and write poetry," she told him. She peered out over the water. In the distance was a layer of white mist separating the sea from the clear blue sky. "The water of the bay is so blue, so serene."

"It's even more beautiful when you are actually out there. I'd like to take you for a sail on my ship soon." He put his arm around her and kissed her cheek. "I'm glad you are here with me and that you are enjoying yourself tonight."

She looked up at him with her dark eyes and smiled. "I am glad too, very much so. And I would love to go sailing with you. However, there is one thing that bothers me about that play."

"What is that?" he asked, nuzzling her hair with his nose.

"The girl is never asked if she wants to marry Sostratos! What if she can't stand him?"

Evander chuckled and brushed his lips over her forehead. "As Menander says, men in love don't always think so clearly."

"But what if *she* was in love with someone else? Was it right to marry her off simply because *he* loved *her*?" she asked.

"That play was written over three hundred years ago; times were different then. A country girl of modest means would have been thrilled to find a rich, city husband. Trust me, she would have been very happy."

"But unfortunately, these things are still happening to women today."

Her comments stirred up questions he had in his own mind about Aurora. She was very self-sufficient and content to stay that way. She obviously had issues with a man making decisions for her.

He wanted to ask her a personal question, but wasn't sure how she would take it. He thought about it for a moment and decided that she needed to be honest with him, the way he was with her the other night. He turned her toward him.

"Aurora, why arc you not married yet?"

She looked taken aback, the way the sails of a ship looked when the wind blows them flat against the masts. "Why would you ask me that? It is an incredibly personal question."

"I'm asking because I have to know. Are you saving yourself for someone? Someone you love . . . but can't have?" He looked directly into her eyes. "Your slave boy, perhaps?"

"Is that what you think?"

"I'm not sure what to think. I can't quite figure you out yet."

"Then let me enlighten you," she said disdainfully. "I am not married because I don't want to end up like that girl in the play, sold off to someone I don't know and don't love. We are living eight hundred and seventy two years after the founding of Rome! Women are educated. We have more freedom now than ever before. We can work and inherit property. We can initiate divorces. Shouldn't women have more of a say in their own lives?"

"Of course they should," he assured her, "as long as they remain under the protection of a male guardian." She crossed her arms and scowled at him. He had done it again, but at least he spoke the truth. "I didn't mean to upset you, I'm just trying to understand who you are."

"And are you really asking me if I am in love with Apollonius?"

"Falling in love with one's slave happens often, actually."

"You are an obtuse man. And right now I am very annoyed with you, but no, I am not in love with my *slave boy*."

Relief washed over him. "And what about your parents? Do they not wish to see you wed?"

"Of course they do, but I have refused every suitor, and they have respected my wishes."

"Refused every suitor?"

She looked away from him.

He walked over to the bench and sat down. A few moments later, she sat down next to him, looking apologetic.

"I'm sorry for being quarrelsome with you." She put her hand on his cheek and made him look at her. "Can't you see how I feel about you? How can you not understand? But we hold different beliefs. I don't know if I can trust you. And things have come between us that aren't easy for me to forget."

"I know, and I'm trying hard to reassure you." He leaned in and kissed her softly on the lips. "You are the one I want to be with."

She stared at him for a moment. "And I want to be with you. But can you imagine how I would feel if a man whom I didn't care for, or despised even, was touching me intimately, kissing me, undressing me?"

His protective instincts flared. The thought of her with someone else was hard to bear, especially if it made her unhappy. "No. I can't imagine."

"*That*, Evander, is the truth about why I am still unwed."

He pulled her up from the bench. "Now I understand." Either she had never been in love before, or the one she loved hadn't asked for her hand. "You have wonderful parents. I am grateful that they never forced you to marry. He gave her a warm embrace. "Come, let's walk."

~

THERE WAS a commotion outside the forum. A group of slaves was blockading the stone water fountain.

"What is going on here?" asked Evander.

Several slaves answered him at once, saying that the water was tainted and people were getting sick from drinking it. A few townspeople holding buckets told them to move out of the way or risk punishment.

"This is spring water; it should be fine for drinking," Evander told them. "But maybe one of the recent tremors broke a pipe, allowing waste to seep in."

"Where are these sick people?" asked Aurora.

"Mostly in the houses down the street," answered one of the slaves.

"Evander, do you mind if I check in on them?"

He agreed, and the slaves escorted them to a house where they found several people, including children, complaining of cramps and other stomach ailments. They all confirmed that their symptoms had started soon after they drank the water from the fountain.

Aurora asked the slaves to procure some blackberry leaves and bark, then explained how they could make a remedy by boiling down the leaves and bark in water. The concentrated liquid had a healing property, especially for dysentery. She also advised them to boil all the water they were going to drink or use for cooking until the town planners figured out what had happened.

They visited several more houses, and she repeated her instructions. Before they left each house, she made a point to sit with all the children and explain why it was important to drink the medicine every day, even if they didn't like how it tasted.

Aurora truly had the gift of a healer, and Evander felt his heart swell. She was a woman of substance, a woman to be proud of. And perhaps that was more important than finding a woman he could dominate.

He linked her arm through his as they headed up the street. "Would you like to see my house? It is very close by."

"I would love to. And where is your vineyard?"

"My vineyard is just outside the Herculaneum gate. We will have a dinner party there soon. It is a lovely estate."

He led her down a narrow lane that was mostly deserted. Before they turned onto the main thoroughfare again, he pulled her under the eaves. "You fascinate me, do you know that? When I watch you taking care of others so adeptly, it is all I can do not to injure myself, just so that I may find myself under your loving care."

She laughed and looked up at him coyly. "I would be happy to have you under my loving care any day of the week."

He leaned down and kissed her tenderly. Her arms came around him and pulled him closer, encouraging him to take it further. He felt his blood heating up in his veins and was desperate to be somewhere more private. "Let's go," he whispered.

CHAPTER 15

$\mathcal{H}$e kissed her passionately in the semidarkness of his room. The tour of his stately residence had somehow ended here. She had helped him light the oil lamps, and then it was just the two of them, gazing silently at each other. She knew she was on dangerous ground, but she didn't care. There were no parents watching over, just his sister, who had gone out for an evening stroll.

His mouth was hot and insistent, and she could feel his member swelling into her. He removed her scarf, then slowly ran kisses down her shoulder and arm. It felt like he was infusing her body with fire, melting away her senses, and it made her feel dizzy and exhilarated.

She pushed at his shoulders. "I know I am in your bedroom, but still, you may not take my virginity."

"Don't worry, there are many other ways I can love you." He kissed her neck and bit her gently. She breathed in deeply and found his lips again, drawing her fingers through his silky black hair.

He picked her up and carried her over to his bed, laying her down on the soft pillows. He pulled off his tunic and stood before her in his loincloth. The muscles of his lower abdomen were ribbed, and his thighs were strong and powerful. What lay in between them took her breath away, even hidden under the cloth.

His skin looked golden by the fire of the oil lamps, and his whole body seemed to shimmer. "You are so handsome," she murmured, running her fingers slowly down his chest and abdomen, then skimming along the top of his loincloth, dipping her fingers lower into his black hair.

"I'll leave this on," he promised.

Venus give me strength.

She wanted to be reckless and give in to all of her desires, but she knew she needed to be careful. He had a power over her that she had never encountered before. Still, love was a gift from the gods, to be savored and appreciated. She told herself to relax and see where the fates took her.

Evander lay down on the bed beside her and brushed his hand over her dress. "May I take this off? I want to feel your skin on my skin. I want to hold you and make you understand how I feel about you."

Before she could reply, he was removing her stola and the light tunic she wore underneath, leaving her naked on his sheets. He ran his hand slowly down the length of her body, over her soft curves and around her hipbones, leaving her breathless.

"Such beautiful breasts." He caressed them, then leaned over and kissed each nipple before sucking on them gently. She inhaled sharply as a sweet sensation swirled low in her abdomen. *Ah, what pleasure.*

He rolled her on top of him and covered them with a light blanket. The heat of his entire body enfolded her, and she closed her eyes to relish the deep and profound sensations that his warm, naked skin provoked.

His strong, sure hands splayed over her back and across her bottom, pressing her hips down into him. "You feel heavenly. Just to feel your weight on me, to feel you so alive and warm . . ." He wrapped his arms around her and kissed the soft lobe of her ear. "You are a garden," he whispered, "beautiful and lush, with the sweetest fruits to discover . . ."

They kissed each other feverishly, then he rolled on top of her, supporting himself with his arms.

> *"Suns may set, and suns may rise again:*
> *but when our brief light has set,*
> *night is one long everlasting sleep.*
> *Give me a thousand kisses, then a hundred,*
> *then another thousand, and then another hundred,*
> *and, when we've counted up the many thousands,*
> *let us confuse them so as not to know them all,*
> *so that no enemy may cast an evil eye,*
> *when he finds out that there were so many kisses."*

He had recited a love poem by Catullus.

She looked into his eyes, so blue and strikingly beautiful, and was overcome with emotion. She was falling, cascading down into deep waters. He was everything she wanted, everything she had ever hoped to find in a man.

She pulled him toward her and kissed him. His lips felt warm and earthy, and he tasted of sea mist and salt. She became aware of his finger slowly slipping into her. He began to stroke her, making her weak with pleasure.

He sealed her mouth with his as he continued to caress her, tickling her skin and reaching deeply into the private recesses of her body. She was filled with indescribable sensations. A tingle swept through her torso and down through her legs and toes.

Suddenly, she gasped and closed her eyes as her muscles contracted, sending waves of ecstasy rippling through her. She moaned in intense pleasure and squeezed his shoulders.

Venus Pompeiana, you have kept your gifts hidden from me for too long. No wonder you are the most exulted goddess of this city.

She inhaled deeply and let herself float, perfectly sated and blissful. A few minutes later, she opened her eyes to find him watching her. He was lying close by her side, his erection pushing out of his loincloth.

He traced his finger around the curve of her jaw and lip. "You are beautiful without a touch of kohl to your eyes or pomegranate juice to your lips." He leaned over and kissed her on the cheek.

"And you, I'm sure, are every woman's dream." She kissed him several more times, enjoying the moist heat of his mouth. She could stay in his arms forever.

"Now it's your turn." She looked into his eyes as she pulled off his loincloth. She stroked her fingers over him, then pulled on him gently. "You will have to guide me and show me what you like. I know many things, medically, about the male sexual organ, but not much about pleasuring a man."

She kissed his neck and chest as she continued to stroke him, eliciting a moan from him. She moved her hand lower and lifted his sac, feeling it's heavy weight. He groaned again and repositioned his body, his broad shoulders taking up both sides of the bed.

"It seems to me that you know exactly how to touch me."

"Your skin is smooth and unmarred, with no visible signs of rash or disease. You look healthy and virile."

"Thank the gods for that!" he exclaimed, making her laugh.

She gently squeezed his sac in her hand. "Doctors say that if a man's testicles are heavy, it is a good sign. That means that they are filled with life-giving seed."

She felt her belly quiver at the thought of his child inside her and looked up at him, all joking aside. His eyes were burning with passion, but his face was filled with tenderness.

Something very intimate was transpiring between them. He felt it too; she could see the emotions playing across his face. He took her hand and clasped it around his shaft, then closed his hand over hers. Together, they began to pleasure him as he showed her how he liked to be touched.

She watched as his eyes closed and his breathing increased. The muscles of his abdomen tightened, and he dropped his hand to the bed, allowing her to continue. After a little while, moisture began to drip from the tip of his cock, and he moaned loudly, his shoulders lifting up off the sheets. She felt him throbbing in her hand and watched in fascination as his seed pumped out.

He reached for her and held her tightly as his body relaxed and his breathing returned to normal. They lay together in the darkness for a while, just holding each other. Then his kisses began again, and she felt her nipples tighten as they brushed against the hair on his chest.

"Gods, how I want to make love to you."

He splayed his hand over her belly and kissed her breasts, teasing each nipple with his tongue. His fingers played with her *kleitorus*, then slowly slipped inside her again. Her body ignited like dry wood over hot embers, and she closed her eyes. She tried to imagine what it would feel like to have all of him inside of her. *Heavenly.* "I want it too," she whispered.

He pushed her back on the bed, arms shaking with passion, and positioned himself at her body's entrance. He kissed her fiercely as he pressed against her.

The thick head of his member probed at her folds. As her body burned with desire, she realized she was at the point of no return. She wanted to know what it felt like to have a man make love to her. What it felt like to have *this man* make love to her. She opened her legs wider for him.

"Do you accept the gifts of Venus?" he asked, voice raw with passion.

"Yes," she whispered hoarsely.

A rap on the door startled them.

"Brother? Open the door!"

Evander jumped out of the bed and scrambled for his tunic. "What in the dark depths of Hades is going on here?"

Aurora gasped and covered herself with the blanket.

"What do you want?" he growled as he cracked open the door.

Helena pushed her way into the bedroom holding a small oil lamp.

"And what is *he* doing here?" Evander roared, gesturing to Apollonius.

"I sent for him," his sister replied coolly. "Are we too late?"

Evander stared at his sister in disbelief, then looked at Aurora. She slipped farther under the covers, pulling the sheet up over her shoulders. "What is going on, Helena?"

The girl looked back and forth between the two of them with a surprised look on her face. "I am here to save you both before you ruin things entirely!"

"Sister, what goes on in the privacy of one's bedroom is nobody else's business!"

"You are wrong, Brother. It is all of our business. You know how things work in Roman families."

"Sister, you are out of line. I am furious!"

"Brother, I find it hard to believe that out of all of us," she held out her hand and waved it around the room, "I am the voice of reason."

Evander let out a snort. "The voice of madness, maybe!"

"Do not trespass on the goodwill of Aurora's parents. They would not want to see their daughter deflowered before a proper wedding. And you know that you must receive permission from Father before a wedding can be planned."

Evander rubbed his hands over his eyes and heaved a sigh. He came to sit on the bed next to Aurora, who felt that she might die from embarrassment.

Apollonius cleared his throat. "If I may respectfully ask a question of you, Dominus?"

Evander looked up at him. "Well, why not? It seems that all social boundaries are being broken tonight."

"Has my mistress surrendered her virginity to you?"

"That is hardly respectful!"

Aurora tried to keep her face as emotionless as possible.

"No, she has not. If she is compromised in any way, it is my fault," he affirmed.

"I am not blameless," Aurora corrected. Fat tears threatened to roll down her cheeks as she realized the gravity of what she had almost done.

"Aurora, my sweet, don't cry," he soothed, then turned sharply to Helena.

"Sister, we were rudely interrupted at the most tender of moments. There is much that needs to be spoken between us. Now please leave this room!"

"I will escort my mistress home," Apollonius announced insolently. He began to pick up Aurora's clothes, then walked over to the bed.

Evander stood up and blocked him. "What do you think you are doing, *slave*?"

Helena intervened once again. "Brother, do you not understand that he is her caretaker? Slave or not, they are family. You have just violated someone that he loves. Now let him attend to her."

"I have not violated her! What hurtful words you say, Sister! This is too much; I am sending you back to father! Aurora, I will come to you tomorrow. Everything will be fine, my love, I promise you." He kissed her, holding his lips to hers for a few extra moments, then got up and stormed from the room.

"Evander!" Now Aurora was truly upset. She didn't want such a beautiful night to end so abruptly, but what could she do? She was naked under the sheets and couldn't chase after him.

Helena walked over to the bed and sat down. "I am so sorry to have ruined your night. I know that you are mortified. But I think that eventually you will thank me."

Aurora looked at Evander's sister and knew she couldn't be angry. "At least one of us was thinking clearly tonight. Now if you both don't mind."

"Shall I help you dress?" the girl asked.

Aurora shook her head, and Helena and Apollonius left the room.

She stood up from the bed, naked and trembling, and slipped her stola over her head, then wrapped herself in the yellow palla Evander had given her. His gift comforted her and made her feel as if she were still wrapped in his arms.

She exited the room and met with Apollonius's disapproving eyes. "I beg you, do not say anything that will diminish one of the most beautiful nights of my life."

He looked at her solemnly and shook his head, and she followed him quietly out of the domus without another word to Evander.

Apollonius's little oil lamp barely illuminated the dark and desolate street. "How can you put yourself in such a compromising position?" he fumed. "Did you not think of your reputation? Did you not think of your father and grandfather? Is this how you honor them?"

His admonishment seemed to go on forever as she followed behind him on the narrow sidewalk. A dog began to bark from inside a domus as they passed.

"Do you not remember our conversation on the night of the dinner party?" he asked in a hushed tone. "You have done a terrible job of resisting him. Mark my words, you will be the cause of your own destruction."

"That's not fair, Apollonius! I care for him!"

"He seduced you, Aurora. And you fell right into his trap."

"He didn't seduce me. We just got carried away . . ."

"And has he asked you to marry him?"

"It's a little soon, don't you think?"

"But not too soon for him to take you to his bedroom?"

Her heart started to sink; he had never actually spoken of a future between them.

"Why are you acting like this?" she cried.

"Because I don't want him to hurt you! He *will* leave Pompeii, Aurora. And he will leave you behind." He was walking briskly now, and she had to shuffle along quickly to keep up with him. He threw a glance over his shoulder, then stopped abruptly, causing her to barrel into him. "Apollonius!"

He grabbed her by the elbow to steady her. "Listen to me, Aurora. There is love, and there is the ocean. If you find a love that comforts you, you will be fortunate, but if you seek an ocean, you will drown."

"And what, by the girdle of Venus, is that supposed to mean?"

"Evander is your ocean. He is a love that breaks through all the rules. He inspires feelings in you that are too deep, too powerful, and too reckless. If you don't learn how to control them, you will fall." He spun on his heel and continued walking.

"If fall I must, then I should desire to fall from the height of heaven."

"How poetic of you. You need to grow up."

"How dare you speak to me like that! You are my *slave!*"

He stopped abruptly and glared at her, his eyes filled with pain.

She couldn't believe that she had just said that to him. She loved Apollonius as if he were her own brother. "Oh, Apollonius, I didn't mean that, you know I didn't mean that. I'm sorry." She linked her arm through his. As much as she wanted to refute him, he was right. Her heart and mind had been pierced with Cupid's arrow from the moment she first saw Evander. Her ability to reason and make good choices had been compromised.

"Do you think I can't feel love?" he asked. "Or that I am ignorant in matters between men and women? I may be a slave, but I am a man, after all."

"I just don't believe that Evander would hurt me."

"Do you love him?"

She remained silent. She definitely had strong feelings toward him, but *love*? How could she measure that? She had nothing to compare it to.

Apollonius stopped walking and held his oil lamp up to her eyes, waiting for her to respond. "Perhaps we don't choose love, Aurora. Love chooses us. Sometimes when we least expect it."

CHAPTER 16

They set sail for the isle of Capri before sunrise. The sky was dusky blue, the water smooth as glass. He wanted to share the sunrise with her, and a beautiful day of sand and water. She stood a short distance from him on the deck, near the towering swan head that dominated the stern. Her eyes were closed; her face was turned into the breeze. He feared that she was still reeling from the embarrassing events of the other night.

The first rays of sunlight began to peek out from behind the eastern hills, lending beauty and mystery to the morning. Helena and Apollonius had joined them out of propriety and stood together on the upper deck, just behind them.

He was still terribly upset with his sister for intruding on his privacy, but if he was truly honest with himself, he knew that she was right for intervening. He could have ruined everything between himself and Aurora if he had taken her virginity. He believed that she might be the one for him, but in order to even consider a proper wedding, he needed his father's approval.

He let out a sigh. He would have to do some convincing, and he wasn't entirely sure how his father would react, especially when he learned of the offer that Trebius Valens had made: an introduction to Emperor Titus in Rome, trade contracts with the vendors of Pompeii, and protection from pirates by the Empire's navy.

Of course, I don't have to tell him.

But if Titus supported him, it would be everything that his father was hoping for, the reason he had sent him back to Pompeii. All of this came at a high price, one that he was not willing to pay. If everything Trebby offered came to fruition, he would have to marry Valentina.

Which meant that he needed a different plan.

"What's the matter?" Aurora looked up at him, her cheeks rosy from the sea mist blowing around them.

He could never tell her what had transpired between himself and Trebby; he had already told her too much. "I'm just thinking about business, and I'm mad at myself as well. I let things go too far the other night in my bedroom. I'm sorry. I never meant to hurt you."

"I have no regrets, Evander. Being close to you in that way, sharing what we shared, it was the most beautiful night of my life."

"Come here." He kissed her forehead and hugged her close. "Look at how incredible the sunrise is from out here in the bay. I wanted you to see this."

"It is spectacular," she agreed. "The rays of the sun cast the hills into shadows, and yet they catch the top of the temples around the bay and make them sparkle."

He gestured to the open sea. "Don't you feel as if the whole world is spread out before you? As though you can go anywhere, do anything? You can leave behind all that ails you—your worries, your sorrows, your frustrations—and wake up new and refreshed, as if it were the first morning of your life."

"Is that how the sea makes you feel?"

"Yes," he admitted. "When I watch the rolling waves, they work some magic in me, they give me hope."

"Who do you want to be, that you're not already?" she asked.

He thought about it for a moment before he answered.

"I want my life to matter. I want my business to prosper; I want to step out from behind my father's shadow. And one day, I want a family of my own." He squeezed her shoulders as he said the last sentence.

"Admirable aspirations. I'm sure you will achieve all of your dreams."

"What about you? Who do you want to be?"

"I want to be a medica so that I may help cure others, but a part of me just wants to play the lyre and write poetry." She paused and looked down at the sea. "I want to be strong, but so often I let my emotions get the best of me."

"You are strong," he assured her. "Stronger and smarter than any girl I've ever met." He turned her toward him. "And I'm sure you will achieve all of your dreams."

They were quiet for a while as they looked at the glassy water and the cities around the bay that were just starting to awaken. He loved mornings on the sea; they felt fresh and unbroken, promising and clean.

"You and I are connected now. Do you feel it?" he asked, holding her close and pressing her cheek to his chest.

"I'm not sure." She shrugged.

"I care very much about you, Aurora."

"But I am not a sophisticated lady who wears makeup and baubles and dresses like an Egyptian."

"Perhaps not, but you are certainly educated and refined." He rubbed her back.

"But do you really know me?" She searched his face. "I relish the sound of the lyre and the wind rustling through the leaves of the trees in my garden. I crave the words of a beautiful poem. I am not in competition with anyone, nor do I want to be. Surely, you would prefer a more worldly girl than I?"

"Actually, I like that you are from a small city by the sea. I find you enchanting; the way you close your eyes when you listen to music, the way you giggle when you've had too much wine. I like you exactly as you are. But what do you mean by competition?"

"I've seen how women look at you."

"It doesn't matter how women look at me, what matters is how *you* look at me."

"You are a man of power and wealth. Your father would never approve of me, not when he has a business to protect. My family has no ties to the Flavian dynasty; I descend from the Samnites."

He looked longingly into her eyes and saw her vulnerability. "I am falling for you, Aurora, really falling. Do you understand what I am saying? But you are right. My father does have certain . . . *expectations* of me."

She shifted in his arms.

"And that is why I need to go back to Corinth. I will leave at the end of summer."

He heard her inhale sharply. "Will you come back?"

"Of course I will come back," he promised.

"How long will you be gone?"

"One month, maybe two."

She remained quiet for a while. "At least it will give me time to devote to my studies. I have been terribly remiss since you arrived in Pompeii." He knew she was trying to sound cheerful, but her voice was strained.

They continued to sail toward the southern coast of Capri, past three towering rock formations that jutted majestically out of the sea, and into a secluded cove, where his slaves threw down an anchor. They would have to take a dinghy to shore. While they hadn't taken the largest of his merchant ships, it still was too big to risk going into shallow waters.

This particular ship had the capacity to hold well over a thousand amphorae filled with wine, oil, or garum, with room to spare for a few slabs of marble. The ship was painted a beautiful red, and its sails were made of brown linen that had been bleached lighter by the sun. The *Corbita* was one of his favorite ships, and he wouldn't risk putting a hole in its hull.

A little while later, Evander watched as his slaves and Apollonius set up a tent and some blankets on the sand for the ladies to recline on.

Apollonius was strong, hardworking, and dependable, but for some reason he didn't want to like him. Maybe it was because Aurora was so fond of him. It still galled him that the slave had witnessed Valentina kissing him on the night of the dinner party.

But even worse was when Apollonius had sauntered into his bedroom with his sister and swept Aurora away, as if he were rescuing her from the Minotaur. Did he think himself to be some kind of hero now?

Gods, it was absurd to be this bothered by a boy! And even as he stood here, Apollonius was casting him the evil eye. Once again, he felt the need to explain himself to a slave. What was life coming to?

"Apollonius, come here!"

The slave dropped the blanket he was holding and trudged over to him.

"Why are looking at me so accusingly?"

"I am not, Dominus."

"But you are. I do not owe you any explanation, and yet I feel compelled to give it. I will be leaving Pompeii within the month to conduct my business in the Mediterranean, and then to return to my father in Corinth."

The slave frowned. "Does Aurora know?"

"Yes."

Apollonius dared not look him in the eye. "She will be crushed if your father refuses her."

"No, I'm the one who will be crushed."

The slave's stance seemed to soften toward him, and Evander looked toward the sea. "You will take care of her while I am gone?"

"Always."

~

EVANDER PULLED Aurora playfully by the hand as they splashed through the shallow waters of the cove, exploring the hidden crannies of the rock formations. "Follow me, this one leads to a grotto. We just need to swim under the arch to get inside."

"Is it safe?" she asked, peering down into the water.

"It's not the grotto you must worry about, but rather the man who wishes to ravish you once we get inside." He laughed, kissing her wet nose.

They waded through the water until it was shoulder deep, then Evander dove underneath the arch. When he was inside, he called for her to come, his voice echoing through the rocks. A few moments later, her head popped up through the water, and her eyes filled with wonder at what she saw.

The grotto was a large, hollowed-out rock formation that let in sunlight from a crevice below them. The reflection of the water danced across the walls and ceiling, creating an otherworldly experience. But most incredibly, everything inside the grotto was bathed in glittering blue that radiated light from within. It was the kind of blue one saw only in a dream. There was no color to match it on any painter's palette.

"This is amazing!" she cried. "I've never experienced anything like it!"

He helped pull her up onto a flat ledge that ran along the side of the cavern. They sat shoulder to shoulder, marveling at the secret beauty of the grotto.

He leaned over and kissed her, then pulled her into his lap. "This is just the beginning of the things I want to show you in the world, the wonders I want you to see."

"It's like our own little world in here. It's so incredible."

"And private." He held her close, his hands caressing her wet skin. He kissed the hollow of her shoulder, then up her neck to her lips. Heat flared between them as it had the night in his bedroom. He wondered at the way she affected him. He had been with many women, but Aurora touched his heart in a different way. She was smart and unwittingly sexy, confident but vulnerable in a most endearing manner.

She was kissing him back now, her hands stroking his bare chest. He closed his eyes and breathed deeply as his body began to stir. He lay back on the flat rock and pulled her between his legs, her wet tunic plastered to her body like a second skin. The nipples of her plump breasts were poking through the fabric. He encircled her body with his arms and pressed her close to him. "I will miss you when I am gone." His throat was tight with emotion.

"I will miss you too, so much."

"I want to make love to you, right here, right now, but I must content myself with simply holding you close to my heart," he whispered. He ran his hands down her back and over her thighs, pressing her hips into his.

"But it's not enough," she whispered.

They listened to the sound of the water lapping gently at the cavern walls and echoing through the grotto.

She ran her finger over his bottom lip. "This is a most enchanting place. And if I believed in magic, I would cast over you a powerful love spell so that you will think of only me when you leave Pompeii. But I don't believe in magic."

"Do you believe in prayers?" he asked.

"Of course."

"The Greeks take love spells very seriously. They use them as prayers as well, as an invocation to the gods."

"Even the Greek men?" she asked.

"All the time. They use spells to make a woman go mad with desire, and women use them to keep their men faithful."

"And lovers?"

"Lovers use spells to bind themselves to each other."

She rolled off of him and looked at the water thoughtfully. "Evander, would you allow me to try an herbal remedy on you? It's from the medical scroll that my mother is making me memorize."

"What is it for?"

"It is just a drink for lovers to share; it can't hurt you. But the scroll says that it can be used for casting a love spell as well."

"That sounds intriguing . . ."

"Shall we try it, then?" Excitement filled her voice.

"I didn't know you were so romantic."

"Half-romantic," she laughed, "and half-driven by medical curiosity."

He looked at her seriously. "I do know that I don't want to lose you. And I don't want you to lose hope while I am away." He scooped her closer to him. "So, yes, Aurora Fortunas, cast your love spell over me and give me a potion to drink. If nothing else, it will be something for us to remember while I'm gone, like a Dionysian Mystery or secret initiation."

"It's settled, then. Let's pick a night and go down by the sea. I will make the elixir for us." She looked into his eyes. "I am looking forward to it."

He leaned closer and kissed her, letting his lips linger for a while. "Let's make the potion together. We can go to the market, buy the ingredients, then take everything back to my house."

"Your house is what got us in trouble in the first place."

"My bedroom, not my house," he corrected. *"And even a god finds it hard to love and be wise at the same time."*

She stroked his chest until her fingers found their way down to his loincloth. She pulled at the wet material until it fell away from his hips. For a moment, he didn't breathe, and he knew he should stop her.

They couldn't go on this way. They needed to stop teasing each other, or propriety be damned, he was going to lose control and plow himself into that sweet virgin body until he had thoroughly loved her. How he wanted to push himself up between those supple thighs, to feel her body sheathe him, to feel her muscles tighten around him as she came.

She clasped him firmly in her hand, causing him to moan, then leaned down and took him into her mouth. The sensations were divine as she stroked and caressed him, licking the length of him with her soft tongue.

"You don't have to be so gentle," he assured her.

She sucked on him harder and stroked him more forcefully. It wasn't long before the heat and wetness of her mouth forced his body to surrender. His seed spurted forth, thick and hot, onto the skin of his belly. He let out a grunt and rested his head back on the slab of rock. When he opened his eyes, she was propped up on her elbow, grinning at him.

"Pleased with yourself, are you?"

She smiled. "I am."

THEY STRODE along the beach arm in arm, kissing each other as they walked. He stopped her for a moment, just to hold her. The warm breezes of the bay blew around them, caressing them, protecting them. It was a beautiful moment, one of the most beautiful of his life, and he wanted to remember it always. He wanted to carve it in stone, like a monument that would stand the test of time.

When they returned to the camp, Aurora picked up her clothes and set off to change in the woods while Evander approached his sister. Helena was sitting under the tent, where a table and four small stools had been set up. The slaves were shuffling around her, setting out fruit, bread, and cheese for prandium.

His sister was watching the slave boy attentively, seemingly lost in thought. Apollonius was sitting on the small boat they had taken to shore. He was pulling up a net filled with amphorae of wine and fresh water that had been kept under the boat to keep cold.

"Why four chairs?" he asked her.

Helena jumped, for she hadn't seen him approach. She stood to greet him. "Brother," she said calmly, "I have asked Apollonius to eat with us."

Evander frowned, his eyebrows drawing together. "Why would you encourage him to overstep his station?"

She looked up at him defiantly. "Did you not overstep your boundaries the other night?"

"That was different. Aurora is my equal in society."

"I know you will not understand, but Apollonius is honorable, wise, and good. If only you knew his story. He should have never been a slave."

"Helena, he *is* a slave, regardless of how it came to be. I think you are just lonely. You need to make some friends in Pompeii and stop socializing with those beneath you."

Apollonius approached cautiously, carrying several amphorae. "The meal is ready, Dominus."

Helena stepped away from her brother and glared at him.

Evander sighed. "Apollonius, I would like to invite you to sit and eat with us. But make it clear to the other slaves that they may in no way serve you. And know that I am doing this not because I agree, but because my sister and Aurora hold you in very high esteem."

Apollonius bowed to him, and a wide smile spread across Helena's face.

"I am honored, Dominus."

THEY FILLED their small plates with chunks of cheese, plump olives, and succulent roasted meat kabobs spiced with ginger and cumin. They laughed and relaxed and drank several glasses of fragrant red wine as they dug their toes in the warm sand.

Apollonius entertained them with stories of Emperor Tiberius, whose Villa Jovis stood on one of the highest peaks of Capri. "Just a little over forty years ago, the former emperor lived here in solitude and hardly ever left the island. Some say he was depraved, and some say he was just a sad and broken man at the death of his son, Drusus."

"Others say he was afraid of being assassinated, and so he built a beautiful castle way up high, on the northeast corner of Capri," Apollonius explained. "It is said that here in Capri he gave in to all of his vices: drinking, feasting, and secret pleasures. In fact, the island is still referred to as 'The Old Goat's Den,' making a play on the name Capri, which means goat."

Evander glanced slyly at Aurora. "Well, being surrounded by the beauty of the sand and the sea, it's not hard to imagine why someone would be given over to secret pleasures."

She looked back at him and smirked. "Yes, it does seem as though the entire island, with its jutting rock formations and secret coves and grottos, was made for lovers."

Later that afternoon, they set sail for Pompeii. The girls napped on his bed in the deck cabin while he and Apollonius manned the sails along with his crew. He had a lot of time to converse with the slave in a more informal manner, and he admitted to himself that slowly, very slowly, he was starting to like the boy.

CHAPTER 17

"Mother? Evander and I are going to the market to buy some herbs."

"Can you buy me some lovage roots?"

"Of course." She kissed her mother's cheek and turned to go.

Teo ran into the atrium. "Can I come too, Sister?"

Aurora looked at Evander as she remembered the debacle that had happened last time she let him come with her. "No, Teo, not today. Evander and I have some private business to attend to." Her mother raised her eyebrows but didn't ask any questions, then wished them a good day.

Evander had been increasingly busy with his father's business since they had come back from Capri. Now that he had set a date to go back to Corinth, he wanted to make sure that his ships were filled with merchandise.

She had seen very little of him over the past week, but they had chosen today to go to the market and make their love potion. Tonight, they would go down to the sea to cast their spell. She laughed inwardly at the wild absurdity of it. She was a medica. She didn't believe in magic or spells, but the love potion . . . now that was intriguing. Could she really persuade Evander to make love to her before he left for Corinth through the combination of specific herbs? Was she hoping it would work? Was she prepared to follow through if it did?

She was worried that he would never come back to Pompeii, especially if his father disapproved of the match. But what if she gave him something to remember her by? The pleasure of her body? The possibility of a baby? Perhaps he would feel more of a tie to her.

She linked her arm through his, and they set out into the bright morning sunshine. A sturdy little mule and driver ambled down the street, and she enjoyed listening to the clickity-clack of the iron mule shoes over the cobblestones as they passed by.

The fruit and vegetable market was filled with people, and they stopped in front of a vendor who was busy weighing apricots on a hanging metal scale. She was one of her father's clients. "Good morning, Celia."

The woman smiled at them, revealing several missing front teeth. "*Salve*, Aurora. I have fresh figs from Herculaneum this morning. Here, take some for your family." She held up a small brown sack in her calloused hand.

"Thank you, Celia. I will also need some pomegranates, pine nuts, and arugula leaves."

"Making a love potion, are ye?" the vendor asked slyly.

Aurora turned red with embarrassment. "Of course not! It is for one of my mother's recipes."

The vendor looked Evander up and down, winked at her, then gathered the requested items and dropped them into Aurora's bag.

"Oh, I also need some lovage roots."

"Sea parsley? Just let me grab 'em from the back."

The vendor returned with a green leafy vegetable in her hand, the roots still covered in mud.

"What is sea parsley?" Evander asked.

"Here, taste it," Celia offered, tearing off a few green leaves and handing them to him. "It's very flavorful. And the bottom of the plant," she fingered the roots, shaking off some of the dirt, "has magical properties."

"Magical?" Evander said disbelievingly as he dropped some *asses* into her coin jar.

Celia let out a raspy laugh. "Magical," she affirmed as she began weighing plums for another customer.

"Come now, Evander, it's *medicinal*," Aurora chided as they walked away. "The roots have medicine in them that bring down a fever."

"Well, what's the difference, if it makes you feel better?" he asked, gesturing with his hand.

"*Magic* is unexplainable—if it even exists—while *medicinal* is a property of various plants. We use different parts of plants to help heal sickness."

"Don't you believe in magic at all, Aurora?"

"No, not really."

"Then why do you believe in omens? Remember the morning of the earthquake? You became very upset when the dogs started to howl."

"Hmmm. I suppose because an omen is a sign from the gods. It's a way for them to communicate with us."

"So you believe in the gods, but you don't believe in magic? Aren't they one and the same?"

She looked at him in surprise and wrinkled her forehead. "Well, if the gods are behind the action, then I don't consider it to be magic. But it does seem as though they are divided by a rather thin line."

Why *did* she believe in omens?

They were just as mystical as any magic and yet . . . she most definitely believed in reading the signs, signs that the gods were sending.

She supposed it was just a matter of habit and tradition. The emperor made decisions that affected thousands of lives based on the direction of an eagle's flight. *But magic?* Maybe she didn't know herself as well as she thought if she embraced one aspect of mysticism but scorned another.

Evander took her hand in his. "Now where do we find wild orchid leaves and spotted lizard skin?"

～

A FEW HOURS LATER, they returned to Evander's house and laid out everything they had purchased on the kitchen table. Evander's slaves were still gone, as he had sent them all to the market to buy food and spices for the cook since Aurora was staying for dinner.

Aurora greeted the puppy Hercules with hugs and kisses as he wiggled at her toes with excitement. She then opened up her scroll and began to read the directions for making the potion. "We are going to need a mortar and pestle."

Evander searched through the many kitchen items stored on the shelves. "Copper pot, strainer, measuring cup, cake pan shaped like a pig . . . mortar and pestle, got it."

"We should probably start with the pomegranates. Roll them over the table to release the seeds and juices."

"Like this?"

Aurora laughed at his ineptitude. "Well, sort of . . ."

A little while later, Helena peeked her head into the kitchen. "What in the name of Jupiter are you two up to now?"

They stopped their mixing and grinding and looked up. "*Salve,* Helena! We are just trying something out," answered Aurora.

"Is my *brother* preparing *dinner?*"

Evander cleared his throat. "Uh, not exactly. We are making a flavorful fruit concoction to drink tonight on the beach."

"Oh, that sounds delicious! Can I help?" she asked, entering into the kitchen.

"I would prefer not," Evander said, shuffling her back out.

Helena pouted and called for Manolo to take her and the

puppy for a walk through town. When the potion was done, they poured it carefully into a small amphora and corked the top. They relaxed for a little while on the couch in Evander's favorite room.

"So what exactly does your mother use this potion for?"

"According to the scroll, it is an herbal supplement that increases sexual drive and fertility. It is also used to promote feelings of love and attraction."

He made a choking sound. "And we are going to drink this tonight, *together*?"

"Yes," she answered mischievously.

"Are you trying to kill me? I really don't need help with my sexual urges, especially around you."

"I just want to see if the potion really works."

"That's what I'm afraid of!"

"Calm down, it's all in good fun." Aurora kissed him playfully, then closed her eyes and fell asleep on his lap. She awoke a few hours later to the smell of a delicious meal.

"Did you cook for me, Evander?"

He laughed heartily. "You are looking at a man who has never stepped foot in the kitchen before today. Let's go eat before our walk down to the beach."

They entered the garden to find Apollonius sitting with Helena in the shade of an olive tree. He greeted them cordially, then pulled Aurora aside.

"What are you doing here?" she asked.

"Your mother sent me. She knows what you are up to, and she urges you not to use the potion. It has strong . . . effects."

"How did she find out?"

"Between your trip to the market and Helena stopping over with the puppy to see Teo . . ."

She let out a sigh. "Helena told her?"

"Only that you two were busy making some fruit drink for the beach tonight."

"Oh gods . . ."

"What are you planning, Aurora?"

Aurora felt heat rush to her face. "Tonight was meant as a way for us to pledge ourselves to each other before he leaves for Corinth." She huffed at him and walked away mumbling about people getting into her business.

A little while later dinner was served, and Aurora and Evander reclined close together on one of the dining couches. Helena lay across from them, alone, as a group of slaves stood behind her, waiting to serve her.

Evander made it a point to explain each dish that his cook had prepared.

"Taste the spices, Aurora. There are at least fifteen different ones in this sauce alone. Do you like it?"

She sipped the sauce from his spoon and closed her eyes as the flavors dispersed on her tongue. "Delicious." When she was with Evander, she enjoyed the little details in life that she had never taken the time to notice before.

Apollonius had stayed and insisted that he would escort her down to the beach later, much to her dismay. He was now serving Helena each of the cook's creations. He placed them before her, handed her dining utensils, and kept her entertained. Aurora imagined that the girl was very lonely living here without her mother or sisters, and she felt sorry for her. She promised herself she would spend more time with her from now on. They only had a few weeks left before the girl would return to Corinth with Evander.

LATER THAT EVENING, they walked down to the beach as the stars came out and found a secluded cove hidden from view. They had managed to sneak away without Apollonius noticing, but she knew she would hear about it later.

Aurora spread a blanket on the sand, then pulled out two cups from her satchel and placed them next to the amphora that held the love potion. So far, her plan of seduction was going smoothly. She sat down on the blanket next to Evander and watched the gentle waves rolling in from the bay.

"So how do we cast a love spell on each other?" she asked. "That is to say, how do they do it in Greece? Around here they scratch the spell onto a metal tablet and bury it."

"For a poet, you're not very good at this," he jested and kissed her on the nose. He popped the cork, divided the potion equally into the two cups, then handed her one.

"I'll begin."

"Are you afraid?" she asked.

"Afraid of what? The potion or the spell?"

"Both! What if they actually work?"

"Isn't that the point?" He leaned over, wrapped his arm around her, and gave her a long, deep kiss.

"I'm ready," she said breathlessly, wondering why she felt so nervous.

"Come closer and face me. Now hold up your cup and inter-twine your arm with mine. Look me in the eyes."

She did as he said, a silly smile spreading over her face.

"I ask Venus, protector of lovers, to bind you to me with a spell that no mortal can ever break. May she keep our love strong and protect us from obstacles that would keep us apart from this day forward." He stared at her intensely for a moment, and those fire-flies began to flutter about in her stomach.

He gestured for her to begin.

"I ask Venus, goddess of lovers, to bind you to me with a spell that no mortal can ever break. May she protect you and return you safely to me each time you must go away."

They tipped their cups to their lips and drank the elixir. When they were done, they kissed and gazed into each other's eyes.

"That was a fiery mixture indeed," he said. "I still feel it burning my tongue."

"Yes, the rocket leaves added a lot of heat." Aurora was quiet for a moment, then looked at him more seriously. "Evander, the elixir can't hurt us, but the spell—at first I thought it was nonsense, but I feel like we just did something unalterable."

"Perhaps in the eyes of the goddess, we did," he answered. "It seems that was more of a prayer than a spell. Aurora, have you seriously considered having a future with me? You *are* the girl who has refused every suitor."

"Of course I have. I have been in your bed. I have let myself get closer to you than any other man. The bigger question is whether *you* have considered a future with *me*."

"I wouldn't be here tonight with you if I hadn't. But I am restrained by my father's will. I feel that we shouldn't go forward until I know that I have his support. And yet, when I am with you, I cannot deny my feelings." He kissed her tenderly, then stood up. "I feel a little light-headed. Perhaps I should bring you home before those herbs begin to burn us to ashes."

The wine and herbs were definitely having the intended effect. She also felt light-headed and giddy, and parts of her body were tingling. She stood up and put her arms around his shoulders. "No, I want you to make love to me before you leave for Corinth."

He inhaled deeply. "Why do you ask this of me? You know I can't resist you."

"I want to know what it's like to be with a man. I want to know how it feels—to be with *you*, Evander. I want to share something deep and profound with you before you leave. I know it's irresponsible—imprudent and unwise. I only know that I want to be with you."

He walked her to the water's edge, then pulled her into his arms and pressed her hips into his. He was already aroused; she could feel his erection through his tunic.

"Right here, then," he whispered in her ear. "In the water. We will be unwise together."

Suddenly her legs gave out, and she fell to the ground, confused.

"Evander—did you just push me down?"

But he was also having a hard time keeping his balance. Had they just poisoned themselves with that drink? What was going on?

Suddenly, she was under water as a huge wave broke over her head. The force of the water sucked her back into the bay. She came to the surface gasping and choking. Evander grabbed her arms and dragged her back to shore.

"It's an earthquake!" he shouted. "It must have struck out at sea. We need to get to higher ground! We have to move before another wave hits us!"

They scrambled over the sand and up the path toward the city gate. He pulled her along forcefully until her legs gave out and she cried for him to stop. They turned and looked back at the sea. The waves were violent now, crashing against the shore and tossing small fishing boats onto the sand.

She stood there shocked, her hair and clothes dripping wet.

In the moonlight, his face was as white as plaster. "It was just so unexpected. I think I should take you home."

HER MOTHER WAS WAITING at the front door with a scowl on her face. "You went swimming in the dark?"

"No, Mother, the ground started to shake and knocked me over. Next I knew, a wave crashed over my head."

"Lady Lucina, there must have been an earthquake at sea. We were taken completely by surprise."

"Where is Apollonius? I sent him to find you hours ago. I don't like what is going on here. You two are getting way ahead of yourselves."

"Mother, please—"

"No, you listen to me, Daughter! I know what it feels like to be young and in love with a man. I know how impatient you both may feel, but you *must* have permission from both of your fathers to continue this relationship. And let's not forget Grandfather; he also has a say."

"Lady Lucina, I—"

"Evander, you may have the best of intentions toward my daughter, but if your father refuses her, what good is it? I will not stand by and watch her get her heart broken. I'm sorry, but these are the rules that we live by."

"And as for you, Aurora, I think it would be wise to devote more time to your studies. Grandfather has been asking for you. Now say good night." Her mother stormed from the atrium, and her heart sank to her stomach. Her mother rarely got upset with her, and when she did, it hurt.

"What have we done?" she asked.

Evander shook his head. "We have done nothing wrong. Love is never wrong—it can't be. Our feelings are too strong to be mistaken. You'll see. Fortune will be with us." He kissed her good night and walked out of the door, leaving her staring at the empty spaces.

Her mother came to her room just as she was dousing the oil lamps. "What were you thinking, drinking that love potion?"

"I was just being carefree, Mother. Enjoying a summer night with Evander. That is all."

"But you know that is a powerful medicine. The combination of those plants is known to help men get an erection and help women conceive. Is that what you wanted?"

"We used it as a spell, Mother."

"Spells are just superstitious nonsense, and you know that! What were you really trying to do, Aurora?"

"He will be leaving soon, and I wanted to bind him to me somehow." She searched her mother's face. "Do you understand?"

"Binding him to you by pregnancy is not the option you want. If he is serious about you, he will bind you with a ring."

"It's not that simple. His father is hoping for an advantageous marriage. That is something I can't offer him. My great-great-grandfather fought against General Sulla; the walls of Pompeii still bear the battle marks. Our ancestors defied Rome, and Rome doesn't soon forget."

"And what would you do if you found yourself pregnant by a man who can't marry you?"

"I hadn't gotten that far. I only knew that I wanted to be with him, more than anything I've ever wanted before."

Her mother embraced her. "My daughter, you can't change the course the Fates have set for you. Good or bad, you must learn to accept what life brings your way. We will not speak of this to your father, ever." She kissed her good night and left the room, closing the door behind her.

Aurora climbed into her bed and buried her face in the pillow, wishing Evander was next to her. She didn't know who she was anymore. She had disappointed her mother and tried to persuade Evander to make love to her against her better judgment. She felt like a stranger even to herself. What had she been thinking?

And that crazy wave that had taken her under felt like a sign from the goddess herself. It had happened right at the moment when Evander had agreed . . . Venus, born of sea foam, had spoken. Was she telling her to beware? Trying to protect her from her own foolish ways? Or saying that she had heard their prayers?

Only time would tell. But something was different now. She felt bound to Evander in a new way. The words he had spoken during the incantation had finally revealed his intention to have a future with her.

And that set her heart on fire more than any love potion ever could.

CHAPTER 18

"Your grandfather is asking you to tend to the wounded gladiators at the next game?" Evander shifted his weight uncomfortably on the marble bench.

It was a hot day with little breeze. They sat in his garden, in a pretty corner shaded by two walnut trees and a trellis of grapevines. Aurora strummed lazily on the lyre as they conversed.

"Yes," she sighed. "He knows that I hate the games, but he needs my help."

"Why didn't you remind him that they upset you?"

She could see that the prospect of her dressing the injuries of the flirtatious and bawdy gladiators was not making him happy.

"You may oppose the games," she said in a deep voice, *"but this is the world you live in, and you must learn to accept it."* She made an expression of distaste. "That is what he told me, but I will never accept it."

"And what about your parents?"

"My parents will be there, but they will be busy politicizing with Titus's newly appointed senator and Trebius Valens up in the podium. Apparently the senator will be visiting Campania that weekend and has let Trebby know that he will be attending the games in Pompeii."

"I don't think your grandfather needs your help at all. I have a feeling he has alternative reasons for making you do this. He may be trying to toughen you up."

"It's possible. He always says I'm too soft." She looked up absently at the almost ripe grapes hanging down above them. "Gladiators, ugh!"

"So you really don't like them? I thought they were every girl's fantasy?" he teased. "They can't be all bad."

"Those murderous beasts! Hardly!" She shook her head vehemently. "I mean, what kind of sport is killing off innocent animals?"

"And criminals and murderers," he added.

"A death for a death. Murderers are easier to justify, but who is a criminal? Someone who steals to put food in his child's belly? That is another issue entirely. What's more, the animals are killed needlessly, and the emperors have been told that it's not necessary. The people would be more than happy to simply watch them run about, but the emperor insists on the slaughter. It's outrageous!"

"Perhaps so, but the crime rate would go up sharply if they stopped killing the murderers and criminals."

Aurora pursed her lips and scowled at him. "What will future generations think of us if all they remember are the bloody games, the crucifixions, the exposure of innocent babies? They will think us no better than the barbarians. The games tarnish us, Evander!"

He started to interject, but she cut him off.

"We are a people who strive to be educated and moral. We love our families and pets, and we are generous with our clients. We appreciate beautiful gardens, art, literature, and music, just to name a few. I worry for my children, I really do. What kind of legacy will we leave them?"

"Future generations will remember us for our good as well as our bad," he assured her. "They will remember us for the contributions we made to the world; they will forgive us our disgraces. Every generation makes mistakes."

"That's a poor excuse!" She jumped up. "If I could only be a lawyer and study Roman law! I would fight these injustices!"

Evander chuckled.

"Put that down," he said, taking the lyre. He put his arms around her shoulders and hugged her close. "Such emotion! You need to have faith in people. We will change the world for the better one step at a time, one person at a time, one *baby* at a time. You'll see."

"Will I?" she asked.

"Yes. You are an amazing woman, and I have no doubt that it will be women like you who will bring about such change in the world."

She wrapped her arms around his waist and held him tightly, allowing his essence to enfold her. "The sound of your heart comforts me greatly."

"Don't worry about the games. I will be right there if you need me."

A FEW DAYS LATER, she found herself at Pompeii's grand *spectacula*, the first of its kind to be built all in stone. Inside the arena, the *velarium* had been drawn to protect the spectators from the intense sun and heat, and outside, vendors were busy setting up their tables with refreshing drinks, snacks, and souvenirs.

The excitement in the air was palpable. Children ran about imitating their favorite gladiator, and crowds poured in, not only from Pompeii, but also from the neighboring cities of Nuceria, Stabiae, and Herculaneum.

To add to the festivities, a group of musicians played triumphant marches on their horns in the center of the square.

A large tent had been set up outside the spectacula where she and her grandfather, along with a large group of slaves, would tend to the wounded, or in some cases, put them out of their misery.

The gladiators themselves were an expensive commodity and were expected to survive their wounds and fight again for many years. The lanista spared no expense for the pampered brawlers, providing them with bathing facilities, excellent food, and medical care. The losers were always spared—unless one was a convicted criminal.

Some gladiators lived long enough to buy their freedom and retire, but this was not usual. Most of them were dead by the age of thirty, either from internal injuries or complications arising from flesh wounds.

Some gladiators were mere boys who had sold their freedom for five years as a means of providing money for their families. But regardless of how they came to be a gladiator, they all had an ego the size of Mount Vesuvius and thought they were the gods' gift to women.

Aurora looked down self-consciously at her rough brown tunic. This was not a day for nice dresses, and she was sure that by the end of the games her tunic would be stained in blood, dirt, and sweat.

She felt exhilarated at the prospect of practicing her medical skills, and she knew she should be proud of her accomplishments, but there was one thing pricking at her like a thorn, and her name was Valentina.

She would certainly sneer if she happened to see Aurora in these rough clothes, hair tied back, and doing a job that many didn't believe was an appropriate discipline for a woman. She would probably seek her out on purpose, just so she could laugh at her, tell her she was dressed like a slave, and taunt Evander over his taste in women.

Evander approached, and she steeled her mind, mentally

preparing for the day ahead. He looked striking in his leather sandals and expensive tunic with gold embroidery. He and Helena had also been invited to watch the games from the podium with the Valens family, Aurora's parents, and the senator.

"Good morning, beautiful!" he greeted.

She raised her eyebrows at him. "You can't mean that."

He looked her over. "The clothes don't matter. You would be beautiful in rags." He took her hands and kissed them. "Are you ready?"

"Ready as I'll ever be. I feel anxious but excited, despite how my grandfather has dressed me." She gave him a reassuring smile.

"And you look handsome, as usual." She walked around him, observing his expensive clothes. "Very nice," she said as she smoothed her fingers over the gold embroidery.

He laughed and kissed her forehead. "Stop teasing, silly girl. I *am* going to meet a senator of Rome today. I have to make a good impression, you know."

"You better hurry along, then; the games are about to start."

"Only after you have graced me with a kiss."

She raised herself up on her tiptoes and planted a sassy kiss on his lips. He wrapped his arms around her, and they both laughed at her playfulness.

"Oh, to be young and in love once more," her grandfather interrupted.

Evander let Aurora go and greeted the stately elder.

"Doctor, it is a pleasure to see you."

"And you." He looked at Evander's fine clothes and whistled. "Now take my advice, son; go enjoy the games, and don't be seen in here again."

"Take care of her," Evander told him with a concerned look on his face.

"My granddaughter? Don't you worry about her; she can hold her own, even with the boisterous gladiators. Now off with you."

~

Aurora heard the roar of the crowd and the clanking of steel swords from inside the arena. There were as many as twenty-five pairs of gladiators fighting at once, all with referees who made sure that strict rules were followed. It didn't take long for the first wave of injured men to arrive.

Aurora sprang into action, cleaning the flesh wounds with hot water and vinegar and binding them with clean linen bands to stop the bleeding. Deeper lacerations were cleaned and sewn together, just as her mother had taught her.

As the games progressed and the gladiators fatigued, more grievous injuries were sustained, some not survivable. She helped her grandfather set a broken arm, then hurried over to another young man who was holding his ribs and trying hard not to whimper.

"What's your name, gladiator?"

He looked at her with deep brown eyes that implored her help. He couldn't have been more than sixteen years old.

"Julius," he answered painfully.

"Lie down, please, and let me look at you."

He lied back on the table with her help.

"I was hit hard by a ball club."

She could feel that several of his ribs were broken, and she ordered a slave to bring some poppy juice.

"Here, drink this; it will take away the pain and let you sleep."

She lifted his head and dribbled the juice inside his mouth.

"I will wrap your ribs while you are sleeping. For the next several days, we will give you poppy juice and unwrap you, during which time you must do breathing exercises to avoid disease from setting in your lungs."

He nodded and grunted something incomprehensible, then fell asleep.

Next she worked on sewing up the brow of a big, burly, curly haired gladiator who thought it funny to grab her between the thighs as she administered to him. She stuck him purposefully with the needle she was using, then grabbed him hard by the jowls.

"Do that again and I will sew your eye shut, gladiator! I am the granddaughter of Vibius Popidius, great surgeon of Pompeii, equestrian class, and you will treat me with respect—especially when I am spending my day taking care of your kind!"

"Yes, my lady!" he shouted back, looking amused. "'Scuse me, my lady, you're such a pretty morsel I couldn't help myself. And the way you are dressed . . ." He pointed to her tunic. "I thought you were a slave girl. My name is Crispis. Pleased to meet you," he continued jovially as if he hadn't just offended her. "What's your name?"

"I am Aurora Fortunas, your medica today."

"I sure appreciate a girl with some fire inside her."

"Is that so?" She finished the last few stitches and put down the needle. "Are you going back in the arena today?"

"No, miss, the gladiators are done. The hunt is about to start."

Aurora sucked in a deep breath and looked down.

"You just turned the color of plaster, miss. What's the matter, don't you like the games?"

"I don't like violence," she answered forcefully. "Or pain and suffering, especially when inflicted on innocent, unsuspecting animals."

"I don't like pain and suffering neither, miss."

"And yet you are a gladiator. Why?"

"Some of us got no choice, miss. Not like you and *your kind*."

"Did you win or lose your fight today?"

"I won, of course!" he bristled.

"Congratulations. Does it bother you to think that one day you may not come out of that arena with just a cut above your eye?" She sponged over his stitches with vinegar, and he cringed. "One day you might suffer mortal wounds, and then what?"

"And then I will die with honor, miss. As do all gladiators."

She stopped and looked at the gladiator, his brawny muscles and tan skin. Underneath his strong exterior, he was just a man, trying to survive.

Although they were from two different worlds, there was honesty about him. She decided that she liked the curly haired fighter.

"Crispis, how would you like to make some extra money today?"

EVANDER WATCHED the last of the gladiator fights from the comfort of the podium. There was ample shade, delicious food, and cool water. Slaves walked around fanning the guests and refilling their drinks. He spoke mostly with his sister and Aurora's parents, as the Valens family was fawning over the senator, even Valentina.

It seemed to him that the fights were especially brutal today, but nobody had been killed, intentionally or accidentally, and the Roman senator almost seemed disappointed.

Now came the animal hunt, and it promised blood. A group of criminals and murderers would fight for their lives against three large leopards, two bears, five wild boars, and a small pack of wolves. He had no desire to witness the carnage.

"How do think Aurora is faring down there?" asked Helena.

"My daughter is stronger than you might think. Trust me, she will be fine," answered Lady Lucina. "She is a bright girl who needs to keep her mind occupied. Practicing medicine is good for her, especially since you both are leaving soon."

A wave of guilt hit Evander, but if he didn't go back to Corinth, he wouldn't be able to get permission to pursue Aurora, nor set things straight between himself, Trebius Valens, and his father's business. Writing a letter just wouldn't do; he had to speak to his father in person.

"I'm a little worried about what she might do when she sees the animals," said Dominus Fortunas. "She is violently opposed to the hunts."

"Then, Dominus, with all due respect," said Evander, "what is she doing down in that tent?"

"Her grandfather insisted. I had to defer to his judgment."

Evander didn't quite agree with him and felt a surge of protectiveness streak through his chest. Aurora was already brave; did she really need to prove herself at a hunt? He looked down to the arena nervously and wondered if he should go to her.

Valentina appeared at that moment and linked her arm through his.

"Evander, you really must relax and enjoy the entertainment. Don't you agree, Helena?"

"Of course." His sister gave her a polite smile.

"You know, Helena, the other night my father threw a symposium for a few of his friends. I'm sure Evander remembers the evening well."

Evander shifted, but she continued to hold on to his arm as she spoke, stroking his skin with her ring-clad fingers.

"Of course, we women were not invited. But a curious thing happened to me." She looked up and caught Evander's eye. "After I ate my dinner with my mother and sister, I was confined to the latrina all night with stomach pains and other ailments that I won't mention here."

Evander saw the blood leave his sister's face.

"Perhaps, *you*, Lady Lucina, as a medica, could offer any explanation as to why that might have happened to me?"

"Perhaps something you ate did not agree with you," Lady Lucina offered.

"Perhaps, but it almost seemed to me as if someone had *poisoned* me."

They all looked appropriately surprised.

"But you were fine the next morning?" Lady Lucina asked.

"A little weakened maybe, but yes."

"There was quite a bit of raw seafood on the menu," Evander added.

"Ah, well then, let me assure you it was not poison," said Lady Lucina. "This is common with raw oysters and sea urchins. Did you eat any seafood?"

"I did actually," she answered contritely.

"Well then, you see, there is nothing to worry about, my dear. You must have eaten a bad oyster. Please excuse me." Aurora's parents walked away with Helena, leaving him alone with Valentina.

"Why did you leave the party so early? I looked everywhere for you, but you were gone," she whispered.

"My head was spinning from the wine, and I had started not to feel well," he lied. "I also ate quite a few oysters and sea urchins myself."

"Well, it all makes sense now." She smiled and looked around to make sure no one was listening. "But you would be wise to consider my father's offer. You would become a very rich man, and I would make you a very fine wife."

CHAPTER 19

Aurora and Crispis tried not to attract any attention as they slipped quietly into the tent where the animals were caged. Only the tigers and wild boars had been released into the arena thus far. The animal master didn't like to release all the animals at once, or they would fight each other instead of the men. They also liked to drag out the gore for as long as possible.

They heard shrieks and cries coming from inside the spectacula, and Aurora fought to keep down the bile that rose up in her throat. She held up her medical bag to a passing guard.

"I am here to check on the animals."

The guard nodded, then smiled when he recognized Crispis. "I heard you fought well today!"

"As always," Crispis boasted. "And, uh, the medica would like me to finish off the dying animals quickly as they return to the tent." He motioned to the sword he wore on his belt.

The guard looked relieved. "Well, you'd be doing us all a favor. They pile the animals up in the back, but sometimes they're not yet dead. Nothing scarier than a half-crazed panther waking up to stalk you again."

Aurora and Crispis walked up and down the rows of animals

locked up inside of small, cruel cages. They were lethargic from the heat, and sickly. She stopped in front of a half-starved wolf that was foaming profusely from the mouth.

"This one looks very sick. Quick, Crispis, find me a small piece of meat."

He pulled a cube of meat from one of the feeding buckets and gave it to her. She opened her medical bag and withdrew a vial of powder, which she sprinkled generously over the meat. She tossed it into the cage, and the wolf gobbled it hungrily, then curled up in a ball and closed its eyes.

"Sleep well, little wolf," she said somberly.

She wanted to rant and rave, protest the cruelty and blatant disregard for life that existed in the Empire, but crying wouldn't change a thing. It was action that brought about change.

"Crispis, I have to return to the medical tent before my grandfather wonders what I'm up to. Here is the vial of opium. Be careful, it is very concentrated. You know what to do?"

"Yes, miss. I will relieve the animals from their misery quickly and gently, as you have asked."

Just as Aurora was leaving the tent, a group of slaves came running out of the arena screaming for a doctor. She ran toward them.

"What has happened?"

"One of the tigers has pounced on the animal master!"

"Go and call the surgeon in the medical tent! Hurry!"

She ran to the entrance of the arena and saw where the animal master was lying, surrounded by a group of men with spears. The tigers were now busy stalking a group of men on the far side of the arena. Bodies of dead men were everywhere, strewn around on the sand.

"Give me passage!" she yelled to a hunter, showing him her medical bag.

He gestured for her to stay behind him and guarded her with his spear until they reached the animal master.

Her heart hammered in her chest as she kneeled down beside the bleeding man. The tiger had slashed across his belly with her fierce claws before puncturing his neck with its teeth. Her grandfather arrived a moment later with an entourage of slaves and supplies. He shoved a handful of linen into her hands.

"You work on the puncture wounds, and I'll take his abdomen," he ordered.

She packed clean linen around the man's neck and applied direct pressure with her hands, using her body weight to help staunch the bleeding.

❧

EVANDER JUMPED as Lady Lucina let out a loud cry. His back was to the arena, as he had chosen not to watch the bloody hunt.

"Great Juno, help me!" she cried. "My daughter is in the arena with tigers and boars!"

Evander's chest turned to stone with fear. "I need to get down there now!"

Lady Lucina threw down her long scarf, grabbed her husband, and ran for the stairs. Evander followed close behind, but Trebby blocked his way.

"The senator is watching. I do not recommend putting yourself in the middle of the crisis; it may not bode well for you or your business."

"Do you think I would put my business before Aurora's life? I would throw myself in front of a tiger if it meant saving her. Now let me pass." He ran down the stairs after Aurora's parents, feeling angry and sick to his stomach. *Why can't she just be a normal girl who stays at home and spins the loom?*

A group of guards blocked the entrance to the arena and told them that entering would be forbidden until the situation was under control. Aurora's mother argued that she was a doctor as well, but the guards didn't budge.

"This is an outrage!" Evander shouted. "Their daughter is in there with a tiger!"

"Dominus! Step back! We have our orders!" a guard yelled.

"Let me pass!" he boomed, losing his self-control.

Three soldiers approached and physically moved him away from the archway. He was so upset, he felt as though he might have an attack of the heart.

~

AURORA WAS NOW COVERED in blood, but it looked like their effort to save the animal master was going to be successful. The flow of blood coming from his wounds was considerably less, and that was a good sign.

She put her hands into her lap, closed her eyes, and breathed deeply, trying to calm herself. When she finally opened her eyes again, one of the magnificent tigers was being dragged out of the arena, leaving a trail of blood behind it.

A feeling of hate and disgust filled her chest, and she fought down the urge to vomit. She felt weak, like all of her strength had suddenly deserted her. Her grandfather helped her up and walked her out of the arena, surrounded by a group of hunters holding long spears.

Suddenly, her parents were there, shouting at her. Everything seemed dreamlike and slow. They took her inside the medical tent and sat her down on one of the tables.

Evander huffed about nearby. He looked like an enraged bull, ready for the kill. "Who brought her into the arena? Who put her in such danger?" he fumed.

"I did," Aurora answered flatly. "Nobody asked me to go. I wanted to help."

Their attention turned to the entrance of the tent, and they all watched cautiously as the senator from Rome approached them, flanked by Helena and the Valens family.

"Who is this girl who ran into the arena to help the animal master without a concern for her safety?" he asked.

Her father stood tall. "This is Aurora Fortunas, my beloved daughter, Senator. She is a medica in training."

The senator took Aurora's hand, even though she had not yet washed.

"She is the bravest young woman I have ever seen. My sincerest praise and commendation are in order for your actions today, *puella*."

Aurora bowed her head respectfully. "Thank you, Senator." She noticed that the Valens family seemed irritated. Valentina and Lady Claudia looked her over quietly and scoffed.

The senator turned to Trebius Valens. "I believe we should cancel the rest of the hunt, as this tragic accident has marred the day. It is surely an evil portent." Trebby's face turned red.

The senator turned to her grandfather. "And thank you, Doctor, for your excellent work today."

The Valens family escorted the senator out of the tent, leaving Aurora surrounded by her family. Evander and Helena tried to approach her, but she looked down at her filthy tunic and shook her head. She did not want to taint them or their beautiful clothes with blood.

"Take me home, Father. I am not feeling well. The heat is getting to me."

Her father put his arm around her and helped her stand. "Come, my daughter." He looked at Evander. "You need to visit with the senator now. Go and promote your business. You can visit her tonight."

"Helena? Are you coming with me?" Evander asked.

"No, Brother. Put your mind at ease. I will stay with her."

"Thank you." Evander looked Aurora in the eyes, shook his head, then walked reluctantly away.

She climbed into her grandfather's decorated carriage feeling that something immutable had happened to her. She could never forget or even consciously blot out what she had experienced today. As they rolled away from the bloody arena, Aurora put her head into her mother's lap and cried.

~

THE PILLOWS of the couch felt soft and comforting, and she let herself sink down into them and relax. She let out a loud sigh and told herself to be strong. Then she tried to push the blackness from her mind.

It had been a tough day.

Mending the brawny gladiators hadn't been so bad, but seeing death up close had shaken her to the core. She would never forget those men, mauled to death by the animals. Who were they? Did they leave behind wives or children? To society, only the life of the animal master had mattered.

Watching the beautiful, lifeless tiger being dragged through the sand had also been agonizing. It was an unfathomable crime when the death of a man or animal was used for entertainment.

She felt a powerful conviction that life was sacred, and that she should work hard to protect it. She had gained a new perspective today. Perhaps this feeling was what had propelled her grandfather to learn about medicine all those years ago. And perhaps that is why he had wanted her to see all these atrocities up close, as devastating as it had been.

She had experienced acutely the bitterness, the emptiness, and the *meaninglessness* of death. Now she just felt numb and tired. So, so tired. She didn't want to feel anything at all.

She heard footsteps approach and cracked open an eye. It was Evander. She turned her head toward the wall as he pulled up a bench next to the couch.

"I have brought you an infusion of chamomile," he said gently. Her throat felt pinched and tight, and his voice made her want to cry.

"Why are you pushing me away?"

She heard him place the tea on the table next to her. "Because I don't want you to see me like this."

"Like what?"

She refused to answer him.

"Aurora," he said more forcefully, "do you not care how *I* feel?"

"Of course I do," she mumbled.

"Do you not realize what you've put me through today?" he asked angrily.

Twenty men had lost their lives violently in the arena, and she should feel sorry for *him*?

He lowered his voice to a whisper and rubbed her back. "Were you not in my bed sharing intimacies with me? Did we not cast a love spell over each other on the beach?"

She shrugged, but didn't speak.

"I want to protect you!" he cried. "And today, while you were in the arena with bloodthirsty tigers and boars, I was helpless to do anything! The guards wouldn't let me pass! If ever we are married, I will *forbid* you from entering that arena again! I don't care who is in there that needs saving!"

"Forbid me?" she cried, rolling over. "So you plan to control me? And you speak of a marriage that will probably never happen!"

His face flushed with anger, and he pulled her up from the couch none too gently.

"Hey!" she cried. "What are you—"

"I have indulged you long enough. You will submit to me when it comes to your safety!" He grabbed her jaw and held it tight while he planted a hard kiss on her lips.

She thrashed his shoulders with her fists and tried to push him away, but he continued to kiss her angrily until he broke through her defenses, and she started to cry. "I'm sorry! I'm sorry!" she sobbed.

"Why don't you want me here?" he asked, wiping away her tears.

She gazed down at the black-and-white patterns of the mosaic floor. "I feel weak and overly emotional. It is not becoming."

"Nonsense. You are allowed to feel all of those emotions, and then some, after what you've been through." He took her in his arms and rocked her back and forth.

"I took care of a mere boy today. He had his ribs smashed in by a ball club. He was trying so hard to be brave, and yet I knew he was in terrible pain. It broke my heart," she sniffed.

"Yet you helped him," he said, "and I'm sure he was thankful."

"Then I met Crispis. The big loaf groped me, so I stabbed him with a needle. After that, we became friends, and he helped me."

He furrowed his brow. "Slow down, you're rambling. Friends? With a gladiator? And he groped you! I thought you hated them."

"I've changed my mind. They're not so bad, just from a different walk of life."

"Obviously. But how did he help you?"

She looked at him gravely. "Promise me you will never tell a soul."

He stared at her, waiting for her response.

"I paid him to kill the animals."

"What!"

She let out her breath. "He walked me through the animal tent, and we saw that many of them were sickly and dying. He helped me kill them quickly with opium so they wouldn't have to suffer more pain in the arena."

"Aurora! I'm sure you broke some law." He began to pace back and forth, stopping to look at her incredulously as if there were no end to her delinquency.

"Then I made Crispis stay in the back of the animal tent to make sure that the slain animals were really dead and not just dying a slow, painful death."

"I just don't know what to do with you," he said, shaking his head.

"Neither do my parents. Are you starting to understand why

I'm not married yet? Now if you don't mind, I would like to be alone."

"You're dismissing me?" he asked in disbelief.

"Yes," she answered, lying back on the couch.

He kneeled down on the floor next to her. "Fine, I'll go. But not before you promise me that you will never, ever shut me out again. I want you to know that you can talk to me, lean on me, depend on me . . . always." He kissed the top of her head.

But how can I depend on you if you're not here?

She buried her face in the pillow and let herself fall into oblivion, praying that tomorrow would somehow bring back her innocence.

CHAPTER 20

Aurora strolled arm in arm with her mother through the narrow paths of Evander's vineyard. The dense green foliage surrounded them, and the plump purple grapes were almost ready for harvest. They were on the western slope of Mount Vesuvius, outside the Herculaneum gate, and the summit of the mountain dominated the landscape above them. Evander and her father strolled ahead of them, discussing viniculture, stopping here and there to examine the vines, and taste the grapes.

Behind them Teo ran up and down the rows of grapevines, sometimes chasing Hercules, and sometimes being chased. His leg was mostly healed now; it had been two months since the accident.

Tonight was to be their farewell dinner. Evander sailed for Corinth in two days' time. According to Evander, he had many things to discuss with his father. She didn't have a mind for business, and she couldn't begin to understand the workings of a shipping and trading company, but her intuition told her there were greater forces at work, and she didn't quite believe it would all turn out in her favor.

So much had happened in so short a time that she scarcely could believe Evander had arrived in Pompeii at the beginning of summer. It was the end of August now, and he was leaving. Soon, she feared, it might feel like he had never been here at all.

She had made up her mind to be busy in his absence. She would help her grandfather with his patients each day, and she was especially interested in learning how to care for pregnant mothers and babies. And even though she wasn't sure that she would marry Evander, she could see her future more clearly. One day she hoped to be a mother too, and she wanted to learn as much as possible.

They caught up to her father just as Evander plucked a succulent bunch of grapes from the vine. He handed them each a few and popped some in his mouth.

The juice burst from their skins inside Aurora's mouth, and she marveled at their sweet, tart taste. "Delicious, Evander. Why do you not produce your own wine?"

He laughed and gestured to her father. "I was just telling Dominus that in my family's absence it has been easier to sell the grapes to local winemakers for a profit. But when I come back here to settle down, I would like to buy all of the equipment needed to make my own wine, like your father does."

They walked a little farther down the path, and Evander stopped abruptly. The shoots of several large vines were dry and withered, and the trunks looked dead.

"Why does this keep happening? This is not the first time I have seen vines withered to such a degree. I'm sure my irrigation system is working properly."

Her parents took a closer look, their brows creased in thought. Her father turned a leaf over in his hand, crumpled it, and watched as it turned to dust. "It's too soon for the leaves to dry out. We don't usually see this happening until the end of October. I don't understand." Her father scratched his chin. "We should consult with some of the other vineyards around here; perhaps they have seen this kind of thing before."

Her mother looked baffled. "We have had the same problem. It started early in the growing season. Our vineyard is on the other side of the mountain, so it doesn't seem to be confined to one area."

Myrrhine came walking down the path with Apollonius. "I have been asked to tell you that dinner is ready to be served."

They walked back to the rustic villa and settled themselves on the dining couches in the garden. Evander reclined with Aurora, across from her parents, and Helena reclined with Teo.

Apollonius played the lyre for their entertainment, and they laughed heartily as the puppy tried to nap on his feet. "Why do dogs love me so much?" he asked with a smile.

"Because you are pure of heart," her mother said.

Aurora relaxed as the beautiful music flowed through the night air. She could feel Evander behind her, his body heat flowing into her like a slow fire. His breath fanned her neck, and she closed her eyes and lost herself in thought as she waited for dinner to be served. What would happen when he left Pompeii?

Tonight, things were wonderful, but life could fall apart in a single moment, destroying all one believed in. It had happened to her before, when Niketus had died. Yet through all of life's difficulties people were still capable of creating something beautiful.

Maybe it is love that inspires us, that keeps us walking forward.

She believed that stoicism had its value at times, but the truth was, the people of Pompeii lived fully and loved fiercely. They held nothing back, not food nor wine, nor passion, nor tears. And if one looked closely, one could see it all, painted in the frescoes, written in the graffiti on the walls. No matter where one went, joy of life permeated the air. It was in their houses and on the streets, in the fragrant baths and seedy brothels.

She glanced over her shoulder at Evander. Gods, how she would miss him. The music continued sweet and slow, stirring up all of her emotions. She realized that she could never survive the loss of him, yet here she was, drawn to him like a moth drawn to the flame of an oil lamp.

Evander held up his wine for a toast. "Wine brings to light the hidden secrets of the soul, and so I shall tell you all how dear you have become to me. I care for you as if you were my own family. It is with a heavy heart that I leave here in two days, but as you know, I have many things to discuss with my father." He turned to Aurora and gave her a knowing look.

"*Sanitus bona*," her father exclaimed and clinked his wineglass against Evander's.

Aurora tried hard to blink back the tears. Evander was so strong, so healthy and virile. She etched his handsome features in her mind, not wanting to forget a single detail about him when he was gone.

Helena's face clouded over. "I have come to love you all as well and cannot bear the thought of being apart. You are like my second family. And so I have decided to stay in Pompeii during my brother's absence."

"I would remind you, Sister, that you have a family. One that is going to be deeply upset if you don't come back to Corinth with me," Evander scolded.

Everyone's head turned to the pretty girl. "What's this, Helena? Why don't you want to return to Corinth?" asked Aurora's mother.

Helena shrugged. "I've only just arrived here, and I was so terribly seasick on the way over. I just can't bear it again."

"This was never meant to be a permanent solution, Sister. I cannot leave you alone with only slaves to watch out for you. It is unacceptable. Father would be furious."

"You may stay with us until Evander returns," Aurora's mother offered. "As long as he agrees to it."

"Great idea," concurred her father. "You and Aurora can keep each other out of trouble."

Helena beamed at Aurora from her couch, and Aurora was thrilled to have Evander's sister move in with her. It would certainly make his absence more bearable.

"This was exactly what she was angling for," Evander mumbled under his breath.

"Come now, Evander, it is a wonderful idea," Aurora said. "As long as you feel your parents would approve."

"Fine, then. My sister may stay with you. Thank you, Lady Lucina and Dominus Fortunas. I know she will be in good hands."

Her father nodded back at him. "But the dog stays here at the vineyard with the slaves." He looked pointedly at Teo, who pouted. "And, Helena, do bring an escort of slaves to assist you."

Aurora raised her glass. "I salute all of you here tonight. My dear parents, my precious brother, Myrrhine and her family, Helena, and Evander, you all hold the deepest place within my heart. To our health," her voice quivered as she finished, and she clinked her glass against Evander's. The music or maybe the wine was moving her to tears. "I'm sorry," she whispered.

"Don't be. I find it endearing." He squeezed her hand, and they held each other's eyes for a moment, then he turned to her brother. "Teo, would you like to say something?"

Teo held up his glass of grape juice and gave a lopsided smile. "It has been a great summer!" he shouted. "Thank you to Dominus Evander for saving me from the earthquake, and, Miss Helena, I hope I can marry you one day. But the best part of the summer for me was Hercules. I love him so much!"

Evander smiled broadly as he looked around at everyone reclining comfortably on the couches of his garden triclinium, in the heart of his vineyard. "This is what makes a house a home, sharing a meal with those you care about," he told Aurora.

They were happy, laughing and chatting lightheartedly as they began to eat the food that was placed before them. Evander was hopeful that things would turn out favorably for him and Aurora. Feelings of warmth filled his chest, and he thanked the gods for sending him such supportive and wonderful people. They were nothing like the vulgar, self-serving Valens family.

The last course was a tasty nut-cake drizzled with honey. Everyone raved over how rich and decadent it tasted, and Lady Lucina asked if the cook would share his recipe. Dominus Fortunas rubbed his belly and said that he needed to walk, so they all rose and took another stroll through the vineyard while the slaves sat and ate their dinner.

The evening continued on splendidly, and darkness began to settle over the vines. When the slaves came out to light the oil lamps, Evander knew their time together was coming to an end. He took Dominus Fortunas aside. "Dominus, before you take your leave, I ask your permission to walk with Aurora privately to say my good-byes to her."

"Permission granted, my son. And know that I will be praying to the gods for you and my daughter. There has to be another way for you to gain Titus's favor; you just need to find it."

Evander was astonished. "You know about Trebby's offer?

"Pompeii is a small city. Of course I know," he said quietly.

He shook Dominus's hand. "You are a good man, the very best, and I hope to be part of your family one day."

Evander found Aurora, and they walked together to a secluded part of the vineyard. "So first I will stop at Salernum and then south to the straits of Messana. The trip home should take me no more than five days if the winds are favorable, seven or eight if they are not."

"It doesn't take as long to get to Corinth as I thought," Aurora reflected. "So why must you be gone for so long?" She looked up at him longingly, and he felt his heart stutter.

"Because I must stop at many ports in the Greek Isles to pick up merchandise before coming back to Pompeii."

"Ah." She nodded.

He turned her toward him and looked into her dark eyes. "Aurora, listen to me. If Valentina should say something to you while I'm gone, if any one of the Valens family says something to upset you, promise me that you will ignore them."

She gave him a confused look. "What do you think they might say to me?

"That is all I can reveal to you right now."

She huffed. "So it comes back to Valentina again. You are worried that your father will believe her to be a more suitable match for you politically, and the Valens family understands this. I'm sure of it; I can see it in their eyes when they look at me."

Evander became very serious. "My father is a reasonable man. He will not make me marry someone that I don't love." He placed her hands over his heart. "Have faith in me. I will not let you down."

He worried that Valentina would reveal her father's offer to Aurora the moment he set sail. The girl had no scruples, and she seemed to delight in hurting Aurora. In a way, he was happy that Helena would be staying in Pompeii; Aurora would need her support if anything happened. He embraced her warmly. "You will wait for me?"

"Do you think I could fall for another man so easily? You are the one who will be traveling the Mediterranean. How many women will try to steal you from me?"

"You have nothing to fear." He hugged her tightly. "I love you, Aurora, you must know that by now. You have captured my soul."

He looked into her eyes, wanting to hear her say the words back to him.

She slowly shook her head. "Don't, Evander. Don't make me say it, not when you are leaving and your father might refuse me." Tears filled her eyes.

"Don't cry, my love. We have many reasons to be hopeful." He leaned down and kissed her tenderly. "I will come back as soon as possible. Remember—let nothing break you. You are strong, brave, and beautiful." He planted little kisses all across her face, making her laugh.

"I will miss you, more than I ever thought possible," she admitted. "Even though you are old-fashioned and a bit overbearing."

"Overbearing? Is it wrong that I want to protect you?"

"No, I suppose not," she answered, kissing his hands. She gazed at him intently for a moment. "Come back to me. Just come back to me, Evander." She stood on her tiptoes and kissed him, and he wished the night would never end.

They returned to the villa, where he said his good-byes to her family. Dominus Fortunas, Lady Lucina, and Teo hugged him heartily. "May Fortune go with you," they wished him.

Myrrhine bowed to him, and Apollonius shook his hand. "I will watch over your sister and Aurora. You have my word."

The Fortunas family loaded into a stately wooden carriage pulled by two mules for the ride back to town. Apollonius climbed up with the mule driver and gave the signal to depart.

As Evander watched the carriage disappear into the night, he wondered when he would see Aurora again. If the Fates were kind, and Venus had heard his prayers, he would be returning with an engagement ring to put on her finger.

CHAPTER 21

OCTOBER AD 79

"*L*upa, where are you?" Aurora called. She walked around the garden wondering where the dog had gone. It was unusual for her not to come when called. She heard a rustling sound in a nearby bush and walked over to it. "Lupa?" The dog was shaking with fear beneath the low branches. "Lupa, what is it? What's wrong? Are you sick?"

The dog crawled over to her and put her head on Aurora's lap. Aurora looked around for evidence of something the dog may have gotten into, but found nothing. She stroked the dog's head and tried to calm her.

"Teo! Apollonius! Come out here, please!" she called.

Teo was the first one to run out to the garden. "She's been under there all morning, Sister. Mother said to leave her, that she must be feeling sick."

"Oh, poor dog. Do you think she ate fish bones again?"

"Don't know. She's just acting strange today."

Aurora kissed the dog's face and smoothed back her ears. "You'll be all right, little wolf." She stood up and brushed off her stola. "Please watch her, Teo. I have to go help Grandfather today. Where are Mother and Father?"

"Father is in his office with a client. He told me not to disturb him. Mother went to Grandfather's house. A messenger arrived this morning and told her she needed to go quickly." He sat down next to the dog and hugged her.

"Hmm. I wonder what happened now."

It was almost the end of October. Evander had set sail for Corinth almost two months ago, and ever since he left, the oddest things had been happening. Cracks had suddenly appeared in the city walls, the road had lifted up in various places around town, and there were continued reports of people getting sick from the air around Vesuvius.

Apollonius came out from the narrow hallway holding a bucket. "I don't know what is happening. Look." She peered inside the bucket and saw that it was half-full of dead birds. Among them were beautiful golden orioles that lived among the fruit trees, black-eared wheatears that loved the grapevine blossoms, and the melodious song thrush.

She jumped back from the bucket, alarmed. "A dead bird in one's house is the worst possible omen. Where did you find them?"

"In the garden this morning. They were everywhere, like they had just fallen from the sky."

"Do you think the dead birds are what's spooking Lupa?"

"It's possible."

"This reminds me of the morning in the forum when I first met Evander. The dogs were all behaving strangely, whining and walking in circles before the earthquake struck." She looked up at Apollonius, who was clearly worried. "Bring me some fresh water."

She walked around the garden looking for signs of anything that might tell her another earth tremor was imminent. She stopped abruptly and swore as another dead bird fell from the sky and landed at her feet. There was a disturbance in the air, she could actually *smell* it, and a feeling of dread trickled down her spine.

Apollonius returned with a glass of water and handed it to her. She sniffed it and grimaced. The smell of sulfur had returned. She set the water on a table and stared absently at the glass as she tried to decide what to do. A curious occurrence caught her eye. Every now and then a large ripple appeared in the water, as if something was moving the glass.

"Apollonius, watch the water. Tell me what you see."

He stared at the glass. "I see water."

"Have you ever noticed how it feels when a centuria of soldiers march past? You can feel the vibrations go up your legs as they are marching."

He gave her a confused look.

"I don't see any soldiers in our garden, and yet there seem to be vibrations in the ground that are causing the water to ripple. Could this mean that another earth tremor is imminent? Could these all be signs? The dead birds, the dog's behavior, that strange smell in the air?"

"I don't see how any of that could possibly relate to an earthquake, but they are certainly strange portents."

"I need to talk to my mother and grandfather. Perhaps they will have an idea as to what is killing the birds."

"Wait for me. I will accompany you. If an earthquake is about to happen, I don't want you caught alone out in the streets."

THEY WALKED QUICKLY along the sidewalks and over the stepping-stones, turning corners and hastening down narrow alleyways until they reached her grandfather's stately house. When inside, they followed the voices to a small cubiculum, where they were shocked to find Valentina vomiting into a bowl. Her mother, Lady Claudia, sat next to her on the couch, wiping her brow with a cloth.

"Grandfather?" called Aurora.

Her grandfather excused himself from the room and signaled for Aurora and Apollonius to follow him. He took them down the hall and into a small garden where he grew all of his medicinal plants. In the corner grew a tall chicory plant, with its bright blue flowers, used for stomach and liver ailments. Next to that was mallow, whose roots were used to relieve a toothache.

Her grandfather began to cut some shoots of the maidenhair fern, whose potent leaves boiled in water would cause an abortion. "Valentina is about three months pregnant."

Aurora's eyebrows shot up. "Pregnant? It really shouldn't surprise me, knowing her. Where is my mother?"

"She is checking on some of the other patients. You know how superstitious these Pompeians are. I was flooded with panicked people, some who thought they were having an attack of the heart because birds were falling from the sky. They think the world is coming to an end."

"It's true about the birds, Grandfather. That is why we are here."

She gestured to Apollonius. "He found many dead birds in our garden this morning, and when I finally found the dog, she was shaking with fear under a bush."

"Doctor, look," said Apollonius, pointing to a dead blackcap songbird in the grass. Just then her mother rushed into the garden. "I thought I heard your voices. We need to talk."

Aurora embraced her. "Mother, I'm worried that an earth tremor will happen today," she said gravely. "There are many strange signs. We came to warn you."

"I'm afraid we have bigger problems to deal with."

"Bigger than an earthquake?"

Her mother grabbed her by the arms. "Aurora, listen to me. Valentina is insinuating that Evander may be the father of her child."

Aurora felt the blood drain from her face and her knees go weak. "You don't believe her, do you?"

"No, *I* don't believe her, but if Trebby finds out, he can easily ruin Evander, whether it's true or not."

Aurora felt her whole body fill with a rage she had never known before. "Is she here to abort the child, Grandfather?"

Her grandfather shook his head. "I don't know. Lady Claudia would see her abort, but Valentina says she is here because the morning vomiting has left her feeling weak. She is asking for medicine to clear the nausea."

"That is not Evander's child, and she is a lying little whore!" Aurora ran out of the garden and down the hall, her family running behind her. She bolted into the room where Valentina sat with her mother.

"You are despicable!" she spat. "You can't stand the fact that Evander doesn't want you, and you are trying to get your claws into him by any means possible! You are *not* carrying his child!"

Lady Claudia shot to her feet. "Lucina, get your daughter out of here!" she screamed, but Valentina tilted an evil brow. "Apparently, Evander doesn't want you either, or he wouldn't have left you alone for so long. And as for the baby, can you prove it isn't his?"

"Evander returned to Corinth to ask his father's permission to marry me. He warned me about you."

"Aurora, you are so naïve. Tsk, tsk." Valentina shook her head. "Perhaps if you had taken better care of his needs, he wouldn't have turned to me."

Aurora gaped at her.

"Valentina! What nonsense are you spouting?" Lady Claudia cried.

"You really should know the truth, Aurora. My father has offered Evander everything he could ever want to ensure his business is a success—contracts, protection from pirates, even an introduction to the emperor himself—all for the small price of my hand in marriage. So you may believe, if you choose, that Evander went home to talk to his father about marrying an insignificant girl like you, but he actually went home to discuss the monumental offer my father has made him."

Aurora was stunned at Valentina's words, and her skin prickled with heat. Why would Evander not tell her? She looked at her mother and grandfather and wondered if they knew if this was the truth.

"Evander has wanted me from the first night he met me," Valentina continued, pointing to Apollonius. "And your slave can even vouch for me. He saw Evander kissing me on the night of your dinner party."

All eyes looked to Apollonius.

"Is this true, *slave?*" Lady Claudia asked accusingly. "Did you see Dominus Evander kissing my daughter on the night of the Fortunas convivium?"

Apollonius looked at Aurora before he was forced to tell the truth. "Yes."

Anything he said to incriminate Valentina might cost him a beating, or possibly worse, and yet here was this scheming shewolf, planting seeds of doubt about Evander's character in everyone's minds.

Aurora saw the look of surprise on her mother's and grandfather's faces, and it hurt her to think they would think less of him. Although she was shaking with anger, she cautiously addressed Valentina's mother.

"Lady Claudia, with all due respect, Evander is not here to defend himself."

"What is to defend?" she answered scathingly. "He is a rogue and a scoundrel. He spent the evening charming you—we all saw it—before he seduced my daughter, as the slave has attested to. When he returns to town, he must do the right thing by my daughter and marry her."

Lady Claudia's scratchy voice grated on Aurora's raw nerves.

Her mother walked over and sat down next to the detestable woman. "Why is she insisting that the child is Evander's?"

Lady Claudia let out a long, dramatic cry. "Trebby won't stand for this. I know my husband! If he learns of this pregnancy and cannot marry his daughter off respectably, he will send her away! The senator will never have her in this condition, but Evander stands to gain much by marrying her. They would both benefit from this match."

"He will send me away because I will no longer be of use to him, Mother!" Valentina spat. "He dangles me in front of his associates like a worm on a hook, and I'm tired of it!"

"So you would publicly proclaim Evander is the father of your child in an effort to coerce him, even though it's not true?" Aurora asked in disbelief.

Valentina threw an ugly look at Aurora. "Who says it's not true?"

"Please calm down and listen to me. Pregnancy in an unmarried girl is not rare," Aurora's mother explained. "You would be shocked to know it happens quite frequently. But it is possible to promote menstruation quickly, before any scandal ensues."

"Shall I prepare the maidenhair brew, then?" asked her grandfather.

Valentina's eyes filled with tears, and she actually looked scared. "No! I will not drink it!" She put her hand over her belly protectively, broke down crying, then vomited into the bowl again. "Please, just give me something to stop the retching!"

As much as Aurora hated her, she also felt the tiniest bit sorry for her predicament. If she and Evander had taken things any further, it could have been her vomiting into the bowl this morning.

Her grandfather poured out a glass of water and handed it to Valentina. She took a sip, then spit it out. "Ugh!"

Her grandfather sniffed the jug of water. "There is an odor of sulfur in the water." He took a sip and grimaced. "Please excuse me, I will ask the slaves to fetch you something else to drink."

Aurora stormed from the room, pulling Apollonius with her. Her mother followed them down the hall. She spoke quietly but adamantly. "We need to find out who the real father is. Apollonius, I need you to speak with your friends in the Valens household today. See what you can learn."

Aurora shook her head in disbelief. This day just kept getting worse and worse. Could Valentina possibly be telling the truth? What if it *was* Evander's baby? The thought made her stomach turn over. Didn't Evander warn her not to listen to anything Valentina said? It was as if he had known this would happen. She felt more confused now than ever.

"It's time for you both to go," said her mother. I will work with grandfather today. Take care of Teo and the household, please."

"But, Mother, what about the dead birds? And if there is another earthquake?"

"I think you're reading too much into things, Aurora. But if it makes you feel better, stay away from public places today."

Aurora and Apollonius stepped outside into the cool autumn air. But this morning, the air had a sulfurous smell to it, and a burnt aroma, like when a piece of food falls into the embers on top of the stove. She leaned back on the stone façade of her grandfather's house and tried to relax.

Several Vestal Virgins shuffled past them, mumbling about the lack of water pressure in their domus. They lived in a grand, posh residence next door to her grandfather that boasted spectacular fountains and a swimming pool.

Apollonius looked at her gravely. "I'm sorry if what I said hurt you. I had no choice."

Aurora closed her eyes in dismay and shook her head. "And what do you know about the offer Trebby made to Evander?"

"I know nothing of that. Let's get back home and tell Helena what is happening. Perhaps she knows something that we don't."

~

HELENA HAD JUST SAT down for a meal in the garden. The girl stood and rushed over to them, embracing them both at once. "It is a most dreadful morning!" she cried. "There are dead birds falling from the sky!" She gestured with a graceful arm to the table set up under the portico. "I can't even sit under the trees for fear that a bird will fall on my head!"

Aurora took hold of her hands. "Let us sit at the table, near the fire. We have much to talk about."

Helena asked Pioppo to bring out one more place setting, and Apollonius stood near the table as they ate. Aurora told her in hushed tones about the situation with Valentina. "Do you think it's his child, Helena?" she asked, barely breathing in anticipation of her answer.

"Well, it's true that—"

"It's true!" Aurora nearly knocked over her glass.

"Aurora, calm down and drink some wine. What I was going to say was, yes, it's true that my brother was very promiscuous in Corinth, especially when he was younger. But since he has met you, he's different. He's in love with you, I'm sure of that. And from everything he's told me, he doesn't care much for Valentina."

Apollonius tapped his thumbs together. "Would you like a man's opinion?"

"No!" they said in unison, and Apollonius looked away and bit his lip.

Helena put her hand over Aurora's. "Do I believe Valentina is carrying my brother's child? Not for a moment."

Aurora let out a sigh of relief. "That makes me feel somewhat better, I think."

Apollonius leaned forward. "The only way for us to truly know who she has been sleeping with is for me to talk to the slaves in the Valens household."

"And what about this offer Trebby supposedly made to Evander?" asked Aurora.

Helena shook her head. "I cannot speak to that. My brother never discussed it with me."

Aurora felt a sharp ache in her breast for Evander. She missed him terribly and couldn't wait for him to come back. But bile rose up in her throat as she thought of how Valentina had already tarnished his return.

THE FIRST TREMOR struck that afternoon as Aurora was pacing the garden, waiting for Apollonius to return from the Valens's house. Her mother was still not home, and her father had gone to a town meeting in the basilica. She immediately threw herself down and covered Teo with her body. Lupa was with them too, whimpering and shaking. Helena, Myrrhine, and her boys ran out from the rooms they were in and huddled together with them.

"Where is Apollonius?" cried Myrrhine. "Why can't he just stay put?"

"I am here! I am here, Mother!" Apollonius ran into the garden and wrapped his arms around the group huddled on the ground. "Just stay calm. It will be all right."

Teo started to cry when the earthquake lasted longer than usual, and several terra-cotta tiles fell from the roof. "Make it stop!" he wailed.

No sooner did one tremor end than another one began, throwing them down on the ground. This one was stronger than the first, and Aurora watched in terror as the walls of the house swayed back and forth like a tapestry in the wind. The shaking went on and on until a column of the portico cracked in half.

When it was finally over, they stood up on unsteady legs, holding each other. Aurora's heart was pounding hard in her chest, and Helena and Teo were crying. She pulled her brother close. "It's over, Teo. It's over now," she soothed, cupping his head in her hands and kissing him. "Why don't you take Lupa to your bedroom and take a little nap while we clean up the mess."

She walked around the portico surveying the damage the tremors had caused, picking up the terra-cotta shards and throwing them into the bucket with the dead birds. *No Evander to come to the rescue today,* she lamented.

"Mistress, why don't you go and rest. We will clean this up," Myrrhine offered.

"Thank you, but no." Aurora held her breath for a moment and tried not to cry. "I need to keep busy. I'm filled with bad humors today."

~

SEVERAL HOURS LATER, they sat in a room off of the garden with her parents and enjoyed the heat of the brazier. Myrrhine served an infusion of chamomile and red valerian flowers to everyone. "This potion will soothe our nerves and help us sleep," she explained.

"Ah, it is just what I need," said Helena. "I am so anxious."

"I must warn you all that there may be aftershocks tonight," her father said grimly. "But usually they are less intense than the original tremor. Just make sure there is nothing placed above you on a shelf that may fall on your head while you are sleeping."

"Good advice," agreed her mother. "We must all be vigilant tonight." She made a face of distaste. "I just wish that burnt smell would go away. By the way, Apollonius, did you find out anything relevant from your friends at the Valens's house?"

"Yes, as I have already explained to Aurora, both Marcus the Younger and a senator from Rome have been seen leaving the house late at night."

Her parents looked at each other with raised eyebrows.

"Lady Claudia would never allow it," said her mother.

"Maybe Lady Claudia doesn't know," her father said.

"Doesn't know what?" asked Aurora.

Her parents glanced back and forth at each other.

Understanding finally dawned on Aurora. "You think Trebby forced Valentina to sleep with the senator?" she asked, riveted.

"I wouldn't put it past him to use his own daughter in such a way," her father replied.

Her mother looked disgusted. "We've known for years that Trebby and Claudia have no morals, and yet we are still *friends*. Why, Aurorus? Why do we put up with them? If this is true, they have acted most shamefully."

"Politics, Lucina. It's all about politics. We must maintain good relations with all families in power—the safety of our own family depends on it."

Aurora sat forward in her chair. "But what if the child belongs to Marcus? Why would she blame Evander?"

"Obviously, she doesn't want to marry the senator, and her father would never let her marry the son of an aedile, a junior magistrate in charge of public works," explained her father.

Helena clanked down her mug on the table next to her. "My brother is too smart to be manipulated, and my father would never allow it."

Aurora's father cleared his throat in a manner that told them he was getting ready to say something important. "Your mother told me what happened today at Grandfather's house. It's true, Daughter, what Valentina said about the offer Trebby made to Evander. He just about offered him the stars in the sky if only he would take Valentina as his wife."

Aurora's face flushed with anger, and she questioned everything she thought she knew about her relationship with Evander. "So he had other motives for returning to Corinth."

"Don't underestimate yourself, my daughter. Evander told me himself that he will ask his father's permission to marry you. He just needs to find another patron."

Aurora drained the rest of her hot chamomile infusion and stood up. It had been a long, difficult day punctuated by two frightening tremors. She wasn't sure her heart could handle any more revelations. "I'm going to bed," she announced. "Where is Lupa?"

"Sound asleep on Teo's bed," answered her mother. "Good night, darling."

She made her rounds and kissed everyone good night, then shuffled down the hall and up the staircase to her bedroom. Her body felt heavy and sore from fatigue, and emotionally she was a shipwreck. She took everything off the shelves and placed them on the floor, then snuggled into her bed for a much-needed sleep.

CHAPTER 22

She dreamt that she was on Evander's ship, being tossed to and fro by a storm at sea. Valentina stood in front of her laughing insanely, while Evander scooped out buckets of seawater from the deck. A huge mountain of water rolled toward the ship, lifting the bow up until it pointed straight to the sky, then slamming it down hard into the turbulent sea as it passed under the stern. She cried out and woke up, her heart thundering inside her chest.

The bed was on the opposite side of the room from where it should have been, the walls were rocking, and the furniture rattled over the wooden floorboards. It took her a moment to realize that she was in the middle of another earthquake. She wondered if she should attempt to run, but she didn't want to risk falling down the stairs.

Stay here, just stay here, she told herself. *It will pass.* Then she heard a scream and a loud booming noise from somewhere downstairs. She bolted out of bed and ran down the dark stairwell as fast as her bare feet could take her. She found her way through the garden, stepping over debris with the help of the moonlight.

"Helena! Oh gods, Helena—are you all right?" she shrieked.

She ran into the cubiculum off the atrium where Helena was sleeping. The girl was crying and moaning in pain, but it was too dark to see what had happened.

"Help me!" she cried in the darkness.

Apollonius arrived in a heartbeat, carrying an oil lamp. They gasped when they saw the thick wooden beam that had fallen from the ceiling lying across her bed, trapping her underneath. She looked at them desperately before her eyelids fluttered shut.

Apollonius rushed to her side and lifted the heavy beam off of her as if it weighed no more than a feather. The rest of the slaves rushed in, followed by Aurora's mother, her night tunic tousled in disarray around her body. "Don't move her, she may have broken bones!"

Apollonius held the oil lamp up while she and her mother examined the girl. Helena lay motionless, her face covered in plaster and dust.

"Is she dead? Oh gods!" he cried, his handsome face twisted in pain at the sight of her. "Domina, is she dead?" he demanded loudly, and Aurora could hear the panic in his voice.

Aurora's mother signaled for her to escort Apollonius out of the room. Aurora grabbed him by the arm and pulled him away. Once in the atrium, she looked fully at his frantic face. "Control yourself, Apollonius! I'm fairly certain she just got the wind knocked out of her. Her skull was not fractured. But you may have saved her life by lifting that beam off of her before it crushed her heart."

Apollonius sat down on the floor and put his head between his legs. "What is happening, Aurora? I feel like the world is falling down around us."

Myrrhine and Giorgio rushed over holding two more oil lamps. "Son, are you hurt?" She kneeled down and embraced him.

"No, just shaken, Mother."

Her father entered the atrium with Pioppo and Teo, who both

promptly climbed into Apollonius's lap. Aurora held on to the dog, who was shaking with fear.

"Was that an aftershock?" asked her father, to himself, more than anyone. "It felt stronger than the others. I don't understand. Each tremor is supposed be weaker than the preceding one."

"What time is it, Father?" Teo asked in a small voice. They all looked up at the sky through the compluvium.

"It seems to be a few hours before sunrise," he answered.

Her mother came into the atrium. "Helena is alive and will be fine, but several ribs have been broken. Myrrhine, I am going to need some long bandages and clean water."

The boys and their mother rushed away to retrieve medical supplies, but Apollonius continued to hold Teo, and Aurora sat down next to him, pressing her body close to him. She felt him tremble. If Apollonius was disheartened, what hope was there for the rest of them? He was her rock.

She fought back the feeling of helplessness that threatened to overtake her. "We will be fine because we have each other." She wrapped her arms around Apollonius, Teo, and the dog and held them tight. "That's truly all that matters. Let the house crumble to dust, I don't care. We will survive. Helena's ribs will heal, Evander will come back, and all will be right with the world once more."

Apollonius grabbed her hand and kissed it. "Thank you," he croaked. "Thank you for being strong when I have failed you. I don't know what happened. After I removed the beam from Helena, all of the strength in my body fled me, and I felt that I might collapse."

"It is a normal response," she assured him. "Now let's go help the others. And, Apollonius?" He looked at her with his big brown eyes. "You could never fail me."

HER FATHER ASSEMBLED all of them in the middle of the garden, away from the walls and falling ceiling tiles. He and Apollonius had carried Helena there as well and laid her on a portable bed. She was sleeping soundly with the poppy seed juice her mother had administered.

Her father ordered that only a few small oil lamps should be lit, nothing large that could be a fire hazard, in case of another earthquake. They also brought out food, water, and medical supplies. They huddled together on the mattresses they had stripped from the beds, wrapping blankets around their shoulders, as the late October morning was cool and breezy.

"The question now is, do we leave Pompeii, or is the worst behind us?" her father asked them. "And where would we go? To Neapolis? To Stabiae? I'm sure the entire bay is suffering through these same earth tremors. Will the mules even cooperate if there is another quake?"

Her mother shook her head. "I think we need to remain here right now, Aurorus. Campania is no stranger to earthquakes. Yes, we are having a rare sequence of them these past few days, but they will pass; they always do. We would put ourselves in more danger out there in the streets with scared people and animals running mindlessly about. Now, children, why don't you all try to get a little more sleep. I know this isn't an ideal location, but it's safer than being under the roof."

Aurora put her head to the pillow and fell asleep on the mattress next to Teo, with Lupa at her feet. She dreamt of Evander again, but this time he was standing on the beach, his impressive fleet of beautifully painted merchant ships behind him, sails blowing in the wind. She called to him in her dream. *Please come back . . . we need you . . . I need you . . .*

She slept peacefully for a couple more hours until a loud explosion startled them all awake. Immediately, the ground beneath them started to rumble and shake. Helena tried to sit up, then moaned in pain. Aurora encouraged her to lie still, but the rocking of the ground was causing motion and discomfort to her ribs.

The shaking of the earth continued so violently that two columns of the peristyle garden crumbled and fell to the ground, and their beautiful statue of Venus Pompeiana toppled into the bushes. When it was over, Aurora looked around the garden in shock.

"Father, something is very wrong here. We must do something."

"Yes." He turned to her mother. "Lucina, I must go out and investigate that explosion and see what the situation is throughout the city. Perhaps there is some kind of plan being formulated."

"And I should go to my father's house and see how he is faring with his patients. He will need help this morning, I'm sure the tremors have caused many injuries," her mother said.

Aurora stared at her parents in disbelief. "You are both *leaving* at a time like this? What are you thinking? What shall we do with Helena?"

"Apollonius will take charge of the household, and Myrrhine and the boys will still be here to help," her father said.

"Mother?" She looked at her beloved mother with uncertainty.

"I don't want to go, but I feel it is my duty to help Grandfather. You are capable of caring for Teo and Helena, and Apollonius is capable of caring for all of you. Just remember—small doses of poppy seed juice when Helena's pain overwhelms her."

Her mother hugged Teo for a long time. "Be brave, my little love, listen to Apollonius and your sister, and do not leave the domus under any circumstance. Understand?"

Teo nodded. "I understand, Mama."

Aurora hugged her parents good-bye and stood alone in the atrium, feeling forlorn. The house was a mess; chunks of plaster had dropped down from the walls, the garden portico was badly damaged, and a wooden beam had fallen from the ceiling.

Helena called to her weakly, and she rushed back into the garden.

"Where is Hercules?" she asked as she tried to look around.

"He is at your vineyard. I'm sure he is fine."

"But he must be scared! He's only a puppy. Can Apollonius go get him for me?"

"I'm sorry, Helena. It is too dangerous for him to go there right now. Another tremor can strike at any moment."

"And my brother? Where is he?"

Aurora realized the girl was very confused and wondered if she had been struck on the head, after all. "He has not yet returned from Corinth; he is due back any day now."

"Oh? How long has he been gone?"

"Two months now, since the end of August."

The girl smiled up at her, then closed her eyes and fell back asleep. Aurora hoped her confusion was due to the poppy juice. She would be fine after she slept for a little while.

Apollonius took charge of the situation, just as he always did, organizing, ordering, and delegating clean-up jobs to his brothers and the other slaves that had come from the Mercurius household.

Myrrhine was busy setting food out for all of them, and Aurora decided she would venture to the corner fountain to get fresh water. She grabbed a wooden bucket and headed out the door. She was distressed to see the damage the earthquake had caused. She looked down the street and realized that her beloved city was falling down around her. She put her hand over her heart. There was so much rubble lying about that the road was almost impassable, and many of the second-floor apartments were damaged to the point of being uninhabitable.

Most people were busy trying to clean up the mess, but some wandered around in a daze, as if they couldn't get their minds to understand what had happened.

Down at the fountain, her neighbors complained about the

lack of water pressure. It seemed the tremors had damaged the aqueduct and water lines. Still, there was a trickle of fresh water coming out, and they all waited patiently for a turn to fill up their buckets. They offered to help one another and organized a group to go house to house to check on each family.

Aurora's heart swelled with love and pride for her fellow Pompeians. How she loved this town and all of the good people who lived here. In times of need, they helped one another, just as they were doing now.

She turned around to make her way back home when she saw a jet of gray-black smoke blowing high into the sky from the top of Vesuvius. "What is that?" she asked the others.

They stopped what they were doing to look up, then shook their heads and shrugged. "Looks like some farms caught fire on top of the mountain."

But she couldn't reconcile how a farm, a vineyard, or a villa would create a plume of smoke that enormous. It looked like an entire city was burning, but there was no city at the summit of Vesuvius. Pompeii and Herculanuem rested on its slopes, and Neapolis was far to the west. Now she was scared, truly scared, and she sprinted back to her house as fast as she was physically able without tripping over the rubble or spilling the precious water.

She banged on the door as hard as she could, and tried to control her breathing. Apollonius flung open the door with a concerned look on his face. "What is it? What is wrong?"

She set down the bucket, swallowed hard, then slid her body down the brightly painted wall to the floor. Tears sprang to her eyes, and her throat was painfully dry.

"They think a farm is on fire," she cried hoarsely. "But it's not—it's not!" She started to cry as a wave of hysteria hit her. "My parents, where are my parents?" She put her head in her hands and sobbed.

Apollonius grabbed her by the arms and pulled her up,

speaking sternly to her. "Aurora, don't you fall apart on me. Not you, not now. I need you to be calm. You are making no sense. You are going to upset the others, and everyone is just starting to calm down. Now what are you trying to say?"

"The explosion—it was our mountain. Smoke is coming out from the top of Vesuvius!"

He pulled her out into the street. "If this is true, then . . ."

They had to walk a little ways before they had a clear view of the summit. When Apollonius saw the smoke for himself, his jaw dropped open, and the color drained from his face. "Damn me to the realm of Hades, it is just as you said."

Aurora wiped tears from her eyes. "I think Vesuvius is a fire mountain. You know, the kind they have in Greece and Sicily. Evander says that the fire moves slowly down the mountain, and people have time to get out of the way."

"I see smoke, lots of it, but no fire. Is there always fire?" he asked.

"The fire is within. Don't you see? The burnt smell in the air, the tremors, the dead birds and vines. I know this sounds crazy, but I think all that rumbling and rocking we are feeling is the fire trying to escape."

Apollonius backed slowly away, pulling her with him. "We need to get everyone out of the house and away from the mountain immediately. We cannot panic; we must keep our wits about us. Now come quickly." He grabbed her hand, and together they scrambled over the debris back to the domus.

They assembled inside the garden once more, where Apollonius laid out the details for an escape plan. They were to pack as much food and water as they could carry in a satchel, along with an extra pair of shoes, a warm cloak, medical supplies, and valuables such as jewelry. He also told them to take as much money as they could fit in their coin pouches. He had the slaves prepare a litter for Helena, who couldn't walk on her own.

Aurora's father came crashing through the front door as they were all packing their bags. "Children, we must leave!" he boomed. "I have brought one of our mules to help carry supplies; the others I have given to my clients who are without. Make haste! The roads are in a difficult state."

She scrambled down the stairs and threw herself into her father's arms, holding on to him tightly. "Oh, Father, thank the gods you came back! I was so worried about you and Mother. Where is she? At Grandfather's house?"

"Yes, I brought her there first, and when we saw the smoke coming from Vesuvius, we decided that we should leave the city as a precaution. She is helping Grandfather prepare his patients. They will meet us outside the Stabian Gate. From there, we will take the path down to the sea and along the coast to Stabiae." He kissed her forehead. "Daughter, we must hurry. We have no idea what the mountain may do."

Teo ran into the atrium and threw himself into his father's arms. "Father, please don't leave us again!" he cried.

"It's all right, Son. We will stay together now."

"Father, can Lupa come with us?" he asked.

"No, Son. She must stay and guard the house from looters. Chain her to the front door and give her plenty of food and water."

"Father!" they both cried.

"We can't leave her behind! And to chain her up, not knowing when we will be able to come back—that's cruel!" cried Aurora.

"Then don't chain her, but she must remain in the house to guard it."

"As if she's really a guard dog . . ." Aurora mumbled. "And what if there is fire, and it reaches our house?"

"Aurora, right now I must concern myself with keeping my family safe," he huffed. "I can't worry about the dog. Let's go. Teo, get your satchel."

Teo ran from the room, and Aurora noticed little splashes

coming from the impluvium as he ran by. "What are those?" she inquired, moving closer.

"What?" her father asked impatiently.

"Those little gray balls falling into the pool?"

They walked over and looked down at the spherical orbs floating in the water. Her father scooped some up in his hand. "They're very light. They must be some kind of debris blown out by the explosion."

The little gray balls were falling in earnest now, the sound of them plopping into the water like giant raindrops. Aurora regarded her father in disbelief. "It's raining *rocks*?"

CHAPTER 23

*I*t was two hours before midday when Aurora stepped out onto the street with a satchel full of medical supplies and a heavy heart. She couldn't believe they were going to leave her home, but a mountain that spouted black smoke was an ominous, terrible omen. The earth tremors had caused too much damage, and they all agreed they weren't safe staying indoors anymore for fear that a ceiling or wall might fall down on them. The best and safest plan was to leave the mountain for a while and return when it had calmed.

The small, light orbs pelted them on the face and head, and they drew up the hoods of their cloaks to protect themselves. She wondered about the fire that Evander had spoken of. Would it come next? And if it did, would it travel down the mountain slowly? Would it breach the walls of Pompeii? She wished with all her heart that he were here to help guide their decisions. He would know what to do; he had seen these fire mountains before.

But she was wasting thoughts on things that couldn't be. She needed to be brave for the others, so she took a deep breath and resolved to stay in control of her emotions. *Let nothing break you,* he had said before he left.

They gathered into a circle on the street, the mule braying in the middle, and watched as the front door closed behind them. They looked at one another with pain in their eyes and the heaviness of their journey ahead, but it was Myrrhine who started to cry.

"This is the only home my children have ever known. They were too young to remember our home in Greece. This house, this family saved our lives," she cried. "How can we leave?"

Aurora's father put his arm around her. "Home is where you are with your loved ones, Myrrhine. A house is only a house. Keep your chin up, all of you. Think positively. We are only leaving as a precaution. I'm sure we will be able to return soon."

Helena's entourage of slaves picked up her litter and waited for the command to go. But inside the house, Lupa was crying woefully, and it broke Aurora's heart.

This is too much. I can't leave my dog! But she also knew that she couldn't contradict her father, especially in front of all these slaves. She held her breath and tried to ignore the falling tears, and the feeling of despair that was creeping down her spine. Then Teo lost his composure too and fell to the ground. "Luuuuupa!" he wailed loudly, striking his fists on the pavement.

Her father turned red in the face and looked at Giorgio. "Get the leash and the dog," he said crossly. He kneeled down to Teo. "We need to be on our way now, Son, and I need you to show me that you can act like a man. This is serious, Teo. Stop crying. You will be in charge of Lupa, and don't make me regret my decision."

The ground started to shake again. "Let's move!" her father yelled. "Down to the Stabian Gate!" He pulled the mule forward and gestured for everyone to follow.

"Hold my hand, Teo, come on!" cried Aurora. Giorgio caught up to them a moment later toting Lupa.

"My Lupa!" Teo cried as he took her leash. "We are going on a journey to Stabiae! You will be our guard dog and protect us from harm." Then he turned and looked up at his sister, his face full of concern. "Who is taking care of Hercules?"

"I'm sure that one of Evander's slaves is caring for the puppy," she assured him. "He is out at the vineyard." *And there's nothing we can do about it now.*

When they reached the corner of their street, they had a clear view of Vesuvius. They were amazed to see a gray-black cloud, spreading out like an umbrella pine, hanging high above the mountain. The wind was blowing the cloud in their direction, and ash began to fall on the pavement.

They moved as quickly as they could along the main thoroughfare of Pompeii, stepping carefully over rubble and debris, stopping here and there to gape in astonishment at the broken walls and collapsing roofs of their beloved city.

Her father stated calmly to everyone he passed that they were headed to Stabiae as a precaution. He also invited people to join them as long as they were willing to help and share food, water, and supplies. Soon there was a large crowd following, and Teo was excited to see that some of his friends from the palaestra had joined their group. Aurora gave him permission to walk with a friend as long as he kept her in his sight.

Once outside the walls of the city, they took a breath of relief and stopped to look for her mother and grandfather. But the cloud of ash grew larger, and the sky continued to darken over Pompeii. Aurora coughed and covered her face with her scarf as the air grew thicker with ash.

Several loud booms were heard coming from the summit of Vesuvius. They echoed powerfully across the sky and shook the air with violence. Aurora was frozen with fear. The vibration of the explosions hit her body a moment later, almost knocking her to the ground.

The shower of light gray orbs intensified, and she wondered what was happening inside the mountain. *Has the end of my days arrived?*

A wave of panic rolled through the crowd.

"Get to the bridge and cross the Sarnus river!" ordered her father. "Stay on the road; it is the safest route to Stabiae," he urged. He came to her and held her hands. "I need to find your mother and grandfather—they were supposed to be here. Maybe they were hindered by the crowd. I can't leave them behind. I need to go back and look for them."

"Father, no! The sky is darkening. It is too dangerous, and you might never find them. They are not foolish; they will flee the mountain one way or another. We need you here with us!" she begged.

"Look!" Apollonius cried above the noise and confusion. "I see sails off in the distance, a fleet of ships, just around the promontory of Surrentum. Could it be Evander?"

They looked out to sea, where the sun was still shining, and saw the brightly painted merchant ships, their towering white swan heads gleaming above the waves. Aurora felt her knees go weak with relief as she recognized Evander's fleet. Tears streamed down her face, and she thanked the gods for his return.

"Father, we must get down to the harbor. Mother and Grandfather will see the ships, just as we have, and will meet us there." Her father agreed and began to lead the group down the hill toward the port. Aurora ran to Helena's litter and opened the curtains. "Your brother has returned! We can see his ships coming around the cliffs of Surrentum!"

Helena let out a happy squeal, then grimaced in pain. "Thank Neptune for his safe return! When will he arrive?"

"Within the hour; we will head to the harbor now." She blew the girl a kiss and squeezed her pretty toe, which was peeking out from under the blanket.

Apollonius came over to address them both. "We need to keep moving. This black cloud is heading our way, and the air is growing thick, making it difficult to breathe. Keep your scarf over your face."

Half of the group had already moved toward the bridge to cross the river, but the other half decided to follow her father to the harbor. Aurora felt a sense of urgency to get as far away from the mountain as possible, and knowing that Evander would be arriving shortly gave her a great boost of energy and purpose.

People began to pour from the city gates in an attempt to flee the mountain, and it seemed that everyone was heading to the water. Aurora's father took them off the main road and onto a well-trodden footpath to the sea. They walked carefully through the accumulation of light rocks on the ground and cleared the ash from their hair and shoulders every few moments. The earth continued to vibrate and shake, and although it was still early, it looked like dusk had arrived.

A large piece of burning rock sizzled through the air overhead and landed in a flowering bush, setting it on fire and striking new terror into their hearts. Another projectile pelted Giorgio on the head, causing him to stumble. Aurora checked him over, but aside from a few singed hairs and a good bump, he wasn't badly injured.

Apollonius ordered them all to carry on like soldiers, to squelch their fear and to stay strong for the children, who set their behavior by watching the reactions of the adults.

When they finally arrived at the harbor, they pushed through the crowd toward the base of a natural cliff, which offered some protection against the falling rocks and ash.

The long wooden piers where Evander's fleet usually docked jutted out into the bay in front of them. The water pummeled the docks fiercely, at times obliterating them from view. She tugged at Apollonius's arm. "Can he safely moor his ships?"

"It won't be easy," Apollonius admitted with concern.

A group of young boys huddled in front of Aurora, and suddenly she realized that she had lost track of Teo. She looked anxiously through the group of people who had come down the footpath with them, but Teo was nowhere to be found.

A wave of nausea hit her hard, and she couldn't breathe. How could she have lost her brother? Was she so preoccupied with her own fear that she neglected to care for him? And Giorgio, his slave, who was always one step behind him, had been pelted on the head by a rock. Could she blame him for losing track of her brother as well?

"Father! Father! I have lost Teo!" she cried, running over to him.

"What do you mean *lost* him? Teo! Teo!" he roared. "He has to be around here somewhere! Who saw him last? Could he have followed the other half of the group over the bridge to Stabiae?"

"I don't know. I gave him permission to walk with his friends as long as he kept me in his sight. Oh gods! I am so sorry!" She was growing hysterical.

Myrrhine and her boys mobilized in an instant, sifting through the crowd and asking if anyone had seen a brown-haired little boy with a black dog. Her father continued to bellow Teo's name.

Aurora found the little boy that Teo had walked with and grabbed him by the shoulders. "Where is Teo? When was the last time you saw him?" she demanded.

"He made me promise not to tell." The little boy started to cry, and his mother compelled him to speak, threatening severe punishment if he didn't reveal what he knew immediately.

"He went to save a puppy in a vineyard somewhere."

Aurora let go of the child and covered her mouth with her hand. *I need to go find him*, she thought desperately.

She returned to her father, feeling a kind of dread she had never known before.

"Father, he snuck away when we weren't watching. He went to save Hercules up at Evander's vineyard!" she cried hoarsely.

They looked up toward the mountain in the direction of the vineyard. The ever-increasing black cloud hung ominously over-head. "Oh my gods. I will go back and look for him," said her father. "I will never forgive myself if something happens to him."

"No, *I* will never forgive myself. Let me come with you, Father."

"Absolutely not. You must stay here and wait for Evander, and get yourself away from here as fast as possible. Go wait under the cliff with the rest of the group."

She embraced him hard. "I love you, Father. Stay safe and come back to us quickly."

"I love you too, Daughter. Have courage." Her father pulled his cloak over his head, and she watched him set off toward the Herculaneum Gate.

I am the most wretched of souls. She put her head in her hands and cried. *I have lost you, my sweet brother. I would gladly trade my life for yours. Gods, I beg you, keep him safe.*

Evander's ships approached the harbor, and Apollonius ordered everyone in their group to stay away from the piers, as the water was wild and choppy, and mooring the ships would be dangerous. Nobody heeded his warning. Driven by fear and the desire to escape, people swarmed the quays, creating more confusion and injuries.

On any other day, Aurora would have felt joy and elation upon watching Evander's hardy merchant ships sail into the harbor. She was finally going to see him after two long, lonely months. But this had been no ordinary day, and at this moment, all she could feel was sorrow and despair for herself, her family, and her beautiful city.

CHAPTER 24

urora stood anxiously against the cliff wall and watched through the darkening sky as a figure approached. A long cloak covered his large frame and flared majestically out behind him in the blowing wind. His movements were strong and powerful, but his face was hidden in shadows. When he was finally close enough for her to discern his features, her heart started to thunder inside her chest, and she pushed her way through the crowd. "Evander!"

He fixed her in his sight, then hurried toward her, his long strides quickly eating the distance between them. She ran to him, throwing her body into his outstretched arms. "Evander! Thank the gods!"

He picked her up as he embraced her. She found his lips and kissed him until she could no longer breathe. The ash was everywhere—in her hair and eyelashes, under her tunic, and in her mouth, but she didn't care—Evander was back.

"How I have missed you!" she cried. She caressed his cheek and twined her fingers in his hair. "But what an unfortunate situation you have found us in! We are fleeing Vesuvius!"

He set her down and cradled her face in his large hands.

"Aurora, my love, we must get on one of my ships immediately so we can sail to safety. You have been living on a fire mountain! I saw the black cloud over the top of the hills as we approached Salernum. I came as fast as the wind would allow."

"No," she lamented, "I can't leave! I have lost my brother!"

"What do you mean *lost* him?"

"He snuck away to save Hercules up at your vineyard. My father left to go search for him over an hour ago, my mother and grandfather never showed up at our meeting point, no one is where they should be, and everything is just a mess!" She broke down in tears, overcome by so many conflicting emotions at once.

"Calm down, Aurora. I will go to my vineyard and search for them."

"But there's no time!" she cried. "The mountain is spitting out smoke, ash, and rock, and the tremors are unbearable. We have also heard several explosions. The last one was so powerful it knocked us down!"

"I will take my chances. Now where is my sister?"

"She was injured during a tremor last night." She led him by the hand to the litter. He pulled open the curtain, his eyebrows creasing when he saw her petite frame wrapped in bandages.

"Sister, I am here."

Helena opened her eyes. "Brother! My dearest brother! You have made it back safely!" She started to cry with relief. He held her hands and kissed her cheek. "Helena, listen to me. I am going to have the slaves bring you and Aurora aboard one of my ships now. I want you both far away from Vesuvius." He looked up at Aurora, his face becoming very serious. "It may get much worse before it gets better."

"Worse than this?" Apollonius asked as he approached, pointing to the mountain.

"If Vesuvius is anything like Mount Aetna in Sicily, the fire and burning embers will come next."

Aurora sucked in her breath. "My gods! Teo and my father are up there!"

"I will go now and look for them. But I need you and Apollonius to stay calm. Take Helena and wait for me on the *Corbita*. It is the last ship down the farthest pier. The crew of each ship has orders to depart as soon as it is filled to capacity. The *Corbita* will wait for me. But if the situation worsens and I haven't returned, you must give my instruction to Manolo and the crew to sail without me."

Aurora scoffed. "Sail without you? We would never leave you!"

"You may have to if your life depends on it. And soon all of these falling rocks, as light as they may be, may begin to clog the harbor."

She bristled at his suggestion that she would leave him here to suffer an unknown fate while the rest of them sailed to safety on his ships!

"Now kiss me good-bye," he ordered.

"Good-bye? You just—" His lips came down on hers and lingered for one soft, special moment. She inhaled his breath and his scent.

He gathered her in his powerful arms once more and held her tight. "Be brave, my love. I will find your brother. Now get to the ship as fast as possible." He recruited a couple of male slaves from Helena's entourage and set off.

Aurora watched bleakly as they hurried toward the dark city and the disaster that was unfolding above them. She was traumatized to her core. Everyone she loved was in danger. Would they all be able to survive this day?

A clap of thunder and flash of lightning shocked her out of her contemplation. The mountain was becoming ever more violent. Her brother was lost, her father and Evander in search of him, her mother and grandfather unheard from. Her world was upside down. Pandemonium was breaking loose in her once beautiful and well-ordered city, and she was powerless to stop it.

Apollonius led them down to the farthest pier. It was at the outer limits of the harbor, an arm curving into the bay. The ash had combined with water, covering the pier with a slippery paste and making each step challenging. But the crowd was thinner out here, and she realized Evander was smart to have docked the *Corbita* last.

She counted at least ten more of his ships anchored throughout the harbor. The port was clogged with boats and ships of all sizes, and some of Evander's ships had not been able to approach the dock. Smaller boats were being used to transport people to the larger vessels.

Aurora climbed up onto the deck of the *Corbita*, and a sense of relief washed through her. She looked back at the city, now cast in shadows due to the large ash cloud that loomed over it. The cloud looked to her like an enormous tree; it rose to a great height on a trunk of smoke, then split off into smaller branches. Part of the cloud looked white while other parts looked gray and dirty. She marveled at the forces that could cause such a strange and horrific apparition.

Evander's crew was busy taking charge of the rescue operation. She made sure Helena was comfortable inside the deck cabin, then set about helping others who were coming aboard the ship. She offered words of assurance to everyone and told the children who were crying to be brave and strong and that together they would survive this.

When the ship was filled to capacity, the crew pulled up the gangplank. It was a little after the midday hour when Apollonius finally approached her with solemn eyes. "It is time to go."

"I will not leave without them!" Aurora cried into the wind.

"We must, those are his orders! We have families on board who want to get their children to safety. We must depart now!"

Tears flowed down Aurora's cheeks, and she started to tremble.

Apollonius gripped her shoulders. "There are still two more of his ships in the harbor. They will make it back before the last ship sails."

"Will they?" she cried.

"What is the alternative?" he demanded. "Wait here until desperate people storm the ship? Until the mountain burns us with fire? We have no choice." He gave a nod to Manolo, and the crew quickly prepared the ship to sail.

"You are forcing me to abandon everyone that I love!" she screamed at him. "You are wretched! I hate you! I hate you!" She sank down to the deck and sobbed. The ship made a rough departure from the pier, then turned into the turbulent waters of the bay.

Apollonius picked her up and carried her into the deck cabin. Her heart and soul were crushed at leaving Evander and her family behind. Helena began to weep inconsolably when she heard that her brother was not aboard.

A little later, when Aurora stepped back outside, she was able to see the situation in the bay more clearly. The cities west of Pompeii—Herculaneum, Neapolis, and Misenum—were all bathed in sunshine. But Pompeii and the cities to the east—Nuceria and Stabiae—were under the dark cloud, being rained on by stones and ash.

Across the bay, Surrentum, with its beautiful cliffs jutting up from the sea, stood like a beacon of hope, a sanctuary from the evils that plagued them. The sun was shining brightly there, and she thanked the gods for their good graces. She turned her mind to her mother and grandfather and prayed that she would find them on the beach once they all docked.

⁓

EVANDER and his slaves moved stealthily along the path that led up to the Old Salt Gate on the western side of the city. They kept their cloaks pulled over their heads to avoid being pelted by the falling rocks. A group of people was fleeing from the city gate, holding pillows over their heads for protection. He told them to make their way to the harbor and his ships and he would bring them to safety. They thanked him profusely and gifted him with some pillows.

I can't save the entire city, but I will save whom I can, he thought with determination as he rushed toward his vineyard, just north of the gate.

He hoped that Aurora and his sister were safely aboard the *Corbita,* and he prayed hard that he would find Teo and Dominus Fortunas. They arrived at the entrance of his property and ran toward the villa. His once beautiful vineyard was covered in white ash, and thousands of small, light rocks cluttered the paths between the rows of grapevines.

He stopped for a moment. "What is happening? Is the entire city to be buried by falling rock?" He scooped up a handful of the light orbs and examined them. "It's pumice. The engineers use it to make concrete for the aqueducts." The slaves nodded nervously and looked up at the mountain. Evander threw down the handful of rocks. "Come on, then."

When they reached the villa, he was shocked at the damage. "It looks like the walls and ceiling in the rear of the villa have collapsed. We need to be careful so that we don't end up under a pile of rubble." They entered the villa through a missing wall and started searching for Teo.

Evander called out to Hercules and heard a bark come from one of the storage rooms. "That way!" he commanded. When he entered the room, Hercules scrambled over to Evander and started whining excitedly. "Hey, little pup, where's Teo? Where is Teo, Hercules?"

The puppy ran back to the corner and barked at a wooden cart.

"He's under the cart!" cried a slave.

"Teo! Come out if you can. It's me, Evander."

The slaves quickly moved amphorae and other equipment out of the way, clearing a path to the cart. They pulled Teo out from beneath it, his eyes wide with shock. Lupa came crawling out next, cowering close to the floor, her hind leg dragging behind her.

"Dominus?" The little boy's voice trembled with fear. He slumped into Evander's arms and began to sob.

"Teo, we need to go now; it's not safe here. Your sister is waiting for you down on my ship, and she's sick with worry. What were you thinking?" he scolded. "Why did you leave her?"

"I came to get Hercules, but there was another earth tremor, and then the walls fell down. Lupa got hurt and started howling, I didn't know what to do!"

"You could have gotten yourself killed! And your father is looking for you too. He should have been here before me. You will not disobey your family—or me—again! Understand?"

Teo nodded as Evander picked him up in his arms, and each slave took hold of a dog. But before leaving the house, Evander decided to grab more pillows from the bedroom for protection. He ordered the slaves to rip some linen sheets into strips to use as ties.

When they each had secured a pillow over their head, they realized that Hercules had scampered away. Evander grabbed Teo by the arm and pulled him into the dark hallway. "This dog is going to be the death of us." He whistled loudly to call the puppy back. "We can't wait any longer—the ships will be leaving."

They heard a bark and followed the sound to the back entranceway. The floor was thick with bricks and plaster and chunks of wall that had crumbled to the ground. The puppy sat whimpering on a pile of smashed terra-cotta roof tiles.

A slave carefully approached the dog and picked him up.

Evander heard the slave gasp and felt his heartbeat quicken. "What is it?"

"Father!" cried Teo. "My father is under there. I see his sandal!" Teo ran to the pile of rubble and began to dig through it with his little hands. Evander was on his heels, and they furiously removed the debris to get to the man buried underneath.

Evander choked back a cry when he realized Dominus Fortunas was dead. "We must go before we suffer the same fate," he said grimly, his heart filled with remorse at having to leave the good man behind. Aurora's father deserved to be buried with dignity, in a beautiful tomb. He hesitated for a moment, then decided it would be too difficult to carry his body to the ship under these conditions.

Teo began to wail. Evander picked him up and carried him out of the house. The slaves followed behind him, each with a terrified dog in their arms.

The return to the harbor was slow and treacherous. Although it was only a little past midday, the sky was growing darker as the ash cloud expanded. Heavier rocks were now pelting them from above, and pumice stones clogged the walkway. Panic and an impending sense of doom were intensifying among the people who hastened alongside him, trying to escape.

They questioned aloud how they could survive such a catastrophe. Some lamented their decision to flee and thought it might have been safer to stay indoors. A baker confessed that he had fled while loaves of bread were still baking in his oven, and his mules were tied up in the stable.

When they finally arrived at the harbor, Evander breathed a sigh of relief when he saw that one of his ships remained. The *Corbita* had sailed, taking Helena and Aurora to safety.

The last ship was anchored alongside the quay, but something was wrong. The vessel was listing to one side, and people were rushing to disembark. Evander pushed his way up the gangplank. "What is going on here?" he yelled at the captain.

"The anchor is stuck in the rocks, Dominus. The water level has lowered, and we are in danger of being grounded."

Evander grunted in frustration. He told Teo to take the dogs and stay inside the deck cabin. "Unload the cargo and lessen the weight of the ship until the anchor is free!" The men and crew rushed to carry out his orders.

The earth tremors continued, rocking the piers, and Evander remembered the night on the beach with Aurora. An earthquake out at sea would eventually cause a large wave to break onto the shore. They would use the sea to their advantage.

He told the men to be ready to pull hard at the anchor when the force of a wave hit the ship. After a while, several large waves finally rolled into the harbor, and the heavy iron flukes of the anchor wrestled free.

Evander ran to the gangplank and signaled for more people to board. They looked at him reluctantly as the ship still listed to one side. "We will sail, I promise you, we will sail," he assured them. Families filed past him holding their children, small animals, and most valuable possessions. They even loaded people down into the cargo bay, but the line was never ending, and he and his crew had to fight men off of the gangplank when the ship was at capacity. They pulled in the ropes and made ready to sail.

Evander promised the people on the pier that he would return to rescue them as soon as possible. It tugged on his heart to leave so many behind, but his merchant ships were fast and safe and would be able to cross the bay quickly. They had large square sails that provided stability to the heavy vessels and harnessed the wind well.

More great waves rushed into the harbor. People cried out in fear as the ship rolled and bobbed, then was finally swept away from the quay as the water retreated to the sea. The crew adjusted the sails, and soon they were heading southwest toward Surrentum and away from the dreadful fire mountain.

AURORA HEAVED a great sigh of relief as the *Corbita* sailed into the harbor of Surrentum. It was sunny here, and she looked at Pompeii across the bay with a feeling of disbelief. Pompeii was so close yet suffering so dramatically under the most horrific circumstances.

She stayed onboard while everyone disembarked. The crew began to unload food and other merchandise onto the docks. "Why are you unloading the ship now?" she asked Manolo.

"Dominus's orders. All ships are to return to Pompeii for another rescue mission. We will use the cargo bays to carry more people."

Apollonius approached her. "I know you are angry with me for leaving Evander and your brother behind, but I wanted to tell you that I'll be going back."

"You? Back to Pompeii?" she cried, alarmed.

"I must, Aurora. The crew needs help."

"Gods, Apollonius! Will everyone I love desert me?"

He embraced her hard and kissed her cheek. "I cannot stay here knowing that people might die over there."

She swallowed the lump in her throat and brushed aside her tears, her heart numb with too many sorrows. "May Fortune go with you," she prayed, as she reluctantly let go of him.

THE GOOD PEOPLE of Surrentum had seen the ships arriving, and many were waiting down at the harbor with donkeys, carts, and water. They helped transport the refugees safely up to the city, especially those with babies and small children.

Aurora chose to stay on the beach with Helena and help set up a camp for those who could not endure the steep climb up to the city. She desperately awaited the arrival of the last two ships, hoping that Evander and her family had made it to safety. Her mother and grandfather might already be here, and she was anxious to search for them.

Another of Evander's vessels sailed into the harbor, and she ran out to the pier where it would dock. She searched desperately through the people who disembarked, but there was no sign of her parents, her brother, or Evander. She returned to the beach disheartened.

Another hour passed. Where was the last ship?

Finally, she saw the large square sails coming toward Surrentum. The ship seemed to take a lifetime to cross the bay. As it sailed into the port, her heart jumped into her throat when she saw Evander moving swiftly about the bow.

She desperately scanned the crowded deck for Teo but couldn't see him. Her throat pinched painfully, and her stomach lurched at the thought that he was lost to her. She waited for the crowd to unload, then sprinted up the gangplank.

"Evander!" she cried. "You made it! You made it!" His face and hair were covered in soot, and he looked like he had been through a battle. She ran to him and embraced him tightly.

"And my brother?"

"He is in the cabin."

A wave of relief swept over her that was so profound all she could do was hang on to Evander's shoulders and pray that she wouldn't collapse onto the deck.

"But there is something I must tell you."

She looked up at him in fear, her heart hammering in her chest.

"It's your father, my love. He didn't make it."

Aurora's face crumpled in pain, and she let out a high-pitched cry. She fought for her breath as she slumped into Evander's arms. "My father, my father . . ." she wailed.

"We found him under the rubble. The ceiling of my villa had collapsed on him. I was too late to save him. I'm so sorry."

She continued to sob pitifully for her father. Her world had just crashed down on her, and she didn't know which way to turn.

"Aurora, your brother needs you now. He is grieving as well." He kept his strong arm around her as he escorted her to the cabin and opened the door. Teo was lying down on the bed whimpering, Lupa and Hercules flanking his sides.

"Teo!" She ran to the side of the bed and scooped him up in her arms. "My sweet brother, my baby, why did you leave me?" she sobbed. "Do you know what sorrows I have endured thinking you were dead? Believing it was all my fault?"

"I'm sorry, Sister! And now father is dead. *Because of me.*" He buried his head in her lap and wept loudly.

Evander interrupted them. "I'm sorry, I know that you both are grieving for your father, but you need to get off the ship now. I *must* go back for more people before it is too late." He nodded to Lupa. "I think her leg is broken."

Aurora turned her tear-stained face to her dog and felt a streak of irrational joy creep into her heart. "Come here, you silly creature. Are you hurt? I'll fix you right up, don't you worry." Lupa whined and wagged her tail. Aurora helped the dog up gently, and Evander picked up Teo and Hercules.

Evander escorted them down the pier. "I want you all to stay together with my sister on the beach. As soon as I return, I will come and find you."

Aurora looked at him thankfully, but sorrow filled her heart yet again. "I cannot tell you not to go, but I wish it wasn't so. I know it is right to save as many lives as possible. You are a hero now, Evander, but just remember"—her face creased in pain—"I need you too." Fresh tears ran down her face, and she wondered that she even had any tears left to cry.

He held them both for a moment within the safety of his arms. "And I need you. Just a little bit longer, and then we'll be together." He kissed them both. "Now go and stay on the beach. I need to sail before all hope is lost for the others."

Aurora said good-bye to Evander for the second time that day and watched him board one of his ships. He was strong and brave, and Fortune was on his side, but for how much longer? One escape from Pompeii was fortuitous, but two? She feared that this time he might not be so lucky.

CHAPTER 25

$\mathcal{E}$vander and his fleet of ships headed fearlessly across the Bay of Neapolis. They lit their torches as they approached the mountain and the enormous black cloud that hovered ominously over the cities east of Vesuvius. The sky grew darker, thicker ash began to fall, and the air grew hotter as they drew near. Embers swirled around them, and black pieces of charred rock pummeled the ship.

The walls of Pompeii appeared eerily out of the darkness at uneven intervals as forked flames and great flashes of lightning lit up the sky. The water level in the harbor looked dangerously low, and the shore was beginning to be blocked by debris from the mountain. The conditions had worsened considerably in the last couple hours.

Evander called out orders to his crew in a strong voice that did not waver at the danger before them. "Cover your head and be prepared to snuff out fires. We need to be quick about this; if the sails catch fire, we must do our best to douse them with water. Get as many people as possible on these ships, use the cargo hold as well, it doesn't matter—we need to save as many lives as we can, gods be willing!"

A few moments later, the ship slammed into the pier, sending them flying. Evander picked himself up and carried on calmly, propelled by an inner strength hitherto unknown to him. Blood ran down his forehead and into his eyes, but there was no time to think or hesitate, he needed to act, and act quickly.

As soon as the vessel was secured and the gangplank was down, frenzied people scrambled onto the ship, and he bellowed at them not to trample each other. He grabbed a woman who was holding a newborn baby and pointed to the deck cabin. "Stay inside there with your baby," he ordered.

Hundreds boarded the ship. As they were fighting off more people and trying to pull up the gangplank, he noticed that another one of his vessels was in trouble. He gave the order to sail, then disembarked and ran toward the next pier.

The sails of the ship had caught fire, and several slaves were trying to douse the flames with buckets of seawater. But the fire was spreading, and soon it would reach the mast. People were pushing back down the gangplank to escape. He realized with a lump in his throat that this was going to end badly, and he ordered everyone to abandon ship. The fiery mast broke in half and slammed down on the deck just moments after the last man had fled to safety.

He ushered people by torchlight down to another quay where his final merchant ship was attempting to dock. The sky was cloaked by a dense darkness, as if an oil lamp had been snuffed out in a closed room. *This is it,* he thought. *I'm out of time.* People tried to find each other by the sound of their voices, and he heard some say that they wished to die.

They crammed as many women and children as possible aboard the last ship. The remaining men stood on the dock and blocked it from those who would try to overtake the vessel. Devoted husbands and fathers who had sacrificed themselves in order to see their families escape were left standing on the pier.

Evander shouted to them to find a boat and row toward the

light of Surrentum. He promised that he would send his ships out in the bay to rescue them but that they couldn't come safely into the harbor anymore. As they pulled away from the dock, he was sick for those souls he was forced to abandon. His heart felt like an anchor dropped to the bottom of the sea.

It was roughly three hours after midday when they approached the sunlight in the center of the bay. Evander saw a fleet of triremes leaving from Misenum, a large military city opposite Surrentum. They were headed to Pompeii. *Thank the gods,* he thought, *the Roman navy is on the way to save them.*

They were almost to Surrentum when they saw the warships row beneath the dark cloud and disappear. He was exhausted to the bone, his clothes were singed, and he was suffering from a head wound. His stomach was empty and raging, but he couldn't stop. He needed to care for these people and offer what solace he could. He wandered around the deck trying to calm them and offered words of hope.

"We will be all right!" he yelled. "We will make it! We're almost there! But listen to me, when we dock, I need you all to proceed calmly and slowly so nobody gets hurt. The worst is over. Please don't trample somebody's child or grandmother! We will set up camp on the beach, and there will be people from Surrentum there to help you. Some will open their homes to you. Be careful, be honest, and take care of each other."

The traumatized faces looked at him hopefully, and some came forward to offer him pieces of bread and water, which he accepted gratefully. Frazzled mothers held on tightly to their children, and cried for their spouses who had been left behind.

How did this happen, he wondered wretchedly, *and why did nobody see it coming?*

Once the ship had docked and unloaded, Evander went to find the crew of the *Corbita,* his favorite ship. Apollonius was busy securing the moorings to the quay. Evander realized that the slave had gone back to Pompeii with his crew. As he walked down the pier toward him, he felt bad for the times he had treated him poorly.

Apollonius looked just as battered and exhausted as Evander felt. He stood before him. "Words don't do justice to the bravery you have shown today, Apollonius. Your deeds won't be forgotten."

Apollonius looked him in the eye, fatigue etched into the lines of his youthful face. "Did you find Teo and Dominus Fortunas? I left Surrentum before you arrived."

Evander sighed. "Teo is fine . . . but Dominus didn't make it."

Apollonius bowed his head and tried to hide his tears. Evander put his hand on the slave's shoulder. "Why don't you come with me now to find my sister and Aurora? Night will soon be falling, and I don't want them to worry about us."

Aurora and Teo were sitting around a small fire eating fruits and nuts that had been unloaded from one of Evander's ships. Helena reclined on her litter, and all the slaves who had stuck with them through this disaster were huddled about. When they saw the men approach, they stood up and cheered.

"Our heroes! You made it!" they cried. Myrrhine ran to her son and embraced him tightly. Evander smiled at Aurora and opened his arms. She ran into them gratefully, and he folded her into a long embrace. "You made it back! Thank the gods, thank the gods . . ." she cried into his chest. "We were sick with worry—your sister was beside herself."

Helena was laughing with joy and crying with relief. "Brother! My brother, the hero!" Lupa and Hercules were barking now, and a small crowd was gathering around them with words of encouragement and congratulations.

Evander walked over to his sister and kneeled down. He took her hand and kissed it, then kissed her cheeks. "I would hug you, but I don't want to hurt you. Now tell me what happened to cause this injury, Sister."

Helena explained everything to him, and when she was done,

Evander looked over his shoulder at Apollonius. "You saved my sister's life and didn't tell me?"

"We've been a bit busy today, Dominus."

"I will never forget that, nor your courage today, as I have already told you. I am indebted to you." Evander stood and gave Apollonius a hearty shake of the hand.

Apollonius finally turned to greet Aurora. "I'm so sorry about your father. He was the most wonderful master a slave could ever hope for." They held each other and cried until Myrrhine bid them sit down by the fire and eat.

Evander sat between Aurora and Teo. He hugged them both close and offered words of support. The slaves brought him food and fresh water, and Aurora tended to his head wound.

It was almost sunset now, and much darker than usual. He couldn't bring himself to stop watching the tragedy that was unfolding just across the water. Broad sheets of fire and leaping flames blazed at several points around the mountain, their brightness emphasized all the more by the darkness. Earth tremors continued, even in Surrentum, causing everything on the ground to rock back and forth.

"How are you faring?" he whispered in Aurora's ear. She looked at him despondently, then looked at Vesuvius. He stood and stretched out his hand. "Let's take a walk."

CHAPTER 26

*E*vander took Aurora by the hand and led her away from the beach.

"Where are we going? Shouldn't we all stay together now? What if the ash cloud blows in our direction?" she asked nervously.

"The winds are blowing from the northwest, toward Salernum. I won't keep you away for long. I just thought we could use a few moments alone."

She realized that Evander really didn't know where he was leading her, but that perhaps he just needed some time away from the crowd to compose himself. It had been a long, exhausting, traumatic day for all of them. He brought her back to the port, then turned and led her down the pier to the *Corbita*.

"You want to go back to your ship?" she asked confused.

"Yes."

When they came to the end of the pier, he whistled until a crew member came forward and lowered the gangplank for them. The sailor gave him an oil lamp, and they exchanged a few words.

Evander took her to the deck cabin and closed the door. When he had secured the lamp, he sat down on his bed and put his head in his hands. He was acting strange, and she wasn't sure what to do, so she sat down next to him and put her arm around his shoulders. "Does your head hurt?"

"It does, but not as much as my heart. Have you heard any word of your mother or grandfather?"

"Not yet, but there are so many people who came across on the ships that it's possible we just haven't found each other."

He looked at her wearily. "Yes, many people made it to safety—and many did not. I had to leave thousands of people behind. I couldn't send my ships back in; the sails were catching fire, and it was just too dangerous. I even lost a ship."

She sucked in her breath. "Were there people on it?"

"No, luckily they escaped before the burning mast came crashing down on them."

"Oh my gods." She squeezed his shoulders. "Evander, there was no way you could save the whole city."

He looked at her angrily. "But you didn't have to look into the eyes of those men on that pier today and tell them they couldn't come with you! I will never forget that moment. I simply couldn't fit any more people onto the ship."

"Do you think my mother and grandfather could have been among them?"

"I don't know. I just don't know," he answered plaintively. "I could only see the faces in front of me by torchlight." He looked so distraught that she began to cry.

"My mother . . ." she choked. "There is still hope . . . I will not give up hope. She is a smart woman. Perhaps she and Grandfather headed west toward Neapolis. And those people that you couldn't take, well, perhaps they found a different way out."

"The only way out was by boat. We saw the Roman navy heading for Pompeii as we approached Surrentum. I pray they were able to rescue more people, but under that ash cloud it was darker than the darkest night. The air was so thick I could barely breathe." He began to cough. "My lungs are burning even now."

She wrapped her arms around him, and he looked at her intensely for a moment.

"I am so glad you are safe," he breathed. He embraced her and held her as if he would never let her go. His lips came down on hers, gently at first, but his kisses quickly became passionate and demanding. He pulled her down on the bed next to him and tugged frantically at her clothes.

Before she had time to consider what she was doing, she was naked in his arms. His skin scorched her like fire, and she stroked her hands up and down his flanks, wanting to comfort him.

He sucked hard on her nipples and squeezed her thighs with his hand. He trailed hot, burning kisses over her breasts and down to her belly, then opened her legs, dipping his tongue into her most sensitive parts. She gasped at the unexpected sensations. The heat between them flared, and she knew this was the right moment to give herself to him, body and soul.

He looked questioningly into her eyes, and she nodded and gave him her consent. There was a moment of pain as he pushed through her flesh, and she winced. She closed her eyes and breathed in deeply until the pain passed. He kissed her and waited until she was ready, then moved inside her slowly and gently, causing her body to go weak with pleasure.

The connection she felt to him was intense. She was inside his arms and under his protection, exactly where she wanted to be. He nibbled on her ear and kissed his way down her throat. She ran her nails over the skin of his strong back and felt the muscles of his abdomen brush across her belly as he thrust into her.

She focused on the hot, moist spot where they were joined. The desire to submit to his body was powerful and hypnotic and swept her away to a place where nothing else mattered.

He put his hand under her bottom and tilted her hips higher. She felt him slide deeper, and they both moaned in pleasure. He cupped his hand around her cheek and kissed her tenderly.

"I love you, Aurora. These past two months have been unbearable without you. I never want to be apart from you again," he whispered.

Tears sprang to her eyes, and her heart was overcome with emotion. "And I love you, more than I ever thought possible. I cannot imagine my life without you."

The ship was rocking wildly now from the churning of the sea, made ever more fierce by the seething mountain across the bay. Still, he made love to her passionately, as if it were the last night of the world.

Suddenly, he grunted and gave one last deep thrust. She cried out as her muscles contracted hard around his member, sending rays of pleasure throughout her belly and down her legs. They remained motionless for a moment, then he dropped down at her side, scooping her close to him.

He pulled the blanket over them. She was exhausted, yet her body felt deeply sated. She had given herself to him completely, without remorse or regret. He made her feel safe and protected, and she remembered shamefully how once she had scoffed at the thought.

"Aurora?" He turned her face toward him.

"Mmm?" She was too tired to speak.

"My father said yes."

She smiled as she felt joy overcome her, then cried as she remembered that her own father wouldn't be at their wedding.

"Shhh, quiet now, my love," he soothed. "We will talk in the morning. Sleep, my love, just sleep."

She snuggled closer to him and tried to forget the unthinkable horrors of the day. *He feels so safe and warm,* she thought, *like a sanctuary from the perils of the world.*

IN THE EARLY hours of the morning, they were awoken by frantic knocking on the cabin door. Aurora jumped out of bed and dressed in her stola. Evander threw his tunic over his head, and they both rushed outside. The sun was shining, though dimly, and the entire sky looked hazy.

"What is going on?" asked Evander.

The crew member pointed to Vesuvius. "We saw a black cloud of fire and ash race down the side of the mountain toward Pompeii, but it looked like it stopped outside the walls."

Evander and Aurora ran up to the deck. There was still a thick column of smoke shooting out from the summit of the mountain, and the ever-present ash cloud now stretched from Pompeii over the hills to Salernum. They heard some strange rumblings echoing across the bay, then a loud boom like a clap of thunder. They watched in disbelief as the column of smoke collapsed and another dense black cloud raced down the mountain toward Pompeii, this time rolling right over the city, obscuring it from view.

Aurora squinted her eyes and tried to make sense of it. "What is happening?" she asked. Evander rubbed his hands over his face but didn't speak. He shook his head, and a feeling of dread trickled down her spine.

"Evander?"

He swallowed hard, his body trembling. "I think we have just witnessed the final destruction of Pompeii."

She whipped her head around and stared across the bay, searching for evidence that what he said was true. She couldn't see anything except for the black cloud that cloaked Pompeii like a death shroud. "No, I'm sure there are survivors, there has to be . . ."

"That surge of fire and ash probably suffocated and incinerated everything in its path, people, animals, buildings . . ." he stated without an ounce of emotion.

She stood frozen for a moment as she tried to comprehend his words.

"Noooooo!" she screamed. She dropped to the deck and let out a heart-wrenching cry. "Nooooo!" She pounded her fist on the deck and started to sob inconsolably. Evander sat down next to her and pulled her into his lap, rocking her back and forth. He held her tight and pressed her head into his chest.

"How many afflictions will be cast down upon us?" she cried bitterly. "How many? But surely the gods have deserted us!"

Evander's chest heaved beneath her cheek, and she felt tremendous sadness for everyone who was stuck in the middle of this disaster. When would it end? How could life ever return to normal? Evander was her only constant in the world, and she closed her eyes and held on to him firmly.

After a long while, they stood up on shaky legs and decided to return to the beach. She could only imagine what everyone would be thinking of her. She had spent the night with a man while she was still unwed, during a disaster of epic scale. Teo would be livid that she had left him after such a traumatic day, with no parents there to comfort him. A wave of self-loathing hit her. *I am truly a selfish, dreadful person . . .*

But the more she thought about it, the more she decided that nothing and no one would ever make her regret the night she spent with Evander. Being with him had saved her soul, had made her believe in the power of love when the world was collapsing around her. Evander was her strength and hope, and as long as he was with her, she could survive anything.

CHAPTER 27

*E*vander felt only slightly guilty that he had deflowered the girl he loved. He had needed her sweet and loving body to save him from the deep sorrows that plagued his heart. He couldn't move past the pitiful faces that he had left behind on that dock, and if he had never bought the puppy Hercules, well, perhaps Dominus Fortunas would still be alive.

He kept Aurora tucked under his shoulder as they returned to the beach, both of them still reeling at what they had just witnessed across the bay. Many people on the beach had seen it as well and were arguing over what it meant. Some were shuffling about in a confused state, and some were sitting in the sand crying.

Myrrhine sat huddled together with the boys except for Apollonius and Manolo. Helena reclined on her litter. They all became strangely quiet as Evander and Aurora approached. "You left us!" Teo shouted angrily.

A wave of guilt flooded Evander as he looked at them. "I am sorry. I passed out from exhaustion on my ship. We both did. We spent the night in my cabin," he explained, daring them to protest.

Aurora sat down next to her little brother and embraced him.

He held on to her tightly and buried his curly head into her dress while Evander sat with his sister and held her hand.

Apollonius and Manolo returned with two buckets of fresh water. They filled up some bowls and passed them around the circle for everyone to drink. Apollonius looked briefly at Evander, then looked away, but not before Evander saw the anger in his expression.

"Surrentum's water supply is still clean and functioning thanks to the underground aqueducts. A group of us went down into the tunnels this morning to have a look around," Apollonius explained.

Evander was happy to see that food from his ships was being distributed in an orderly manner to the people on the beach. He ate some dried fruits and nuts, and they discussed the black surge of ash that had overtaken Pompeii.

"Do you think people have survived inside their houses?" asked Myrrhine.

"It's hard to say," Evander replied. "The tremors must have caused many houses to collapse." He didn't want to alarm them any further by voicing his opinion that *nothing* had survived that rolling cloud of fire and debris.

"We felt many quakes during the night, Brother. Even here," added Helena. "I don't think this is over yet."

They looked at Vesuvius and the fearful black cloud that hung in the air, surrounding it.

"I must get out into the bay with my ships and see who made it through the night on smaller boats. Apollonius, would you come with me?"

The slave stood and nodded. "Of course."

Helena cried out. "Brother!" She pointed to the mountain. The dark, dense cloud was sinking down to earth. It started to spread over the water like a flood.

"Oh my gods, it's coming straight for us!" Aurora jumped up, pulling Teo with her. "Run!" she screamed.

Evander grabbed them. "There is nowhere to go! We are stuck between the cliffs and the sea. Now get down! Everybody—cover your face with your cloak!" He helped roll his sister onto her stomach, threw a blanket over her head, and closed the curtains of the litter.

He gave one last glance over his shoulder as the black cloud approached.

Perhaps the final endless night has come upon us. He threw his body over Teo and Aurora. When the darkness arrived, it was as if someone had extinguished the lamp in a closed-up room. He could hear the shrieks of women, the wailing of children, and the shouts of men. They cried for help, and they cried for death. They called to the gods, bemoaning their fate and the fate of those they loved.

Evander felt the intensity of his love for Aurora and wished they'd had more time together. Right or wrong, he was happy that they had finally consummated their love.

The air became hot and dry and burned his nasal passages. He thought of his family in Corinth, and moments of his life flashed before his eyes. *This is it*, he mourned, *my final moment.*

A gleam of light broke through the darkness. *Perhaps it is the fire approaching . . .* Darkness again, then ashes began to fall, and he waited for the end to near.

Several more agonizing moments passed, and he prayed that the gods would take them quickly. A burnt rock pummeled his arm, and he began to tremble at the thought of perishing by fire.

But somehow, someway, the darkness began to disperse, and Evander realized that the flames had remained at a distance. He opened his eyes and saw that the thick cloud of ash was no more. They were going to live!

He sat up and pulled Aurora into his arms. She was pale with fear. "We have survived, my love! We have survived!" He brushed the ashes from her hair and kissed her. Teo stood up and looked around. Evander embraced him tightly. "It's over Teo. We will be all right."

Evander peeked inside the litter. "Sister?" He ran his hand down her back.

"Is it over?" she squeaked. "Am I still alive? Or have we passed to the realm of the shades?"

"We are alive." He climbed into the litter next to her, and she cried tears of joy in his arms.

They all walked to the water's edge and looked out over the bay. The black ash cloud had dissipated, and the sun was shining an eerie yellow, as through an eclipse. They were terrified to see that the landscape had changed dramatically. The cities around the bay were buried deep in ashes, and the water was clogged with burnt rocks and floating debris. They might have survived the storm, but their lives would never be the same.

CHAPTER 28

*A*urora attended to her physical needs as best she could, then spent an anxious day wavering between hope and fear as the tremors continued. She took her medical bag and searched for her mother and grandfather all along the beaches, providing care to many of the children that she passed.

She was tired and felt disconnected, as if she were outside of herself, watching her life from a distance. When she sat down on a rock and closed her eyes, several women rushed over bearing bread and water and asked her if she needed help. She gave a description of her mother and grandfather, but they only shook their heads.

Evander and his fleet sailed in and out of the harbor all day, depositing more ragged survivors onto the piers. Many had spent the night out in the choppy, debris-filled water, tossing to and fro on tiny boats, and they were seasick and vomiting. She decided that her energy was best spent helping those in need and returned to the location where the newly rescued were being delivered.

More and more of the townspeople from Surrentum descended to the beaches bringing food, water, and clean clothes to the survivors. The men helped sent up tents and organized camp; the women brought as many provisions as possible for the young children and babies. Everywhere Aurora looked she saw people helping each other, and so in the midst of this great disaster, a spark of hope ignited in her chest.

They all slept on the beach that night, under tents that had been set up with the help of the townspeople. Aurora held her brother's hand until his eyes were closed in a peaceful slumber, but sleep evaded her. There would be no sneaking away tonight, no private and tender moments between herself and Evander.

She felt guilty for her selfishness, but she desperately craved his touch. Ever since their encounter last night, her body had been on fire. She felt feverish and hot, consumed by desire for him. He had awoken her body to something unexpected, and she felt closer to him now than she had ever felt to anyone before.

She sat up quietly and peered out of the tent. Evander was still sitting by the fire with Apollonius and Manolo. She slipped over to him in the darkness and touched his shoulder.

"My love, why are you not asleep?"

"I can't . . ." her voice trailed off as a lump formed in her throat.

"Come," he said.

Apollonius stood and blocked them. "With all due respect, Aurora. Have a care."

"Our lives have been destroyed, my father is dead, and we've lost our entire city! Do you think anybody is worrying about my *reputation*?" she snapped.

"Well, *I* am," he answered bitingly.

"I will only keep her a few moments," Evander promised.

He walked her down the beach a short length, then turned and embraced her. She wrapped her arms around his solid strength, as she had done so many times before, and just held on.

"I want you," she said simply.

"I want you too. More than I thought possible. But Apollonius is right. Regardless of the situation, it doesn't give us license to act on all our impulses."

He leaned down, found her lips, and kissed her sweetly. She felt a flutter inside her belly and held him closer, splaying her fingers across his muscular back. She pressed her cheek against the skin of his chest, closed her eyes, and exhaled. Desire flooded her body, and she allowed herself to burn for him.

He kissed the tender spot where her neck met her shoulder. She could feel him growing hard through his tunic. "Soon," he promised. "Soon I will love you again."

He walked her back to the camp and bid her good night.

THE NEXT MORNING, she awoke from a strange and upsetting dream. She quietly left the tent and sat down by the water's edge, looking across the bay at Pompeii. The morning air smelled briny and reeked of dead fish. The waves hissed and crackled as they broke against the shore. The once green and vine-clad mountain was blackened and charred by fire, and only the tops of the highest temples peeked out from the blanket of ash. How was it possible?

Ash so high it buried an entire city?

She sucked in her breath at the inconceivable reality and wondered if she was still dreaming. Evander came out from his tent and sat down next to her, taking her hand in his and kissing it. "How did you sleep?" he asked.

She snuggled close to his warmth. "I slept, but I had the most unnerving dream."

"Oh?" he asked, putting his arm around her shoulder.

"Last night, I dreamed that I was eating my shoes."

He exhaled and looked across the bay. "It's not hard to understand why."

"Do tell; I haven't quite figured it out."

He looked at her somberly. "You put on your shoes when you

have somewhere to go. You want to go home, but you can't. There is no home left to go to."

Silent tears ran down her face, and her throat felt pinched and tight. "You are right. My home is gone, buried under a mountain of ash. It's too much to comprehend. I feel like I'm in the midst of a nightmare, and I can't wake up."

He tilted her face toward him with a gentle finger.

"I will buy us a new home wherever you want. I know it's near impossible to think about that right now, but we can't stay on this beach forever. So I want you to think about where you would like to live. And when this is all behind us, we will marry and live there together. It will be a new day, and we will have a new life."

She looked up at him, at the morning sun shining dimly in his hair and on his skin. He was so beautiful it made her heart ache, and she loved him fiercely in that moment. But there was still one unanswered question. After everything they had been through, she needed to know, she needed to clear the air between them.

"Evander?"

"What, my sweet?" he answered, resting his head on hers.

"Did you sleep with Valentina?"

He looked hurt and a little angry as he pulled his arm away from her. "Why are you asking me this? Have I given you reason to doubt me?"

"Two mornings ago, although it feels like a lifetime now, I went to my grandfather's house. Valentina was there, vomiting into a bowl. She is three months pregnant."

"Pregnant? And you think the child is mine!"

"That is what she planned to declare publicly, at least before all this happened."

Evander's head dropped down. "I told you not to listen to her."

"She was most vicious about it!"

"Those are lies," he said vehemently. "Yes, I kissed her, but I didn't sleep with her, not on that night, not ever."

"My parents believed that Trebby would try to ruin you if you didn't agree to marry her."

He shook his head in exasperation. "Trebby made me several outstanding business offers. They were all things that my father was hoping for, the very reasons he had sent me back to Pompeii. But he wanted me to reciprocate with a marriage of convenience to his daughter."

Aurora frowned. "I learned all that two days ago. Why didn't you just tell me everything before you left?"

"I didn't want to give you anything more to worry about."

"So how did you respond to Trebby?"

"I told him that I couldn't partake in such an arrangement. I even told Valentina on that very same night that I wouldn't marry her. She promised to make me regret it."

"Ah," Aurora said as everything fell into place in her mind.

"It's a moot point now; the city and port are gone, and we can't be sure that they even survived," he added.

They stared silently out at sea for a few moments.

"So who is the father of Valentina's baby?" he asked.

"I don't know. Both Marcus Tiburtinas the Younger and an old Roman senator were seen leaving her house late at night. However, assuming they survived this nightmare, there may not be a baby anymore. Lady Claudia tried to make her drink an abortive tonic."

Evander cringed. "You would never do that to *our* baby, would you?" He rubbed her belly with his large hand and kissed her cheek. "You could very well be pregnant at this moment," he said softly.

She thought about the way he had loved her, the way it had felt so right. Everything they had shared on his ship had been so raw and beautiful. She wanted to love him again and again, to feel the soul-deep connection they had forged.

"Pregnancy is possible, but not likely. Women don't usually conceive during times of stress," she explained.

"But if you did conceive, you know that I would claim that child?"

She tilted her head toward him and found his lips. They were warm and solid, and his kisses gave her hope. They leaned on each other for a while in silent comfort.

"And our child would be so beautiful . . ." he mused.

"How can you think about that now?" she scolded.

"He will also be smart and mule-headed, like his mother . . ."

She couldn't help but smirk. "And a dreamer like his father. One step at a time, please. *You* have a home and a life in Corinth. But *my* life has just come crashing down. Don't think of adding a baby to this mess."

"You're right. I'm getting ahead of myself. But I do want you to know how much I love you. And I felt it so intensely when I thought I might die. You are mine, and I am yours, and nothing will ever change that."

The warmth of his words spread through her body like a summer day. "I will hold you to it."

Evander stood. "I am going to Neapolis and Puteoli today. Many people have asked me to take them across the bay because they have friends or relatives to stay with. I will inquire about your mother and grandfather while I am there. I may not return for a few days, as I would like to bring more provisions back with me for the camps on the beach. Will you be all right?"

"I will be fine." She stood up next to him. "I think I saw Crispis walking along the dock. I am going to find him to see if he would help me set up a medical tent."

"Your friend the gladiator?" he asked.

"Yes, him," she answered, ignoring the jealousy in his voice. "And I need to make a saline solution from the seawater to treat skin wounds, and boil various infusions of herbal remedies. Do you think you can bring me some poppy plants and chamomile from Neapolis?"

"Of course." He smiled. "Now there is the girl who makes my heart pound."

They embraced again and gave each other a kiss good-bye, and she felt the heat flare between them.

"Let him perish who knows not love . . ." he whispered.

"Let him perish twice over whoever forbids love . . ." she answered.

She thanked the gods for him as they parted and thought about the love spell they had cast that night on the beach before he left Pompeii. It seemed like so long ago. But Venus had unquestionably heard their prayer. Evander had come back to her safely and had saved her from certain death.

She realized how much better she always felt after being around him. She was strengthened and encouraged and willing to put her own sorrows behind her in an effort to help others. *Maybe that is what love is all about. Someone who makes you feel that you are more than the sum of your parts.* Aristotle had explained the concept of synergy over four hundred years ago, yet never did it feel so true as on this gloomy morning.

CHAPTER 29

*A*urora was busy under the makeshift medical tent, cleaning out a child's burn with seawater. She was short on many medical supplies and anxiously awaiting Evander's return. He had gone to Neapolis several days ago to transport people from one port to another and gather supplies and information on the situation around the bay.

She had indeed found Crispis and asked if he would like to come and help her. He was overcome with happiness to see her again and told her sorrowfully that he didn't know the fate of many of his friends. Most of the gladiators had left when the tremors became violent, but some had decided to remain in the barracks and wait out the firestorm, as he called it.

She had cleaned up his wounds and offered him a healing broth to drink made from vegetables and salt. His sunny disposition was a welcome addition to the camp, and he was also a diligent worker. The children loved him and listened eagerly to his entertaining stories of fights in the arena. He encouraged them to be brave like gladiators and to help out as much as possible in the camps.

When Aurora thought about the gladiatorial games and the

trauma that followed, she felt as though someone had stolen her youth. But nothing compared to what she was dealing with now. She had aged several lifetimes since then.

What weighed on her the most was the uncertainty of her mother and grandfather. Had they made it out alive? She would not allow herself to mourn them until she had proof of their deaths. *Death. The word burns bitterness through my heart.*

At least with her father, there was no question. He was gone, and she would have to come to terms with his passing, as difficult as that would be.

She heard a commotion out on the beach, then Myrrhine entered the tent and told her that Evander's ships had been seen approaching the harbor. She fought the urge to jump for joy and instead let out a happy cry. "That is wonderful! I can't wait to hear what news he brings us."

"Apollonius and Crispis are gathering a group of men to meet him on the dock. They will help unload the provisions he has brought."

Aurora walked over to the women's tent to find Helena. She was worried that the pretty girl was slipping into melancholy.

"Helena? How are you feeling?"

Evander's sister smiled faintly. "Pretty much the same, although I don't feel that I need as much poppy juice to keep me comfortable."

"Good. I don't want you to become dependent on it." Aurora helped her stand up. "I have good news. Evander is back from Neapolis."

The girl let out a sigh of relief but didn't say anything.

"Helena, are you homesick for Corinth? Though I would hate to see you go, after all that has happened here, it is probably wise for you to return home."

"You are right. I do miss my mother and all the comforts of a house. I want to get as far away from here as possible. But the thought of returning . . ." She looked down to the sand and frowned.

"Well, I know something that will make you happy. You are ready to start moving around and walking on a regular basis. How about if Apollonius escorts you down the beach several times a day?"

Her face lit up like the golden flame of an oil lamp. "I would like that."

~

A LITTLE WHILE LATER, Aurora was chopping vegetables for a healing broth that would be cooked over the fire. She sensed that someone had entered the tent.

"Aurora?"

It was the sweetest sound she had ever heard. She turned around and dropped the knife into the sand.

"Mother?"

Relief and joy struck her body so intensely she almost lost her balance. She ran to her mother on unsteady legs and embraced her hard, a torrent of tears flowing from her eyes.

"Mother! My dear, sweet mother! You are alive!"

"And you, Daughter. Please forgive me for leaving you," she cried. "I could never have known the disaster that would befall us."

Her mother smoothed back Aurora's hair. "How I love you, my child, how I love you!"

"Mother," she choked, "I am sorry for all the sorrow I have ever caused you!" They held each other and sobbed until Pioppo and Giorgio brought Teo and the dogs into the tent.

"Mama?"

Teo's face was wide with surprise as he ran to her, throwing himself into her arms.

"Teo! My beautiful curly-top boy!" she cried. "I thought you were lost to me like Niketus." She held him close and buried her face in his hair. Aurora threw her arms around them both and thanked the gods for her family. The dogs joined in the chorus with whines and barks of excitement.

Her mother hugged Pioppo, Giorgio, and Myrrhine next and told them how much she loved them all and how grateful she was that they had survived and stayed together. Then her face turned dark. "Your father didn't make it," she whispered. "Evander told me all."

Aurora's face crumbled, and she began to cry.

"What shall we do without him?" her mother asked.

They held each other and cried for a good long while. Finally, Aurora pulled herself together. "Mother, what about Grandfather?"

"He is in Neapolis. We escaped by ship with one of his friends."

"Grandfather is alive!" Aurora cried.

"Yes, he is fine, but he decided to stay in Neapolis, where many of our neighbors ended up. He is organizing a hospital there with the help of the local government. There is word that the emperor is on his way to help with the rescue operation."

"But who is left to rescue, Mother? We have not seen a single light coming from Pompeii or Herculaneum, only the mountain itself that continues to puff smoke and spit fire."

"It's not just about rescue. The survivors, like us, will need to be relocated. Land that belonged to the deceased will be reclaimed by the government and redistributed to the survivors. And there is still hope that some people may have survived inside of their homes."

Myrrhine herded them all out of the tent and bid them sit down by the fire with Helena. "What a brave girl you are!" Her mother cried as she leaned down and embraced the girl, being careful of her injuries. "I am so proud of you for being strong and pulling through this, even with broken ribs."

Helena smiled graciously. "Lady Lucina, it so wonderful to see you alive and well. The past week has been quite an ordeal. Thank the gods for your daughter, who has kept me quite comfortable."

"And thank the gods for Evander, who has saved you all, and so many more! He has been combing the coast with his ships, gathering supplies and news and trying to reconnect families. He is the true hero!" her mother exclaimed. "The emperor will hear of his bravery."

A procession of slaves arrived by mule from Surrentum, carrying loaves of freshly baked bread in their large baskets. Evander had paid the bakers generously, and they were sending a daily supply of bread down to the camps on the beach.

Finally, Evander arrived with Apollonius.

Her mother embraced the eldest slave brother tightly and began to cry. "My dearest Apollonius, I have heard of your bravery," she sniffed. "Thank the gods you are all right."

Evander promptly swept Aurora up in his arms. "I have so much to tell you," he said, planting a kiss her on her lips. "Is there any food?"

Aurora swatted him on the arm. "You haven't seen me in days, and all you can think about is food?"

"Not true, but everything else on my mind would be indecent and inappropriate at this moment," he jested. "Now hug your man."

She wrapped her arms around his neck and squeezed. He smelled of sea pine and salt, and she inhaled his scent into her lungs. "I missed you."

"I missed you too." He looked around the camp and saw the new medical tent she had set up. "I see you have been busy."

"Yes, I have much to thank Crispis for. He is an excellent worker and very popular with the children."

"I met him down at the docks. Perhaps I will offer him steady work."

She smiled at him. "That would be wonderful. Now go and say hello to your sister. She has been feeling sad."

~

MYRRHINE CALLED everyone to sit by the fire and eat. Her mother led them in a solemn prayer of thanks to Jupiter, father of them all, for sparing their lives and reconnecting them.

Myrrhine and her boys ladled hot soup into wooden bowls and passed them around. They all dipped the fresh bread into the soup and ate heartily. Teo and the dogs were huddled at her mother's feet. Apollonius sat close to Helena, and Evander threw his cape over Aurora's shoulders, then sat down at her side and began to speak.

"Word has arrived in Neapolis that Emperor Titus is on his way to lead the rescue effort. He is going to send soldiers into Pompeii to dig the city out from under the ash."

Sounds of amazement went around the circle.

"Do you think that is even possible?" asked Apollonius.

"I don't know." He shook his head. "I was able to do a preliminary survey of the coast on my way to Neapolis. It has been completely altered. There is no longer a visible harbor at Pompeii, and the rock and hardening ash from the mountain has pushed the coastline outward considerably. It is like a different world all together."

"And what of Herculaneum? When we look across the bay, all we can see is darkness lying over the city like a blanket," said Aurora.

"Let me first assure you all that many Herculaneans made it safely to Neapolis. But Herculaneum itself, beautiful city once overlooking the sea from its windy outcrop, has been buried by molten rock." He became quiet for a moment, and Aurora swallowed back tears.

Helena covered her mouth with her hand.

"There is no ash cover, as in Pompeii, just liquid rock that hardens over the entire city as we speak. As with Pompeii, we cannot see the harbor, so we cannot dock. But even if we could, the ground still seems to be on fire. The sea and the coast are forever changed, and the unfortunate creatures of the sea float lifelessly on the water. Their carcasses clog the beaches and ports of Neapolis and Puteoli." He let out a sigh.

They listened in morbid fascination as Evander described all that he had seen around the bay and what was left of Campania, most beautiful land in the world.

"I also learned the grim news that the Roman navy had been unable to sail into Pompeii. The water had receded, and the river was not navigable. They ended up at the port of Stabiae instead." He looked pointedly at Aurora, and she could see that this caused him grief.

Night descended, and they talked about how they longed for the comfort of their domus. "It's all so unbelievable," said her mother. "I feel so grateful that you are all alive, and yet so destitute at the loss of life and our beautiful city."

"Lucina?" A deep voice came out of the darkness. "I heard you were here."

They turned and saw Marcus Tibertinus the Elder and his son, Marcus the Younger, standing behind them. Her mother stood up quickly and threw her arms around the handsome aedile.

"Marcus! You made it out! And what of Bertus and Lady Julia?"

"Bertus is fine, but my wife—" He choked on a sob. "The roof came down on her. We couldn't save her," he said hoarsely. "And your family?"

"My husband. He didn't make it either . . ." They embraced again and cried in each other's arms.

Aurora stood and hugged Marcus the Younger. "Thank the gods!"

Marcus gripped her shoulders. "Have you seen or heard from Valentina? I have been searching for days." His voice sounded desperate.

"No. I'm sorry. We have not received any word about them."

Marcus dropped his head.

"Come and sit with us," urged Aurora's mother.

Father and son sat down by the fire. Myrrhine brought them some hot soup, which they gladly accepted. When they were done eating, Marcus the Elder shook his head and heaved a great sigh.

"On the morning of the dead birds, terrible omen as it was, I went to talk with Trebby about a plan to evacuate the city should the tremors begin again. He told me there was nothing to worry about, that everyone should stay in his domus. He derided me for wanting to flee and told me that I should stay to enforce public order and instill faith and calmness in the citizens."

"That's terrible, Marcus," said her mother. "Trebby never did treat you well."

"No. To him, I am just the man in charge of latrines. But anyone could see the situation was quickly becoming urgent. Everyone knows that a small problem becomes larger if you ignore it. So when the tremors began in earnest, I took the boys, and we went from house to house urging people to leave."

"Yes," agreed Evander. "In retrospect, that was the wisest choice."

"Early the next morning, after we heard the explosion, a nasty tremor shook our house from its foundation," continued Marcus. "The second story came down on my wife, trapping her underneath. We tried to save her, but—" his voice cracked as he spoke. "The boys and I barely made it out alive. We ran to the Valens's house and urged them to flee with us, but Trebby refused. He said that Valentina was not feeling well and they were going to stay inside and wait it out."

Aurora glanced at Apollonius.

"You did the right thing," said her mother. "If you had stayed, you would be twenty cubits under the rocks and ash by now."

"Still, Lucina, I would have thought that by the second morning of earthquakes and tremors, houses collapsing, and rocks falling from the sky, Trebby would have reconsidered, if only to save his girls!"

"I agree," said her mother. "But you can't control the actions of others, only yourself."

Marcus the Younger was visibly upset. "I begged Valentina to come with me, but she was scared, not knowing whether to stay or flee, and she didn't want to disobey her father. I was hoping that Trebby would have eventually changed his mind and gotten them out of there."

"And perhaps they did escape," said Evander. "But if they stayed in their house, I don't think they survived." Evander put his hand on Marcus the Younger's shoulder. "I will inquire about them as I travel around the bay."

"Where is Bertus?" asked her mother.

"He is at the next camp over," answered Marcus the Elder. "I have kept him busy with my efforts here on the beaches, helping to organize the camps into functioning units with food and fresh water and setting up makeshift latrines. And, Evander, thank you for the food you have provided from your cargo," he added.

"Marcus, please tell Bertus to come and see us tomorrow," said her mother. "We would be very comforted to see him again."

Father and son stood up and bid them good night, assuring everyone they would visit tomorrow. The rest of them sat around the fire for a while until her mother called them all to bed. She told them there was much to do on the morrow, and most importantly, they needed to stay rested during this difficult time.

Teo kissed Aurora, then rubbed his eyes and shuffled toward the tent with their mother. "C'mon, doggies."

"Hey, Teo," called Helena. "Do you think that Hercules can sleep with me tonight?"

Teo picked up the puppy and deposited him on the sand by her feet. "He will keep the fire monsters away from you."

"Thank you," she whispered.

Apollonius helped Helena stand, ever so gently, taking care not to touch her healing ribs. He walked her into the tent, the puppy following close on his heels.

Myrrhine and the boys did a quick clean up, leaving Aurora and Evander sitting alone. "Did I tell you that my parents are coming for Saturnalia? They will take Helena home with them."

"I am looking forward to meeting them. As for your sister, she doesn't seem to want to return to Corinth, but I think it is best for her. Your parents are expecting to arrive at Pompeii. How will you notify them?"

"I have sent word back with some merchant friends of mine who were leaving Neapolis for Greece. At any rate, they will see my ships in the harbor of Surrentum as they come around the promontory."

He paused and looked at her seriously. "So Valentina may be dead, and I think we can say with certainty whose child she was carrying. Do you think she was in love with Marcus?"

"Perhaps, though I wonder whether she was truly capable of loving anybody but herself. And as for her death, I cannot feel happy about it, no matter how much I loathed her. It all seems so petty now, doesn't it? The things women do and say to hurt each other."

He put his arm around her and pulled her onto his lap. "And the stupid things men do to prove to one another they are strong and virile."

"You mean like getting drunk and allowing a prostitute to fondle you?" she asked dryly.

"Exactly. Those things don't lead a man to happiness."

"So what does lead a man to happiness?"

He snuggled close to her, holding her tightly within the embrace of his wonderful arms. "The love of a beautiful and intelligent woman." He kissed her, and she opened her mouth and felt his tongue dance with hers, igniting the usual fire inside her veins.

"I want more of you," he breathed. "I want all of you, and I don't want to wait another day." He opened up a small leather bag attached to his belt, pulled something out, then held out his palm to her.

"An iron ring?" A wide grin spread across her face. It was the traditional ring of betrothal.

"Will you marry me?" he asked, his face illuminated by the flickering campfire.

"Yes!" she cried without hesitation. She rested her head in the crook of his neck, and allowed herself to be perfectly content and giddy for one moment. *Marriage. To a man who is more than worthy of my respect. A man that I love.*

He slid the ring onto her finger. "How about tomorrow?" he suggested.

She popped her head up. "Tomorrow? What are you saying? I've just been reunited with my mother today, and we don't even have a house to live in!"

"It doesn't matter. We will go to Surrentum and be married at the Temple of Juno. We will stay on the *Corbita* at night until I have found us a new home."

"Evander, look at me—I haven't had a proper bath in days!"

"So I will take you to the bathhouse. I will buy you a beautiful dress, or you can wear rags for all I care. I just want you to be my wife."

She let out a giggle and hugged him tight.

"And I want you to be my husband, but not tomorrow. We are still in mourning, we have no home, and I need my grandfather's permission in the absence of my father."

"Already done."

"You talked to my grandfather about this?"

"Yes, in Neapolis. In fact, I told him everything, including how I took your virginity on the night the mountain exploded."

"You didn't!" she gasped, blushing bright red.

"I did. I wanted to make sure he said yes. And he wasn't nearly as surprised as you would think."

"What about your parents? Don't you want them here for the wedding?"

"They will come for Saturnalia. Hopefully, we will have a

house by then. And speaking of houses, I have been inquiring about some villas that are for sale in Neapolis and Cumae along the coast toward Rome. Where do you prefer to be?"

Her face fell. "Are there no properties for sale here in the bay?"

"Here in the bay? But why? It is no longer beautiful. It is a tomb, cities buried under ash and rock. Is that what you want to look at every day?"

She cast her eyes downward and shrugged. "I want to be near my father—wherever he may be. I want to look across the bay and remember Pompeii, its labyrinth streets and colorful walls, the smell of baking bread in the ovens, the slaves rushing past, their baskets filled with food."

Her tears began to fall. "I will miss seeing the taverns full of people, the baths full of lavender, and the sound of different tongues in the forum. And how I loved the flowered garlands that adorned the city during the holy days. What a beautiful city we had. How can I leave it?" She asked sadly, "Do you understand?"

He looked at her soberly but didn't answer.

"I like Surrentum," she said. "It is small but pretty. And when you return from Greece, I will see your ships as they round the promontory and know that you will soon be in my arms."

With that, she stood and bid him good night, holding her hand toward the fire to observe the iron ring around her finger.

CHAPTER 30

DECEMBER AD 79

*E*vander stood on a small balcony overlooking a quaint little street in Surrentum. He breathed in deeply, enjoying the fresh and salty air blowing in from the bay. Today, on the *nones* of December, he would marry the girl that he loved.

The world and all its crushing needs would have to do without him, at least for a little while. He had saved as many souls as he could save, had fed as many mouths as he could feed. He had combed the coast looking for survivors and had reunited families around the bay.

Now it was his turn.

But there would be no grand celebration, no joyous procession of the bride from her ancestral home to her new one, no flaming torch lit from her parents' hearth to light the hearth of their new home.

There would be no wax tablets to sign about property or riches, no dowry agreements to be made. She and her family had lost everything. Her grandfather was *paterfamilias* now and had given him consent to marry Aurora.

His own father had agreed to the wedding, although somewhat

reluctantly, preferring that he hold out for a more "politically advantageous" match.

But none of that mattered anymore, as the goddess Fortuna had given him his own path to gaining the emperor's favor. He was a true hero now, and he tried to contain his pride.

Upon his second arrival in Neapolis last month, several soldiers of the Praetorian Guard had greeted him and escorted him to the emperor. In a life-changing moment that he would never forget, the emperor had commended him for his bravery, and on behalf of the Empire had awarded him the noble Crown of the Preserver.

This crown was usually reserved for soldiers who had saved the lives of citizens of the Empire. But because of the unusual circumstances, Titus had made an exception and bestowed it on a civilian. It was greatly symbolic and honorary.

The emperor also granted him and his fleet of ships protection by the navy, repaid him the cost of his lost ship and cargo, and awarded him trade contracts with the Empire. As if that wasn't enough, he was also given fertile land and vineyards north of Campania to replace what his family had lost.

The only matter that had needed to be resolved was where they would live.

After Aurora told him that she wanted to remain in the bay, he had found a beautiful villa high in the hills of Surrentum. It was spectacular in every way, with luxuriant baths, refreshing pools, and flowering gardens.

This was where he would take Aurora tonight, their first night as a married couple. He hoped she would love it. It was time to move forward; they had waited long enough.

They had spent more than four weeks down in the camp on the beach, and the weather was turning colder. Most of the survivors had found more permanent lodging with the help of the townspeople and the emperor's relocation plan.

Lady Lucina, Teo, and Helena would live in the villa with

them, as would all of the family slaves from the two former households.

At this moment, the slaves were busy decorating the villa for the arrival of the newlyweds, and he supposed it was time for him to go and gather up the wedding party. They had been staying in this crowded but lovely inn for the past week in the heart of beautiful Surrentum.

He went inside and rapped softly on the door across from his room. Lady Lucina greeted him, smiling widely. "Good morning, Evander."

"Good morning, my lady. You look beautiful, as usual. Is my lovely bride ready?" he asked, peering behind her.

"She is."

Aurora came to the door looking like Venus herself. She was adorned in a long white robe with purple fringe and ribbons. Her dark, curly hair was piled high on her head and held in place with gold bands. And as was the custom, she wore a wreath of flowering verbena.

Golden bracelets of intertwined snakes wrapped around her arms. The snakes, long associated with rebirth and healing, were appropriate charms on this important day. And for the first time, she was wearing makeup. Her lips were a shimmering red, her almond eyes seductively accented with a lining of kohl.

He couldn't take his own eyes off of her. She wore a belt of rope tied in a knot of Hercules, and he smiled as he thought of unknotting it this evening in the privacy of their new bedroom. Suddenly, he was a teenager again, nervous and tongue-tied and worried about tripping over his clumsy feet.

Looking at her now, one would never know all that had befallen them. Like Proserpina, Goddess of Spring, they had been to the underworld and back again.

"You are a painting of beauty and grace, my love."

"Thank you," she said cheerfully. She surveyed his clothes and touched the gold brooch that fastened his expensive ankle-length cloak. He held out his elbow, and she laced her arm through his.

Helena came out to the hall looking more than elegant for one so young. She was healed from her injuries now and able to walk by herself.

"You look so dignified, Brother. And is your bride not equally exquisite?"

"She is everything I ever hoped for and more. Words fail me, Sister, on this auspicious morning. I only hope that you will also find such happiness." He leaned down and kissed her cheek.

Dominus Popidius and Teo came out of the adjacent room looking clean and handsome in bright white tunics and brown leather cloaks. Their winter sandals were soft and new. Everything they wore were gifts he had given them. Dominus shook his hand and gave him a nod of approval.

Evander took a deep breath. "Shall we depart, then?"

They strolled through the charming and narrow streets of Surrentum. The townspeople, and many others that he had saved from Pompeii, recognized him and rushed over to greet them. The people bestowed prayers and good wishes upon him and his bride. An elderly lady pressed a small amulet of a phallus into his palm for good luck.

When they arrived at the temple of Juno at the edge of town, they were laughing with joy. A priestess came forth and led them in a prayer to the goddess of marriage and hearth. A cool breeze blew threw their hair and rustled the leaves on the trees around them.

"We ask for Juno's blessing, and her presence here today, as we witness the consent of marriage between this lovely bride and groom. We also wish to honor the memory of Auroras Fortunas, beloved father of the bride."

Evander looked into Aurora's eyes and smiled. She was holding her composure well, even at the mention of her father.

"Please stand in front of the altar and clasp your right hands."

He guided Aurora to the altar, then took her hand. The priestess smiled at him. "You may begin."

Evander nodded confidently. "On this beautiful fall day, the *nones* of December, during the first year of the reign of Titus, I, Maximus Evandrus Mercurius the Second, pledge my life, my love, and my fidelity to you, Aurora Fortunas. I ask you to be my wife from this day forward."

Aurora beamed and squeezed his hand.

"On this day, the *nones* of December, I, Aurora Popidia Fortunas, agree to become your wife. I pledge to you my love, my support, and my fidelity."

Lady Lucina handed him the wedding ring.

It was a stunning gold ring etched with a picture of his ship, the *Corbita*. He had brought it back from Corinth, not realizing the powerful emotions it would come to represent. He slipped it on her fourth finger and kissed her hand.

"My wife," he began, "let this ring be a symbol of all we have endured together and a promise of a bright and happy future. You are a woman of great intelligence, whom I respect. I vow to protect you and to provide for you for the rest of my life. I love you."

"My husband," she looked up at him with those immense dark eyes brimming with tears, "I am honored that you have chosen me to be your wife. You are a man of *gravitas,* fully deserving of my love and devotion. I will endeavor to please you always. I love you."

He clasped her right hand again, then leaned down and kissed her lips to seal their promises and felt her lips tremble.

Teo handed them a wooden birdcage with two songbirds inside. Aurora opened the cage door, setting the birds free as a gift to the goddess.

"May Juno protect us, and may Pompeian Venus love us both," she said as the birds flew away.

They exchanged warm embraces with their family members.

"No greater man could ever marry my granddaughter," Dominus Popidius said.

Lady Lucina hugged him tightly. "I knew you were marked for greatness when you saved my son. It was an omen of what was to come. Congratulations on your marriage to my daughter. And good luck," she jested lightly. "The mules await—now onward to your new home."

They all piled gaily into the carriages, laughing and singing loudly. As the mules conveyed them ever higher into the hills, Evander smiled widely. Just like the goddess whom Aurora was named after, a new and rosy-fingered dawn was upon them.

AURORA BURST out of the carriage, filled with excitement and anticipation. She inhaled the fresh sea air and looked around her.

A new home. It was bittersweet. After almost a month of living on the beach in a tent, and another week at the inn, she was ready for the luxuries of a house. And not just any house, but a beautiful villa set high on a hilltop overlooking the sea. Evander had described it to her in detail, but now seeing it for herself, its beauty overwhelmed her. She put her hand over her heart as she surveyed her surroundings.

The façade of the villa was painted white, and six Corinthian columns marked the entranceway. All around her stood flowering bushes, green gardens, creeping vines, and beautiful marble fountains. Her jaw dropped open, and she looked at Evander.

"Do you like it?" he asked.

She threw her arms around his waist. "I love it! Oh, Evander, this is truly paradise! Never did I ever imagine living in a villa such as this. I am in awe."

The rest of the family stood nearby and complimented Evander on his choice of property. But she continued to admire the view. Out in the distance was the sea. She looked west, toward Capri, with its towering rock formations. At least that was still a beautiful sight. But straight across the bay was black Vesuvius.

She let go of Evander and walked out to the edge of the hill. As the weeks had passed, it became evident that Pompeii was gone forever. And somewhere over there, under the dark, deep ash, lay her beloved father. She missed him terribly and regretted that he had not lived to see her get married. He would have been so proud of Evander.

The mountain was a grim reminder of their loss, like a soldier's battle scar. But for her, she decided, it would be a reminder that they had survived the battle, and survived together. It was a reminder of her strength and endurance. She was alive. And every day that she looked across the bay, she would be reminded of her blessings, of all the goodness that still existed in her life, and she would not be bitter.

They all walked toward the entrance of the house, where her grandfather stopped them. "As we are short on female attendants, we shall all carry Aurora over the threshold of her new home. Except Evander, of course."

Evander stepped into the house. "Myrrhine! Apollonius! We are here!" he shouted. "Aurora is about to enter—come quickly."

Her grandfather swooped her up in his capable arms and told her to flatten herself out like a board. She was laughing now but tried to obey. He told Teo to hold her under her shoulders and Helena to take her legs.

"Don't drop me!" she cried.

Teo was about to collapse in a fit of laughter, and Helena thought it funny to tickle her feet through her sandals.

"Stop!" she giggled, her body shaking.

When they finally had a tight grip on her, they slowly proceeded headfirst over the threshold, Teo leading the way. They put her down carefully onto the floor of her new home.

"There," her grandfather pronounced proudly. "We did it."

Aurora fixed her dress and smoothed back her hair, feeling happy and exhilarated.

Evander put his arm around her and turned to Apollonius.

"Please hand my wife the keys to the house, as this is now her house to do with as she pleases," he ordered.

Apollonius stepped forward holding the heavy lead keys and put them in Aurora's hand. He bowed before her. "Congratulations, my lady. Would you like a tour of your new home?"

They all followed behind Apollonius as he led them from room to room and through a beautiful peristyle garden with an outdoor pool.

Everything was breathtaking, but she especially loved the private bath suite and its beautiful mosaic of sea animals and dolphins. All kinds of sexual thoughts crossed her mind as she looked into the caldarium and felt herself blush. The water had been heated in anticipation of tonight's nuptial celebration, and steam rose up off the top of the pool.

Apollonius led them back to a cheery indoor dining room that was warmed by an iron brazier and told them that dinner would be served shortly.

After a delicious meal, and many toasts of wine to the bride and groom, Evander stood up. "Please make yourselves comfortable and enjoy our new home. I would keep my lovely bride to myself now and see you all in the morning."

Her family smiled knowingly to one another, and Aurora's cheeks flared red with embarrassment. Evander shuffled her off to the master's quarters at the far end of the house.

"I thought this night would never come." He pulled her into his arms. "Alone at last, married, and in our very own bedroom," he breathed into her ear.

He trailed hot kisses over her jaw and down her neck. "Shall we start with a hot bath?"

"Yes." But she hesitated and leaned away. "I just need a moment to relax, all right?" She glanced up at him and saw him frown. "I know you are anxious, my love, but it has been a long day. I can't just . . ." her voice trailed off, and she examined the fresco on the wall instead.

He lay back on the bed and gestured for her to lie next to him. "I know you, Aurora. And I know when something is bothering you. Talk to me."

She removed her sandals and scooted up on the bed, putting her head on the pillow next to him. She looked into those glittering blue eyes that reminded her of that day in the grotto. For a moment, her throat felt tight and she couldn't speak, so she just caressed his cheek with her palm.

He stroked her bare arm as he waited for her to respond, and his hand felt warm and comforting. Those beautiful hands that she loved, that she had imagined caressing her a thousand times. And now here they were, together, in their new home, and she felt . . . confused. She was consumed by so many emotions at once that she couldn't sort them all out.

"I think I know how you're feeling," he said, "because I'm feeling it too."

She stared into his eyes and willed him to continue.

"You're blissfully happy that finally our time has come, that the ordeal is behind us, and yet you feel guilty. Guilty for surviving when so many others didn't, like your father."

She squeezed her eyes shut as burning tears came forth and heaved a heavy sigh. "Yes," she cried softly.

"You think that somehow it is wrong to feel happy, to feel *pleasure* even, in the aftermath of such a great disaster." He twirled a curl around his finger.

"I feel so many things, elated and crushed in the same moment. Sometimes it doesn't feel real, and I hope that I will wake up to learn this has all been a bad dream. And you, you are the last person that I would ever want to hurt. But now I am your wife, and I am afraid. Afraid of allowing myself to truly bond with you for fear of losing you too." She looked him over, his face, his skin, his hair—every piece of him was precious to her.

"Aurora, do you remember that morning in the forum when we first met again? I was supposed to be on my way to the garum shop, but instead I turned toward the smell of freshly baked bread. I caught a glimpse of you in the canine booth. I turned around, walked past you a few times. Then inexplicably, I found myself walking toward you."

She listened to him intently.

"I never had the chance to tell you my name or to ask yours, but after our eyes met, I knew that I was supposed to follow you that morning as you went about your errands. I felt compelled to do so, especially after the dogs started whining and behaving strangely. Then the earthquake struck, Teo fell, and suddenly it all made sense."

"So even if the gods desired you to be my protector, if somehow, someway, we were destined to be together, what now? What does it all mean?" she asked.

"It means that while we are alive, our lives have meaning and direction. We should not let the rainy days taint our sunshine. Enjoy all the goodness life has to offer, savor it, and when the rain comes, allow yourself to cry. But don't deny yourself happiness when it is your turn."

He put his finger under her chin and tilted her lips toward him. "It is our turn." He leaned in and kissed her, and the taste of his lips on hers was sweet nectar of the gods. The fact that he had listened to her, had talked with her, had let her know that he really understood how she felt, had warmed her soul and made her feel much lighter.

She rolled out of the bed and stood before him, holding the knot of Hercules in her hand suggestively. He sat up and unraveled the knot in a blink.

"Fine work, sailor," she teased, then began to remove the pieces of her clothing one by one. When she was done, she stood before him naked.

"One more thing." He gently pulled the pins from her hair, allowing it to drop in ringlets over her shoulders. He quickly threw off his clothing, then gathered her in his arms. They stood like this for a moment, savoring the warmth of each other's body.

He wrapped her in a light bath tunic. "Let's not forget our bath clogs," he reminded her. "The floor will be burning hot." They put their feet into the new wooden shoes Evander had purchased, then he led her down the hallway to the caldarium.

When she stepped inside the room, hot, steamy air hit her senses. She inhaled deeply. "Ah, lavender, so wonderful."

The bath was dark but for the flames of the oil lamps, which twinkled and danced in his eyes. She knew he was proud that he could afford her such a luxury. She kicked off her wooden shoe and dipped her toe in the water to sample the temperature. "Perfect."

He came up behind her and wrapped his arms around her waist and breasts. "Perfect, like my beautiful wife." She felt his hardness pressing into her back, and her insides began to melt like a candle left in the sun. She pulled him down the steps into the pool. They both let out their breath as the hot water engulfed them.

He wrapped his arms around her. "No more talking," he ordered. "Kiss me. Kiss me like all you've ever wanted to do in your life is love me, because I'm going to love you in every way."

He swept her up in his embrace and sealed his lips over hers. She surrendered to his desire, pushing all other thoughts from her mind. She opened her mouth and wrapped her legs around his waist.

The fires of love flared between them, hot and demanding.

In a moment, she was desperate for him. His member pressed against her covetously. She squeezed his shoulders and dug her nails into his back. "Take me now," she begged.

He positioned himself at the entrance of her body and thrust up.

She moaned as his thickness filled her and focused on the sublime sensation of his body connected to hers. She gyrated her hips against him and brushed her erect nipples across his chest, causing him to shiver.

His masculine body was a banquet of delights that she had wanted to feast on from the moment she met him, from the dark, wet hair that covered his chest and ran down to his navel and beyond, to the muscular arms and wide shoulders that seemed to effortlessly carry the weight of the world.

He held her close and continued to move inside of her. She felt the sweetness of his love, the gentle slide of his skin over her tender parts. *I am drowning in him, and it is beautiful.*

The water carried them gracefully, as if they were one body, one soul, and she thanked Venus for him. She loved this man with her whole being; he had saved her life, had given her everything. What could she possibly give him in return?

He sank his fingers into her hair, drawing her thoughts back to him, to his kisses, his passion, his needs. She was his now, and she reveled in the domination of his body. She felt his hand slip around her back and down over her bottom, pressing her to him, harder and tighter. She saw the veins bulge in his neck and knew he was getting close to his breaking point.

"Let it go!" she cried.

She tightened her thighs around his hips as she felt the first wave of pleasure wash over her. Her breasts were pressed against his chest, his curly hair tickling her nipples. He ground his hips into hers, and she cried out as the fiery sensations of climax swept through her.

He kissed her one last time before thrusting deeply and exploding. He grunted in pleasure as he climaxed. She could feel the quiver of his muscles locked around her, and a deep, penetrating pulsation high inside her core. His eyes were closed, and he was panting.

In that moment, she knew without a doubt that he ruled her, body, mind, and soul.

She would do anything for him.

For a while, she just lay limply in his arms before separating her body from his. They stared at each other in the dim light for a few wordless moments, struck dumb by the way their bodies had responded to each other.

"My wife," he whispered hoarsely, "your body has scorched me tonight, hot as the embers of Vesuvius." He looked into her eyes and drew his fingers down her length, from her collarbone to her navel. "I believe you and I have found a new understanding."

She smiled at him shyly. She wanted to tell him that his blue, blue eyes had the power to take her for everything she was worth. That his touch made her tremble, that she lost her breath when he walked into a room.

How could she explain that the sound of his name made her heart beat faster and her throat go dry? That when he took her in his arms and loved her like he did tonight, the whole wide world and all its heartache disappeared?

She stared at him and wondered.

Perhaps he already knew.

She was taken by a capricious, joyful whim. She raised her arms in the air and began to undulate her hips, clapping her hands in rhythm like a dancing girl from Cadiz. His surprised reaction made her burst into laughter.

As she wrapped her arms around his neck, her body shaking with mirth, she decided not to tell him of the power he wielded over her.

Some words are better left unspoken, some feelings unrevealed.

CHAPTER 31

$\mathcal{A}$urora awoke peacefully, nestled in the warm bed coverings, her head pillowed on Evander's arm. Her husband was sound asleep and breathing deeply.

It was Saturnalia, the best time of the year.

The household was filled with happy shouts, and a feeling of festivity permeated the air. Schools and public businesses were closed, courts were not in session, and no one bothered to go to the palaestra to exercise.

From December seventeenth until the twenty-first, the winter solstice was celebrated. The streets were filled with merrymakers, social roles were reversed, and rules were broken. The taverns were filled from morning to night with wine-drinking, dice-playing revelers.

Aurora had always loved Saturnalia, when master and slave traded places, and friends and family exchanged small gifts with good-hearted intentions. There were wonderful feasts and parties to attend and the liberation of all to do and say as one pleased without fear of retribution.

At least that's how it used to be every year in Pompeii.

Still, she could feel the spirit of the holiday bubble up even here in her new home in Surrentum.

Evander's parents had arrived a few days ago on a stately ship with enough clothing and provisions to last them several months. Both Evander and Helena had seemed very happy to see their parents, but Aurora could tell that they felt most comfortable with their mother. Their reunion with their father had been cordial but strained.

Lady Dulcia was beautiful, with dark hair and blue eyes like her children. She had held out her arms and welcomed Aurora into the family with a warm embrace; the same way Evander always greeted her. "The woman who makes my son happy makes me happy as well," she had proclaimed.

Aurora had liked her immediately and could tell that Evander had inherited many of her fine qualities. His father, however, had been more reserved. He was taller than Evander, with dark hair and penetrating brown eyes. He had intimidated her greatly.

He had greeted his own children with a brief hug, then gave Aurora an awkward embrace. "We are glad you are all safe," he had said soberly. She'd felt a twinge of disappointment that he hadn't shown more enthusiasm over meeting her. *Maximus Evandrus Mercurius was definitely not a man to warm up to.*

But tonight they would celebrate the feast of Saturnalia, and she hoped the spirit of the season would bode well for her acceptance into the family. She scooted her body quietly to the edge of the bed and sat up to get dressed when a muscular arm wrapped around her belly, pulling her back.

"Not so fast, Wife." Evander was grinning roguishly.

She rolled back over to him and snuggled down under the covers, skin on naked skin. "Good morning to you." She kissed his cheek. His body was blazing hot and ready. He fondled her breasts, then pulled a plump nipple into his mouth, drawing on her until she felt moisture drip between her thighs. His kisses moved lower, and suddenly his face was between her legs. He slipped his tongue inside of her, probing deeply through all of her folds. He stroked and tickled and teased her sensitive skin. When she thought she couldn't handle any more pleasure, he planted his mouth over her *kleitoris* and sucked. "Oh Venus . . ." she moaned breathlessly and thought that she might faint.

"Turn over," he ordered.

He pulled up her hips and penetrated her with his long, fine fingers until her body was aching for more. Finally, he positioned himself over her and pushed into her from behind. She inhaled sharply as her body adjusted to his size.

"You feel sublime," he whispered.

He plunged in and out, filling her with raw pleasure until her muscles trembled and a tingling sensation ran down her spine to her toes. His hand came under her, fondling her breasts, teasing her nipples. He leaned in and nibbled at her ear.

She gyrated her hips, pushing back on him until she felt him lose control. He thrust into her wildly, and she cried out as her muscles contracted, a fierce climax raking over her. Evander groaned and stiffened, and she felt his seed pump into her.

She fell to the bed, happy and sated, and said a prayer to the goddess.

He ran his hand down her belly and between her legs, pressing gently on her most sensitive parts, causing more ripples of pleasure to flow through her.

He kissed her navel, then dropped down next to her.

"Did I please you?"

"Do you have to ask? Look at me . . ." She giggled as she gestured to her spent and naked body. "I'm useless."

He chuckled and kissed her neck. "You are hardly useless, my love, but you are entertaining. That luscious body of yours gives me more pleasure than I can say." He closed his eyes, folded his arms behind his head, and exhaled.

"So . . . how are you getting along with my parents?"

"Your mother is a jewel, I really like her, but your father . . . well, I think it's going to take a little time."

"He will come around, you'll see," he assured her. "He's not a man who shows his feelings easily. My father has to find something about you that he really likes or respects before he's willing to invest himself. He was never one for superficial relationships." He kissed her on the head. "Let's take a bath and get downstairs; they are most likely waiting for us."

~

SHE HEARD Teo running through the domus, dogs on his heels, saluting everyone with a shout of *"Io Saturnalia!"*

"Come here, you little imp, and give me a hug good morning."

Teo threw his arms around Aurora. "What gifts did you buy me, Sister?"

"You'll just have to wait until tonight and see. And no snooping!"

"Aw, you're no fun, ever since you got married . . ." he sang out the last word like it was a song. Evander swooped in, picked him up, and dangled him upside down. "No fun? Aurora, get him!"

Aurora tickled her little brother, making him scream with glee.

They entered the atrium like this, where her mother and Evander's parents sat around a warm brazier, conversing as old friends do and drinking spiced wine.

"Good morning, *Io Saturnalia!*" they greeted.

"Io Saturnalia!" their parents shouted back.

Aurora and Evander sat down, and Teo scampered off with the dogs.

"Helena hasn't come down yet?" Evander looked at his mother. She shook her head and gave him a look of concern. His father looked away and put his hand over his belly, as if reacting to physical pain.

"Father Mercurius, are you unwell?" asked Aurora.

"No, I'm fine, just fine," he answered gruffly.

Apollonius entered with more spiced wine and handed it to them.

"Father, there is something you should know," said Evander. He gestured to Apollonius. "This fine man, faithful slave to the Fortunas family, was the one who saved Helena from death. He was the first to arrive in her room on the morning of the earthquake. He lifted the heavy beam of wood off of her before she was crushed beneath its weight."

Dominus Mercurius shifted his weight uncomfortably on the chair and looked at Apollonius, who bowed respectfully and promptly left the room.

"It would be appropriate to give him gifts tonight to thank him for his loyalty; it is Saturnalia, after all."

His father nodded, then held his belly and winced.

"Father Mercurius," Aurora said tentatively, "I can see that you are in pain."

He grimaced and looked irritated.

Her mother reached out and patted her hand. "Aurora, Maximus just explained to me that he has been suffering from intermittent pain in his abdomen for the last month. The journey by ship has made him worse."

Aurora scooted her chair closer to him. "Father, indulge me. Hold out your hands, please." He did as she told him, and she examined his palms, noting that they were red. She pinched at his swollen fingers. "Look me in the eye, please," she continued.

He looked at her as she requested, and they stared at each other for one awkward moment. "It's my belly that hurts, child, not my eyes or hands or fingers."

"Correct, but your eyes and other body parts tell a story. We need to look at the whole body to understand what illness may be afflicting you. Is your belly swollen as well?"

Her father-in-law let out a sigh. "Yes, it is swollen."

Aurora looked at him resolutely. "I believe you are suffering from sickness of the liver, as noted by the fact that your eyes and skin have a yellowish tint, you are retaining fluids, and you have red palms and swollen hands and feet."

Her father-in-law looked unimpressed.

"My grandfather taught me that these things happen when the liver is not cleansing the blood properly and the humors are out of balance."

Then he did something totally unexpected: he laughed in her face.

Aurora felt herself getting angry. He may not like her, but she was not going to let him insult her beloved grandfather, renowned surgeon and medic of Pompeii.

"You do not believe me because I am a woman?" she asked bitterly.

"What do you mean by this, Father?" Evander asked sharply.

Dominus Mercurius gesticulated dramatically with his arms. "Settle down, my children. I am laughing because that is exactly what Lady Lucina told me right before you both entered the room."

Lady Dulcia shook her head at him. "Maximus, you could try a little harder to be nicer to our new daughter-in-law. She doesn't know you very well, and you are not doing a good job of making her feel comfortable," she scolded.

"Aghh." Dominus waved his arm, made a sound of annoyance, then acquiesced. "Aurora, what is your remedy for what afflicts me?" It was the first time he had addressed her by name.

"Your liver will need to be washed out with an herbal elixir that will purify and heal. I will make the remedy myself right now with chicory, hypericon, parsley, and verbena—all herbs that grow in the garden."

"If it pleases my new daughter, I will give her remedy a try." Dominus Mercurius nodded to her, then looked at her mother. "My compliments, Lucina. I can see why my son so stubbornly defended his choice of bride. She is a beautiful, smart, and confident young lady."

Aurora smiled, then stood and excused herself, leaving them all discussing the benefits of herbal medicine.

~

AURORA STOPPED at Helena's room before heading to the garden. Her sister-in-law was sulking on her couch, her eyes red from crying.

"You can't avoid your father forever, you know."

"Why not?" the pretty girl answered in a cheeky tone.

"Because it is Saturnalia, and he is here from Corinth to see you!"

"My parents are here to see you and Evander. *Not me.*"

Aurora sighed. "Come now, walk with me to the spice garden. And put on a wool palla; it's breezy outside." They walked through a long corridor, down a set of wooden stairs, and out a back door to the gardens.

"At least you have a father. What I wouldn't give to see my own father again. I still can't believe he's gone." Aurora picked up a small basket by the outside wall and began to pluck at the leaves of various plants. Her sister-in-law shrugged and looked defiant.

"Helena, why did you come to Pompeii? What were you running away from?"

Helena's face tightened. "My future husband."

Aurora's eyes opened wide in surprise. "You're betrothed?"

"Yes."

"Where is your ring?"

"I refuse to wear it."

Tears filled the girl's eyes, and Aurora understood.

"Your father is making you marry him?"

The girl nodded, tears running down her cheeks.

"But still, how did you come alone to visit Pompeii? Why did your parents allow it?"

"I fell into melancholy. I couldn't eat or sleep. And so they decided to send me away for a little while."

What could she say to her beloved new sister? Such was the fate of many women, especially of the equestrian class. Marriages were only business contracts, and love, as powerful a force as it was, was blatantly disregarded. It wasn't fair.

She realized anew how fortunate she had been to marry Evander.

And who was she? *Just a simple girl from Pompeii.*

"Don't lose hope, Helena. Go back to Corinth; you are only fifteen. And I know I shouldn't say this to you, but hold out for as long as you can. Perhaps your father will change his mind after everything that has happened to you here."

Helena wiped at her eyes with her palla.

Aurora put her arm around the girl's shoulder and walked her through the spice garden. "Tonight is the feast of Saturnalia, and Apollonius will be king. We shall have a load of fun!"

She finished picking the leaves and roots that she needed for her father-in-law's medicine, and they went into the kitchen to prepare the brew.

AURORA'S GRANDFATHER arrived from Neapolis a few hours before the feast was about to begin. He threw off his toga and donned a wildly colorful tunic, as was the custom of dinner parties during this holiday. Aurora also dressed in a manner that would have been laughable during any other time of the year. Her stola was dark green, her palla red and orange.

Marcus Tibertinus and his sons joined them for the festivities, along with some other families they had reconnected with since the destruction of Pompeii. Still, there had been no word about the fate of the Valens family.

Apollonius had borrowed one of Evander's togas that had a

dark crimson border, traditionally worn by male citizens during a religious ceremony. He was reclining on the couch in the triclinium, surrounded by his family and the rest of the household slaves. They were dressed in their finest clothing and chatting amicably. They had cooked up tonight's long-awaited feast, but as custom dictated, the masters were the ones to serve it to them.

Helena descended from her room in high spirits, dressed in bright, eye-popping colors, and led the procession into the dining room holding a bowlful of perfumed water. She stopped first at the king and washed his hands. Apollonius gave her a wry smile and burst into laughter.

"I shall take good care of you tonight, my king," she advised him.

"I am looking forward to it, slave girl," he jested.

Aurora whistled under her breath and prayed that Dominus Mercurius was not listening to their exchange. She sat down in the corner, under the hanging oil lamp, to play the lyre. The large room had been decorated with beautiful winter garlands and greenery and warmed with a cheery brazier.

The dinner began with a mouthwatering *gustatio* of marinated octopus cooked in leeks, and continued with a *mensa prima* of hearty vegetable soup. After that came roast duck and chestnuts, a traditional dish from Neapolis.

Aurora's mother and Lady Dulcia carried in the platters of food and set them in the middle of the couches. Dominus Mercurius was charged with pouring the water and wine, and Evander's task was to clean away the dirty dishes, much to everyone's amusement. Teo walked around with a linen napkin, dabbing at the dribbles of gravy on the slaves' lips, and sometimes "fixing" their hair and clothes.

Smiles and laughter abounded, and as she strummed the strings of the lyre, Aurora's heart was filled with joy knowing they had survived a most terrible nightmare, and yet here they were, slave and master, not only living, but *thriving*.

It proved to her that people were resilient, that they could overcome the highest obstacles, if they had each other to lean on. It affirmed in her mind the value and sanctity of life and how life was never to be taken for granted.

Meanwhile, Helena washed everyone's hands again in preparation of the next course. Silver bowls filled with figs, dates, nuts, apples, and pears were brought in, but what looked most delicious were the quinces boiled in honey. Her mouth started to water just thinking about eating the aromatic, tart, and floral-tasting fruit.

Aurora almost choked as Helena sat down on the couch next to Apollonius and began to spoon the delicious dessert into his mouth. *That girl is brazen!*

After the last course, the tables of food were cleared away.

Apollonius stood and made a request. "Since I am the King of Saturnalia, I command that all unwed girls dance for me now."

Helena joined a group of pretty girls, freeborn and slave, on the floor between the couches and began to dance. Aurora's grandfather sat down next to her with an African drum on his lap. Together they beat out a lively dancing song, and the maidens danced and giggled.

She caught Apollonius's eyes burning into Helena so hotly that she expected to see the girl go up in smoke. She prayed that her in-laws were too busy enjoying the festivities to notice what she had failed to see for so long: his infatuation with their daughter.

Now everyone was clapping to the rhythm, and Apollonius commanded that all the masters should dance for the pleasure of the slaves.

"Does that include us, Grandfather?"

"Well, why not?" the distinguished surgeon answered. They passed off their instruments to the Tiburtinas brothers, and he grabbed Aurora by the arm and began to spin her around. Evander and her mother danced gaily toward them, and she praised her mother for joining in the festivities so soon after the loss of her father.

Aurora held on to Evander's hips and pulled him close. They danced body to body and rocked back and forth suggestively. "And this is why Saturnalia is my favorite time of the year!" She laughed, then planted a seductive kiss on her husband's lips.

When the music ended, Evander announced that it was time for the masters to give their gifts to the slaves. Lady Dulcia helped him hand out the gifts. He gave useful items such as warm stockings, new shoes, and writing tablets. The gifts one gave at Saturnalia were not meant to show wealth, they were supposed to be tokens of one's appreciation for one another.

Then Evander's father stepped forward and everyone held their breath, for no one knew what to expect from the stern and domineering man. He stood before the king.

"Apollonius, faithful slave and servant to the Fortunas family, I would like to recognize your strength and bravery for all that you did to help my son save the good people of Pompeii. But tonight, most of all, I thank you for saving the life of my most precious treasure, my dear daughter Helena."

Lady Dulcia also spoke. "When we heard of the great disaster that had befallen Pompeii, we were ever more grateful and humbled to learn that our own children were safe. We now know that you had an important role to play in our daughter's survival."

Dominus Mercurius moved even closer to Apollonius. "And so tonight I gift you with enough gold *aurei* to buy your freedom, and that of your mother and brothers as well. With the permission of Lady Lucina and her father, the illustrious Vibius Popidius, you are a freedman." He handed a large sack of coins to Apollonius.

There was absolute silence in the room as everyone turned to Apollonius to see his reaction. His handsome face had gone as white as the snow she had once seen on the top of Vesuvius. He arose from the couch and kneeled down before his benefactor. "I am forever in your debt, Dominus." He kissed each of his hands but kept his head bowed until Evander's father bid him rise.

Then everyone let out cheers and cries of congratulations. Myrrhine ran into her son's arms, followed by Giorgio and Pioppo. Aurora looked to Helena and saw that she was beaming.

Aurora squeezed her husband's hand. "Did you know about this, Evander?"

"No. And if I speak truthfully, I didn't think my father had it in him. He must have his reasons."

"He surprised all of us. Apollonius and his family are free!" She began to cry from joy, but also from sadness because she couldn't imagine her life without them. Aurora stepped over to Apollonius and embraced him warmly, her tears wetting his neck.

"Congratulations. I love you, Apollonius, my brother, my truest friend."

"And I love you, Aurora. Freedman or slave, nothing will ever change that."

⁓

THERE WAS much goodwill and gaiety as the rest of the slaves finally served dinner to the masters. When dinner ended and darkness fell, Aurora's and Evander's family exchanged gifts with one another. Teo received new wooden toys, miniature gladiators, and a new drinking mug carved with a funny face. The women exchanged small beauty items—earrings, makeup, and curling irons.

As a belated wedding present, Evander's parents gifted them with a beautiful and very expensive Persian rug for their bedroom. The border was decorated with griffins and deer, and the interior with lotus buds and intricate geometric designs.

Evander gave Aurora a small scroll of poetry that he had found in a library in Neapolis, and Aurora was certain that no one had ever given her a more beautiful or thoughtful gift. But when it came to choosing a present for her husband, she had been at a total loss. What could she possibly give him that he didn't already have?

She had finally settled on a beautifully crafted wooden box filled with fragrant oils, razors, and a new strigil for the baths. She had purchased it from an artist in Surrentum, a kind old man who took great pride in his work. The box had copper fittings and intricate bone relief carvings across the front. Aside from its artistic beauty, she loved the fact that the craftsman had created it with passion. That was where its true beauty lay.

Evander was duly impressed with her thoughtful gift and passed it around for everyone to see. Then he hugged her and kissed her good night. "Don't wait up for me; my father has challenged all the men to a game of dice. It's going to be a very late night."

Aurora smiled. "Enjoy yourself. It's the only time of the year the slaves can play dice with the masters. Have fun. I'm sure Apollonius is looking forward to it, especially now that he is a freedman and has some money to spare."

CHAPTER 32

MARCH AD 80

Several months had passed since Saturnalia, and Evander's father was slowly feeling better. Her grandfather had advised him to give up all but very watered-down wine and to drink instead the herbal infusions Aurora was preparing for him each day. *Well diagnosed, well cured,* she thought. She felt that he was slowly warming up to her, and often referred to her as "my daughter."

Now it was time for Evander's family to return to Corinth, and they would set sail in the morning. Dominus Mercurius and Evander were down at the harbor overseeing the preparation of the ships, and her mother and Lady Dulcia were shopping in Surrentum.

Helena had asked Aurora to set up a discreet meeting between her and Apollonius so she could say good-bye to him without being under the scrutiny of her parents' watchful eyes. After everything they had been through together, she thought the request was justified.

Aurora led Helena through her private bath suite and into an area of the house reserved solely for husband and wife. They arrived at a small atrium surrounded by thin Doric columns. In the center was a shallow pool decorated with a mosaic of sea creatures. Beyond that was another room painted with beautiful frescoes of red and gold, and in the center, a comfortable couch adorned with pillows.

Apollonius stood by the couch, waiting. Helena's face lit up like fire when she saw him, and she flung herself into his outstretched arms. "My dearest Apollonius, how I shall miss you," she cried.

Aurora saw the look on their faces and realized that since their escape from Pompeii, they had developed feelings for each other that went deeper than friendship. "I will wait out here for you two to say your good-byes, then."

She sat in the small atrium by the pool and thought about the possibilities. Apollonius had saved Helena's life, after all. With his handsome looks and kind heart, he was an easy man to fall for. But even as a freedman, did he actually stand a chance with Evander's sister?

Marriage to a former slave was permissible under Augustan law, but there was a stigma associated with these unions. The stain of servitude was hard to erase in the eyes of the elite. She couldn't see Dominus Mercurius, a wealthy equestrian man, ever giving his consent.

The couple emerged from the room a short while later; Apollonius thanked Aurora and walked quickly away. Helena held out her hands. "Look at what he gave me," she said, smiling.

In one hand was a small burnt rock, in the other a large pink-and-pearly conch shell. Aurora looked at her questioningly.

"One represents the past; the other, the future," she explained. "If I become disheartened, I am to hold the conch shell to my ear, listen to the sound of the ocean, and know that one day he will come for me."

❧

THE NEXT MORNING, the mules and carriages arrived, and they all said their good-byes as the slaves loaded up the Mercurius family belongings. Aurora had the hardest time saying good-bye to Helena. "My dearest sister, my heart. What shall I do without you? In whom shall I confide?" Aurora couldn't stop the flow of tears.

"You must come and visit me in Corinth this summer. Promise me, Aurora. Oh, how I will miss you! I feel like I shall cry forever." She dabbed at her eyes with a small piece of linen, then held out her arms to Evander. "And you, Brother."

Evander embraced his sister for a long time. "I am on your side, Sister. I will help you," he told her. "Now be good, and I will talk to Father on your behalf, to save you from an unhappy union."

As the carriages rolled away, Aurora felt the sting of her father's passing strongly. She looked at her mother, who seemed to understand. Her mother put her arm around Aurora's shoulder to comfort her.

"We have said too many good-byes these past few months, Daughter. It is too much to bear. I feel it too. But the good news is that Myrrhine and her boys will stay on and work for us as freedmen and woman."

"That is wonderful, Mother! And Apollonius?"

"Apollonius will work for me," answered Evander. "He will help run my business. I will make him a very rich man."

Aurora smiled at Apollonius's good fortune. "I will miss him terribly."

Her mother nodded. "So will I, Daughter, so will I. What we need around here is some joy. We need children to fill up this beautiful home."

Evander looked at her hopefully, but Aurora remained silent. She had done nothing to prevent pregnancy, but still she hadn't conceived. After all the stress she had endured these past few months, she didn't even know if it was possible, but perhaps a little herbal remedy might help.

Later that day, she asked her mother to help her procure the ingredients needed to make the love potion she and Evander had drunk together on the beach so many months before. She remembered specifically that along with sexual desire, it was supposed to be helpful in promoting fertility and conception. She and Evander certainly desired each other, but maybe they needed a little help with the rest.

THE NEXT NIGHT, Aurora and Evander sat shoulder to shoulder on the hill overlooking the water. The once verdant Mount Vesuvius that had given so much beauty to the bay was covered under a blanket of ash.

And under that ash sat Pompeii, that beautiful, lively city that once was home. Buried in their silent tomb were the houses they had lived in, the bedrooms they had loved in, the gardens they had planted with such care. *What is life and what is death?* she pondered. It seemed that one could slip so easily between the two.

An entire culture of art, music, sculpture, and poetry was now underground and hidden from view. Efforts to resurrect the city had been abandoned by the emperor when he had seen just how much devastation the fire mountain had caused.

But now the days would grow longer, and the sun would slowly return to replenish the land of gardens and grapevines. She hoped the light would return to their lives as well.

She looked at her husband, his strong form, his deep blue eyes, and dark silky hair. Her heart flooded with gratitude. "Where do we go from here? she asked him. "There is nothing I can give you. No land, no home, no dowry."

"You are wrong, Aurora. You have given me everything." He looked tenderly into her eyes. "I love you. I have never felt this way about any woman. If I hadn't returned when I did, you would be buried under that detestable ash. May I die if the gods should ever wish me to go on without you."

She swallowed hard and held back tears.

"And I do believe that you should continue to practice medicine with your mother. It is part of who you are, part of what makes you happy and unique. Perhaps the two of you can open up a medical clinic in Surrentum."

She wanted to tell him that she loved him so much it made her heart ache. That he made her want to live each moment as fiercely as the flames that spewed forth from Vesuvius on that fateful night when she had lost everything. She put her hand to his cheek. "I would like to give you a child, my love, maybe even three or four. You have given me hope and a new home. Now it is my turn to make you a happy man."

His warm hand gently enfolded her own.

She held up her cup to him, then drank the last drops of the love potion her mother had mixed for them, in the hopes that it would work some magic. She leaned over and kissed him with all of her breath and passion.

He smiled roguishly, pulled her up by the hand, and led her into their warm and cozy bedroom. He slowly stripped away her clothes and teased her playfully with his kisses. In a matter of moments she was burning for him.

"Love conquers all things, so we too shall yield to love," he whispered as he doused the oil lamp and took her into his arms.

THE END

AUTHOR'S NOTE

The Eruption

Most of what we know about the eruption of Mount Vesuvius in AD 79 comes from an eyewitness account from Gaius Plinius Caecilius Secundus, commonly known as Pliny the Younger. Pliny was an author, lawyer, and magistrate in Ancient Rome.

Pliny was raised and educated by his uncle, Pliny the Elder, who was an author, naturalist, and naval commander of the Roman Empire. Pliny the Elder is credited with writing *Natural History*, one of the world's first encyclopedias.

On the day of the eruption, Pliny the Younger was about seventeen years old and living with his mother and uncle in Misenum, a naval base west of Naples. After the midday meal, they noticed an unusual cloud in the sky across the bay, which Pliny described as looking like an umbrella pine, a common tree in Italy.

Pliny the Elder decided that the phenomenon warranted a closer inspection and invited his nephew to come along and investigate. Pliny the Younger refused, saying that he preferred to stay home and study. As Pliny the Elder prepared to sail, a message arrived from a friend begging him to come and save her from the mountain. This tells us that the eruption had already been under way for quite some time.

Pliny the Elder and his fleet of Roman warships set out on a rescue mission, but due to the winds, choking black ash, and hot embers, they were unable to sail into the port of Pompeii and landed in Stabiae instead. Through it all, Pliny the Elder commanded a scribe to write down each phase of the eruption exactly as he observed it.

The next morning Pliny the Elder is said to have collapsed on the beach as the smell of sulfur approached. He reportedly died from dense fumes that choked his breathing, as he suffered from a narrow and inflamed windpipe. In modern terms, we might say that Pliny the Elder was an asthmatic, based on his nephew's description. We assume that Roman sailors who were with Pliny the Elder brought back his notes and described all they had experienced to Pliny's nephew and sister.

Years later, Pliny the Younger was asked by the historian Cornelius Tacitus to describe everything that had happened surrounding his uncle's death. Intrigued by the story, he then asked Pliny for another letter describing the events that had taken place at Misenum during the eruption.

The phases of the eruption in my story follow the general timeline that Pliny the Younger laid out in his letters. I surmised that when the black column of smoke and ash finally collapsed, spreading out over the water to Misenum, it would have spread out in a circular fashion, thus appearing the same to a witness in Surrentum.

Date of the Eruption

The commonly held date for the eruption of Vesuvius is August 24. This date comes from a medieval translation of Pliny's letters, but may have been a mistake. When the first large scale excavations began of Pompeii and the surrounding areas, emerging evidence pointed to a late autumn eruption:

- Freshly harvested autumn fruits such as pomegranates and walnuts.
- Fruits harvested during the summer were already dried, such as prunes, dates, and figs.
- The grape harvest was over, and wine production was ongoing. Large *dolia,* (wine-fermenting jars) were found full, sealed, and buried in Boscoreale.
- Tephra deposits (rock fragments and ash) show a southeasterly dispersal pattern, which is a common wind pattern as the seasons change from summer to autumn.
- Winter clothes were worn by many of the victims and portable heaters known as braziers were found in use in many of the houses.

I have chosen the end of October as the date for the eruption, based on this archeological evidence. The year of the eruption, AD 79, is widely accepted and based on legal documents from the reign of Titus Flavius Vespasianus, who became emperor on June 24, AD 79.

Women in Ancient Rome

Ancient Rome spanned a time period of over twelve hundred years from its founding in 753 BC to its end in AD 476. Most of what we know about Roman women comes from the writings of men or tombstone epitaphs. I relied heavily on a book called *Pandora's Daughters* by Eva Cantarella, for the following information.

Early in the Roman Republic (509-27 BC) a woman had no political rights and remained under her father's control until she married. Her husband then acquired power over her and the property she inherited. In legal matters, a woman had to remain under male guardianship for life. During this time period, a woman could be put to death for adultery and was not allowed to drink wine. Women were praised for their devotion to their family and home and played a fundamental role in the transmission of Roman culture and values to their children.

Toward the end of the Republic, new laws were passed, and marriage and divorce changed in the woman's favor. Marriage was considered an equal relationship based on the will of two people to stay together. When they no longer desired the relationship, they were free to divorce. No legal act was necessary to end a marriage, and the woman's dowry was returned to her. Legal guardianship was abolished for freeborn women. Many women began to rebel against the practice of arranged marriages, as well. We also know that abortion was widely practiced, which may have contributed to a population crisis.

In 27 BC, Augustus (Octavian) became the first Roman emperor and ushered in the *Pax Romana*, a period of peace and expansion spanning more than two hundred years. In 18 BC, Augustus attempted to increase the morality and population of the upper classes by passing several new laws that promoted marriage, fidelity, and children. He made adultery a public crime and imposed heavy taxes on unwed men and women. His social laws were not well received, and nine years later the laws were modified.

Meanwhile, Roman women kept up their march toward independence. Two writers, Juvenal and Martial, writing in the first and second centuries, tell us that upper-class women were allowed to educate themselves, drink wine, go to the public baths, wear makeup, and divorce as often as they liked. We know that many women worked as dressmakers, moneylenders, shop owners, teachers, and physicians.

There is much evidence of female midwives and physicians in ancient Rome. Midwives were usually slaves, while *medicae* were either upper-class women or freed women who had been taught by their fathers or husbands.

According to literature of that time period, Roman men were

not happy with the ever-increasing autonomy of women and preferred to keep their wives and daughters under their control.

In my story, I decided to create Aurora as one of these highly educated women who delighted in intellectual pursuits. Her beliefs about a woman's independence and place in society clash with Evander's, who hopes to find a more traditional female.

Slavery

Slaves in ancient Rome were often gained through military expansion as spoils of war and were not limited to any one race. Thousands of people were often captured in each war. Slaves were considered property under the Roman law and were subjected to beatings, torture, and sexual exploitation.

Over time, laws were passed that gave slaves legal protection, including the right to file a complaint against their masters. Educated philosophers also encouraged the fair treatment of slaves.

Household slaves often had a high standard of living, and their children were brought up with the children of the family. Some Romans lamented that the household slaves were better cared for than many of Rome's free, poor citizens.

Educated or skilled slaves were allowed to earn money in the hopes of buying their freedom. Often, once they were freed, they became clients of their master, who became their patron. Clients and patrons were expected to help each other. The act of freeing a slave was known as *manumission*. The freed slave took his or her former owner's last name.

In my story, I decided to have the slaves well treated and thought of as part of the family. Many educated people in ancient Rome understood that it was mutually beneficial to treat their slaves well. If the slaves were happy, they would feel more loyalty to the master and work harder.

Herbal Medicine

The ancient Greeks and Romans used medicinal plants extensively in their everyday lives. We know that many herbal remedies were in use in ancient Pompeii as well. Pliny the Elder describes hundreds of plants in his *Natural History* and tells of their medicinal properties.

In a fascinating book called *A Pompeian Herbal* by Wilhelmina Feemster Jashemski, she describes many of the live medicinal plants she encountered while excavating the gardens of Pompeii. The Pompeian workmen eagerly dug them up and explained how the plants were to be used. As Wilhelmina gathered more information about these medicinal plants, she discovered that almost all of them had been in use in ancient times as well and that knowledge of these herbal remedies had been passed down through the centuries.

Many of the herbal remedies in my story come from Wilhelmina's book. Some interesting examples of herbs used in ancient Pompeii that are still in use today are: hollyhock, used for children's stomach ailments; verbena, used for detoxifying the liver; and of course, chamomile flowers, which are still prescribed in Pompeii today for sleeplessness.

Love Magic

The ancient Greeks and Romans were very superstitious and believed in all sorts of omens, evil spirits, amulets, charms, incantations, and prayers. According to Christopher Faraone in *Ancient Greek Love Magic,* men were more likely to cast a spell on a woman that made her burn with sexual desire for him, while women were more likely to cast a spell on a man that made him want to remain her partner in love or marriage. Often these incantations would use a phrase that asked the gods to "bind forever" the unwitting person of desire to the person casting the spell.

In my story, I decided to make the love spell a reciprocal prayer that invoked Venus, goddess of love, to aid the would-be lovers during a period of separation. The love spell was used in conjunction with a love potion, also very common at this time, and based on ingredients described by Pliny the Elder in his *Natural History* to aid sexual function.

Pompeii Today

Ancient Pompeii was rediscovered in 1748, when the first excavations began. It is part of Vesuvius National Park and was declared a World Heritage Site by UNESCO in 1997. The ruins of Pompeii attract millions of visitors each year, including many archeologists and scholars.

During the summer of 2016 I had the wonderful opportunity to volunteer with an archeological group called The Pompeii Food and Drink Project under the direction of Betty Jo Mayeske, PhD. We were able to work inside of the ancient houses and see first-hand the beautiful frescoes and graffiti carved into the walls. Some of the love poems found in Pompeii are featured in this book.

One morning we got locked inside of a house when a tourist came along and accidentally fastened the lock. This house was very interesting because in one of the rooms we found stone balls the size of large grapefruits. The archeologists explained they were ballista balls, the projectiles thrown at the city walls when Lucius Cornelius Sulla besieged Pompeii in 89 BC.

For those of us who love Pompeii, the ancient ruins are mysterious, intriguing and provocative. They instill a sense of wonder and sadness for the people who endured such a terrifying natural disaster. This book was my attempt to bring the people and beauty of Pompeii to life again, if only for a little while. Thank you for spending your time with my imagination. I hope you enjoyed the story.

ACKNOWLEDGMENTS

A special thank you to my editor and cover designer, Jennifer Quinlan. Your patience and guidance was greatly appreciated as I brought this book to life.

Thank you also to my family and friends who encouraged my efforts, and to the RWA chapter of Western New York. Your support and dedication to writing is inspiring.

ABOUT THE AUTHOR

Carmela Dolce is an emerging author who loves to travel and study archeology.

Fascinated by natural phenomena, she has trekked to the top of volcanoes, been caught in several earthquakes, and is no stranger to lake effect snowstorms.

Carmela lives in Buffalo, New York with her husband, two kids, and a playful golden retriever who begs to go outside whenever Carmela sits down to write.

This is Carmela's first book.

Visit Carmela at www.CarmelaDolce.com or on Facebook, Twitter or Instagram.

9 781732 053106